Found

By

Vampires

Joy Mosby

Found by Vampires
1st edition

For Mom,

Who told me once to tell myself a story when I couldn't sleep.

Thanks Mom, I still do.

PROLOGUE

100 A.D.

Asteria stretched after a long sleep. She thought that she should feel refreshed but she felt sleepy and sluggish. Where were her followers? They should be building her power, not weakening it.

She sent her essence out into the world to gauge the state of the world. There was a new cult taking root in both the Greek and Roman cultures. It was built on the basis of the Hebrew's monotheism, something about the son of God making an appearance and promising to forgive all sins. Asteria shook her head in disgust. It would be a lot of work for one god, but when she looked for her creations, her blood drinkers, she found that many of them were following this new religion.

Where was Tadeas? He should be teaching the new disciples her ways not letting them fall for Christianity and their one god theory. She looked for him everywhere but he was nowhere to be found. Did the first of her creations finally take a trip across the river Stix?

She had to do something to regain her power, and bring her

vampires back to her. She had never spoken to any of the vampires Tadeas created, only him. Now that he was gone she was going to have to reach out to her people. She pondered long and hard on the best way to do it. Taking a page from Christianity she would bring a daughter into the world who would bring all of her creations back to her bosom.

To create a half-mortal daughter, she was going to need more power then she currently had. She could only think of one way to generate enough power and give her vampires a hint of what was to come. She sent them a prophecy, detailing who and why she would send a daughter to them.

The prophecy helped, it did not generate as much power as she hoped, but it would be enough. There was a buzz in the ears of her creations. What she had not planned on was the time it would take to transform herself into her human form.

CHAPTER 1

PRESENT DAY

Miguel stood on the balcony looking down at the hordes of humans gyrating against each other in the hot, sweaty bar below. He stifled a yawn, and pondered why they found such an inferior activity so entertaining. It was a very human thing to do, a way to forget about their petty problems and have a good time. He had nothing to complain about, he owned most of the city, and he had a retinue of followers who were ready and mostly willing to do his bidding. He was the patron of the city, the unspoken king, it had taken over a hundred years to get where he was today, and a year ago he would have said it was worth it. Tonight though, he was bored. He was tired of waiting for the prophecy to become reality. He had been ready for years, he was anxious to begin his real reign and bring Europe to its knees before him. In the back of his mind though, there was always an uneasiness that someone else would discover 'The One' first.

He spent years studying the prophecy and the tapestry. All of the signs pointed to San Sebastian, but there were other bays on the east coast of the Atlantic the text could have been referring to. What if he had missed it? He scowled and shook off the thought. This had to be the place, he needed to have patience and diligence, the reward would be worth it.

He closed his eyes and inhaled deeply trying to find someone to have for dinner. The bar smelled as it normally did of sex, alcohol, smoke, a few drugs, and something else. Something he had never smelled before. It was like blooming lilacs and female, delicious. He opened his eyes and followed his nose, looking for the source. He watched the door on the women's restroom close and the smell faded with it. She must be inside, he thought.

"Master," a voice behind him said.

"Vince, what can I do for you?" he asked, not bothering to turn and look at his underling but keeping his eyes on the bathroom door.

"Everything for the finale of the film festival has been set," Vince said, with his head bowed in supplication. "It will be the same as last year at Castillo de la Mota, I have the big box set up for your entourage."

"Very well," Miguel said, only half listening. "Was there anything else Vince?"

"There has been talk that the prophecy has been confirmed on the Ivory Coast," Vince said, stepping up to the railing next to his master and catching a whiff of the distinctive smell.

"Interesting," Miguel said, barely stiffening at the remark. There must be some mistake. He would call his sister as soon as he found the source of the amazing smell. "I am sure it is nothing. I will look into it. Thank you for keeping me up to date on the situation." He froze as the air became saturated with the smell of the female leaving the ladies room. "If you will excuse me. I think I have found my dinner for the evening." Miguel dismissed Vince with a half wave of his hand, not taking his eyes off the female making her way back to the dance floor.

Vince's nostrils flared, zeroing in on the female and taking a step back. "Enjoy, Miguel."

Miguel watched the female with short dark hair make her way through the crowd. The cut fit her heart-shaped face and when she glanced around he caught a glimpse of her ice-blue eyes. He was surprised he was able to make them out in the smoke darkened club. They must be electric under normal light, he thought. Her skin was an olive color, but he thought most of it had come from the sun. Under her spaghetti-strap, red tank top and short black skirt, he thought she would have skin the color of milk. She was strong; he could see the cut of her biceps, they were not big, but toned and she curved in all the right places. Miguel had seen it all before. The only thing that stood out to him about her was her smell; to him everything else was average.

He watched her stop in the middle of the dance floor, she placed both of her hands on her hips with her legs spread and yelled at a man caught in an embrace with another woman. Miguel leaned against the railing to watch the show with a small smile on his lips.

CHAPTER 2

"He's lying to you," a voice with a Spanish accent whispered in my ear. I looked around, ignoring Mark, to see who had snuck up on me, but no one was there.

"Are you listening to me?" Mark asked, trying to maintain eye contact. "I was just dancing with her nothing more."

"He's lying to you again," the whisper said, louder this time. I fought the urge to look around again for the source of the voice that was trying to distract me. Not giving up on the situation at hand I just stared back at Mark.

"The next thing I knew she was kissing me," he said, trying to take both of my hands in one of his, like he always did when he was in trouble. I pulled my hands away not ready to talk about it in a crowded bar.

"Whatever, I'm not going to have this conversation in this place," I said, waving my hands around the noisy crowded bar in San Sebastian, Spain. "I'm going to head back to the room. When you are ready come back, we can talk," I said, turning and heading toward the door. Maybe I had too much to drink tonight. Hearing voices? Come on.

Out on the street I took a cleansing breath getting rid of all the smoky, sex-driven air of the bar and began to walk toward the hotel Mark and I were staying in.

Some trip this was turning into, I thought while making my way up the sidewalk. I hated being a babysitter and it felt like that is all I had been so far. Whether I was half-carrying Mark home, drunk from a bar, finding his lost passport, or making sure he had dinner when he needed it, all I had done was take care of him. Finding him playing tonsil hockey with some girl on the dance floor while I was in the bathroom was the last straw. Things had to change, or we would have to go our separate ways.

I wound my way through the streets, trying to figure out how to save this trip. I had been dating Mark for three years, and we had been planning this summer in Europe since the beginning of our junior year of college. I thought we had a great relationship. This trip was going to be our last hurrah before settling down with careers and family. We were only on our second week and I was having second thoughts about everything I thought I loved about him.

Turning the corner onto the street of my hotel I felt the hair on the back of my neck stand up. I stopped and look around. There was a man standing in the shadows of the building. I could only see that he was large, and his eyes almost seemed to glow. He creeped me out.

"Good evening," someone behind me said, and I watched the man in the shadows dip his head in greeting. I spun around to see who was behind me but no one was there. I turned back to the man only to find he was gone. My flight or fight instinct kicked in and I ran down the street and almost tripped through the door of my hotel.

Antonio, the night clerk, looked up from behind the desk with a concerned look on his face. "Señora Hunter, are you alright?"

"Si, I am sorry, I thought someone was chasing me," I said, looking around at the empty lobby.

"You have nothing to worry about in San Sebastian, Señorita, this is a very safe town."

"I know. It's been a long night." I headed toward the elevator then to my room.

I flipped on the lights, checked the bathroom, the closet, and under the bed. I wanted to make sure no one was hiding in my room.

It had been a strange night, I thought, as I undressed and put my stinky bar clothes in a plastic hotel laundry bag. I headed toward the bathroom, the shower was calling to me. As the hot water beat on my back I thought about the voices I heard. The one at the bar, and the one on the street. They were different sounding. I didn't think they came from the same person but each time, they sounded like someone was behind me even though when I looked no one was there. Maybe I had too much to drink. I shut off the shower and dressed in boxers and a t-shirt before turning out the lights and going to sleep.

CHAPTER 3

Miguel watched the exchange between the female and Vince from the roof of the building across the street. Something was off. Why did Vince not take advantage of the female? Miguel was sure she must have smelled as good to Vince as she did to him.

Miguel was surprised he had not taken what he wanted from her yet either. This was not how he normally operated. When he found a meal he took it quickly without any fuss and got on with his night. Why was this female affecting him so?

After the female had taken off down the street, Miguel jumped off the roof and landed softly on the pavement next to Vince.

"Master," Vince said, watching the female run through a doorway. "Stalking your prey?"

"I was until you chased her away," Miguel said.

"Yes, that one smells delicious," Vince said, lifting his nose in the air, and breathing deeply.

Miguel fought the urge to take his head off. She was his. "I think I will have some fun with this one, Vince. It has been a while since I played with my food."

"As you wish, Master," Vince said, sounding unhappy, his prey was no longer his to prey upon. "Ah, there is another scent almost as good as hers," he said and took off in a different direction.

Miguel watched Vince leave then resumed his pursuit. He walked up the street and stopped outside the doors she had entered. Looking up at the name over them he smiled, it was one of his hotels. He waited outside the front door, listening as the elevator came down to the main level and went back up. He walked in the door and headed to the registration desk.

"Good evening, Señor Herra," Antonio said. "What can I do for you?"

"Good evening, Antonio," he said, placing both of his hands on the desk making eye contact with him. "Tell me who the girl was who went up in the elevator."

"Oh, that was Katie Hunter. She and her boyfriend, Mark Hudson, are on a backpacking trip across Europe. They are staying here until Monday Sir."

"And how do you know so much about them, Antonio?" Miguel asked, wondering how he was able to get so much information about two of the hundreds of guests he dealt with weekly.

"Oh, she is really nice and wanted to know what the locals do for fun, where they hang out. That kind of thing."

"Show me their passports."

Antonio nodded, went to a drawer, pulled them out, and handed them to Miguel. He glanced at them quickly, memorizing the information and gave them back to Antonio.

"I want you to keep an eye on her for me," he said.

"Sir?" Antonio said, not understanding what his master

wanted from him.

"Do what you can to make sure she stays safe. Do anything you can to make her happy," he said, thinking for a minute. "I want to make sure she does not leave town." He looked at the phone that just began to ring.

"Yes, sir," Antonio, said trying to ignore the phone.

"I will require a report of what she does tomorrow and anything you find out about her. If you need help keeping her in town let me know." He backed up a step and looked at the still ringing phone. "You had better get that."

"Front desk, how may I serve you?" Antonio asked, quickly picking up the phone and looking up at Miguel. He nodded, turned, and left through the front doors.

CHAPTER 4

From the roof of the building across the street from the hotel, Vince watched Miguel leave the hotel making sure he was down wind so Miguel could not smell him. He knew spying on his master had horrific consequences, but he could not help himself. There was something about the female that made him want to protect her. Miguel was a good king, fair and just, but humans were only food for him. Somehow, this female was more than just food. The fact that she saw him standing in the shadows on the corner baffled his mind. Ten other people had passed him by, and none had given him a second glance. She should have been like the rest of them.

How was he going to protect her from Miguel? Why did he care? She smelled good but what did it mean? He had smelled humans who smelled good before and they normally tasted better than they smelled. So why did he not want to just sink his fangs into her neck and have a sip? Taking a deep breath of the salty air and all of the human scents around, he realized he must feed, and soon.

He rounded the corner to see the human that the lovely female was fighting with at the club. His pants were down around his knees and he was fucking the same parasite who he had been making out with in the bar. I could make this so easy, he thought to himself. Just take him out now and maybe the female would be Vince's for as long as he wanted her. He thought about it seriously for a moment. If he killed the male, the female would worry about him, mourn him, and blame herself for leaving the bar without him. It would not get Vince anywhere. Still, this male needed to suffer; he needed to pay for hurting her.

Vince waited and let his hunger grow as he watched the male pump into the whore. It seemed to Vince that it would never end. The male must be too drunk to finish, Vince thought to himself. He looked at the whore, she was too drunk to know what was going on. Finally, the male pulled out and pulled up his pants.

"I can't finish out here in the open," the male said to her, staggering a step then regained his balance. "Can we go to your place?"

"You know what, Mark? I better just head home on my own," the whore said, while pulling down her skirt. "Thanks for the bang, but I have to work tomorrow."

"What? No, we can't be done yet," Mark said, trying to grab her arm.

"Get over it, lover boy," she said, walking down the alley toward the street. "Go back to your girlfriend, maybe she can get off with your whiskey dick."

"What in the fuck are you talking about?" he asked, beginning to trail after her. "I'll give you the best fuck of your life. Whether you like it or not." He ran to catch up with her and pushed her to the ground. She cried out as her body met the cold cobblestone street, and she began to try to crawl away.

What a piece of shit, Vince thought. Could he really allow this to happen? He knew he could not. The female did not deserve to be raped. Why was he thinking like this? He had never cared about anything that happened to humans unless one of his kind was involved. He walked silently up to Mark and pushed him hard against the wall. Mark's head bounced off the brick and he slumped down against the wall. Shit, Vince thought to himself. He was not trying to kill him. The whore got up and dusted off her now soiled clothes.

"Hey, thanks," she said, finally looking up at him. "I think he was starting to go crazy on me. I'm going to call the cops on his ass," she said and continued on her former path.

Vince's hunger got the best of him at that moment. "Just a moment," he said and took her hand. She looked up into his eyes and smiled.

He bent his head to her neck, bit down, and began to drink. Her blood was hot, metallic, and seductive since the endorphins from her sex with Mark were still racing through her system. This was his favorite kind of blood. Under normal circumstances, ingesting the endorphins got him off as well as the victim but not this one. He let go of his vise grip on the girl, only then realizing she was not a whore or a parasite, she was just a girl. Running his tongue over the bite to stop the bleeding he moved her so she would be steady on her feet again and took hold of her mind.

"Go home," he told her, taking a step back and using his will. "You had too much to drink and need to sleep it off."

"You're right, I just need to go home and sleep," she said, turning, and heading down the alley toward home.

He watched her in her drunken state and smiled to himself. She would not remember anything from this night, and she would think the bite marks on her neck were a hickey from Mark.

Vince turned to leave but saw Mark slumped against the brick wall and went to check on him. It would be bad if he had killed him. He placed his fingers on Mark's neck and felt for a pulse. It was there, strong and slow. He was out cold but he would be fine. Vince was sure Mark would not remember most of the night considering how drunk he was.

CHAPTER 5

I was standing on the cliff, high above the town of San Sebastian where the old fort protected the town below. I was watching the waves crash into the base of the mountain far below me.

I felt someone take my hand and squeeze, drawn out of the trance the waves put me in. I looked over at the woman who had taken my hand.

"Mom?" I asked the woman whom I had never met, yet had known since the first time I dreamt of her when I was little.

"It is time," she said, squeezing my hand, and looking out at the ocean.

"Time for what?" I asked.

"Time to become what you were meant to be," she said, turning toward me, and smiling. "You will be tested and you must be strong. The road before you is not easy, but I know you will become a great queen," she said, placing her hand on the side of my rib cage and squeezing.

"Mom, what are you talking about?" I asked, taking her hand off my side and bringing her in for a hug. "I miss you so much," I said as tears fell down my cheeks.

"Be brave and strong," she said, hugging me close.

I started awake in my dark hotel room with my face wet with tears. I tried to roll over but I felt an arm around my waist pull me back. Confused I realized it was Mark, and he was snoring in my ear.

"Mark, roll over. You're snoring," I said, trying to get him to let me go. He didn't stir. I tried to pull his arm from around my waist only to have him pull me to him harder. Finally, I elbowed him in the chest and as he startled awake I jumped off the bed.

"What's wrong, honey?" he asked with a groggy, sleepy voice.

"Go back to sleep." I headed into the bathroom and closed the door. Now was not the time to have it out with him since he was likely still drunk and half asleep. It would accomplish nothing.

In the bathroom, I used the facilities and looked at my tear stained face in the mirror. I turned on the sink and waited for the water to warm up before splashing my face. I hadn't dreamed of my mother in years, and the dreams had never been as foreboding as that one had been. Yet, every time I dreamed of my mother, I would wake up crying. Which at times infuriated me since I had never met the woman.

My parents were killed on the way to the hospital to give birth to me. They ran a red light and were hit by a semi-truck. My father died instantly, while my mother held on until they had her on the operating table for an emergency C-section. From what I had been told, my mother died right after I took my first breath.

It wasn't fair that I dreamed about a woman I couldn't remember. Not that I had a bad time growing up. I had adoptive parents who loved me and raised me as if I was their own. The dreams made me realize I would never really know the people who had created me, and it hurt.

When I was eighteen my adoptive parents explained to me that my parents had left me with a trust fund and, an estate consisting of enough money for college. They also left me a storage unit with everything from their home. When I went through it, I fit everything worth anything to me in a small box. It included some jewelry, which, while not expensive, was very expressive of what my mother liked to wear. It also included photos of my parents, and a sketchbook of my mother's. The book contained the same drawing of a quail on every page. There were small changes here and there like she was trying to get it just right, but instead of erasing the small error she started over. It looked very old, almost ancient, before too much depth in drawing had been mastered. The quail was in mid-flight turned, with his head cocked allowing for the detail on the side of his head, wings, and back to be visible.

The first time I saw the drawing I fell in love with it. I searched high and low for the best tattoo artist in the Denver area, and on my twenty-first birthday I had it tattooed on my side wrapping around from the front to the back over my ribcage. My mother had been right. The quail in her drawings had never been quite right until I had it tattooed on my side. With the bird wrapping around my side it was finally perfect. Looking at it in the mirror, I wondered if the quail was why my mother had grabbed my side in the dream.

Done with the bathroom, I went to the closet, took the extra set of blankets and pillows from the top shelf and settled in on the floor. I wanted to be as far from Mark as I could get.

CHAPTER 6

Miguel arrived home and headed straight for his office where he closed the door and sat down at the computer. He needed to know more about this female. He typed her name into the standard search engine to start with and found almost nothing. She had a social media page but she did not share any of her information with the public. He was not going to get far there. He brought up his special search engine that dove more deeply than standard ones did and typed in her information.

After reading everything he could about her he pulled his cell phone out of his pocket and called his second in command.

"Master?" Vince asked when he answered the call. "What can I help you with?"

"The female you were hunting tonight. I need you to gather all the information about her for me that you can," Miguel said in a stern voice.

"You mean the one you were following?" Vince asked, pausing a beat. "You did not take her already?"

"No, not that it's your job to question me," Miguel said,

sounding more irritated with every word. "I do not answer to you. You answer to me last time I checked. Your response should be . . ."

"I will begin at once," Vince replied dryly. "Is there anything in particular you want me to report back on?"

"I want to know everything about her. There is nothing too minuscule I do not wish to know," Miguel said, turning around in his chair to look out over the pool and manicured lawns surrounding it.

"When would you like your report, Master?" Vince asked, trying to sound excited about following a female around during the day and learning something about her.

"Tomorrow at dusk should give you enough time I would think."

"Very well, Master. I will be at the villa shortly after sunset tomorrow," Vince said and ended the call.

Miguel spun his chair back to his desk and placed his phone on it. Vince would detest following the female around. He would feel it was beneath him, but Vince was the only vampire he could trust other than his sister at the moment. Since Lolita was not there he was going to have to trust Vince to gather the information he needed. He still had a kingdom to run, and having feelings for a human female would make him look weak and cause him to neglect his businesses.

CHAPTER 7

I awoke to the sound of Mark's snoring and rolled over on the bed. My eyes shot open realizing I had gone to sleep on the floor not the bed. Mark must have moved me back to the bed while I slept. Pissed that I was back in bed with Mark, I slid out of the bed and once again escaped to the bathroom.

I looked in the mirror and realized it was time to go. Time to leave Mark and head out on my own. The idea scared the crap out of me, but I needed to do it. After I packed my makeup bag, I went into the bedroom and packed up my meager belongings using the light from the bathroom to see.

After my bag was packed I opened the desk drawer and began writing a letter to Mark explaining that we were over. I heard him roll over and make a noise. I turned to look at him, he was awake.

"Hi," I said, turning my body toward the bed. At least I wouldn't have to write the letter now. "We need to talk."

"About what?" Mark asked, rubbing his eyes with one hand. "If it was about the girl last night. I told you she just grabbed me and started kissing me," he said, running his hand through his hair and wincing.

"How could it not be part of it? When we planned this trip we planned to see the sights of Europe. It feels like all we have done is see the inside of bars and hotel rooms. I thought we were going to experience the history and culture not an extended spring break. All I have done is babysit you," I blew out a frustrated breath. "I am done. I am heading out on my own and I would appreciate it if you just let us go so we can both move on with our lives."

"Wait, what?" Mark asked, sitting up in bed and grabbing his head. "Are you breaking up with me?"

"Yes," I said, knowing there was no easy way to put it. I stood up, picked up my backpack, put my arms through the armholes and buckled the chest and waist straps. "Take care of yourself Mark," I said and opened the door leading out of the room.

"Fuck off, bitch!" Mark said, throwing a pillow at the door. "If you only knew how many women I fucked while we were together. You're just a doormat. Good luck getting around Europe on your own."

I walked out the door, slammed it at his last remark, and tried not to cry. What had I seen in him to begin with? I couldn't think of one thing I liked about him anymore.

I walked down the hall, feeling like this whole situation was bitter sweet. Mark had, as far as I knew, always treated me kindly and until this trip had been a great partner. This trip had brought out his true personality, and I had to be happy I saw it before it would be harder to leave him.

When I entered the lobby, it dawned on me I had nowhere to go, and with the film festival going on finding another place to stay was going to be all but impossible. I hoped Antonio was still at work. He was a nice guy and I was sure he would be able to help me find another place or a train ticket out of town.

"Hola, Antonio," I said, walking up to the front desk.

"Hola, Señorita Hunter," he said, noticing my backpack. "Are you and your boyfriend checking out early?" He did not look very pleased.

"Well, I am. I have no idea what Mark is going to do." I lowered my eyes to the desk suddenly scared to be in a foreign land on my own. "I was hoping you would be able to help me find another place to stay or help me catch a train to Portugal."

"Let me see what I can do," Antonio said, turning to the bookshelf behind him and pulling out a binder. "Why don't you leave your bag here and go grab some breakfast. This will take a little time."

"Okay," I said, unbuckling my pack, shrugging it off my shoulders and pulling my daypack out from the top flap. I zipped it up, then secured my luggage lock. "Thank you so much Antonio. You'll keep this safe, right?" I asked, handing him my thirty-five-pound backpack. He winced as I released the straps into his hands.

"Do not worry, Chica, I will make sure no one touches it," he said, placing it in the room behind the front desk.

"Thank you so much, I'll be back in a few hours. And I'll take anything I can get," I said, turning and heading toward the front door.

I wandered down toward the plaza to find a café, eat some breakfast, and contemplate what I would do without Mark dictating my life. It was early and only the locals seemed to be out making deliveries and opening their shops for the day. The air was cool and smelled of what I had come to know as typical Europe smell, car exhaust, humidity, and fresh baked bread all with an undertone of garbage. I never realized how clean the air in Colorado was until I came to this continent. Maybe it was because civilization was so much older here, the smells permeated everything.

I walked around the plaza for a few minutes before finding a seat at a café that had just opened up. I ordered a café Americano and an omelet. I rarely sprang for expensive food, but I was going to need the energy today. Leaving Mark and striking out on my own with no plan of what to do next was going to require some major energy, especially if I had to sleep on a park bench.

I pulled out my smartphone and logged into my favorite travel website to see what I could find without Antonio's help. I stared at the blank search screen and thought about where we had planned to go. We were going to stay here through the weekend then head over to Portugal for the rest of the week before hitting the southern coast and working our way back up toward Switzerland.

When we set up this trip we had planned on not making any reservations so we could make our way was we pleased. We found out how difficult our idea proved to be in London. The Queen's Day Festival was going on and there was almost no place to stay. We ended up staying at one of the seedier hostels. We didn't even feel comfortable leaving our bags in our room while we went out during the day. We quickly decided we needed to set up at least a few reservations so we weren't stuck in something similar again. With that in mind, we planned our trip and split up the reservations.

I made the reservations for the hostel in Lisbon and we were due to arrive in four days. I had forty-eight hours to cancel the reservation to get my money back. Did I really want to go to Portugal?

We had agreed to skip Madrid; Mark wanted to see Portugal because some of his distant relatives had come from there to America.

The entire trip seemed too centered around where Mark wanted to go. I had made a dozen reservations and every time I used one of those reservations I would think of Mark. Time go where I want to go, I thought and canceled all of them.

With the cancelations done, I started looking for a place to stay tonight and plugged San Sebastian into the search screen. There was nothing. The grand finale of the film festival was going on over the weekend and there were no rooms, no matter how much money I had to spend. I tried to book a seat on a train but they also were booked. I was stranded with no place to go. Frustrated I paid my bill, hoping Antonio had been luckier than I had been, and headed back to the hotel.

CHAPTER 8

Miguel pulled away from his breakfast when he heard Juan knock on his bedroom door. "Stay where you are," he said to the naked woman lying across his bed. He did not think she would have the strength to move if she could, but no reason to take any chances.

Rising from the bed he pulled on his robe and loosely knotted the sash to hold it in place on his way to the door. "Yes, Juan?" he asked. He hated to have his meal interrupted.

"Antonio needs to speak with you," Juan said, holding a cordless phone out to Miguel. Miguel took the phone and closed the door in Juan's face.

"Antonio?" Miguel asked, thinking this had better be important.

"Sir, the girl, Katie, she is leaving her boyfriend and asked me to help her find another place to stay until Monday."

"Is that all you have to tell me? Just let me know where she ends up," Miguel said, wondering why he was always surrounded but incompetent humans.

"No, sir I'm not sure what to do," he said, hesitating.

"Everything in the city is booked. I can find nothing for her. I believe she will leave town if I cannot get something figured out."

"I am glad you called then," Miguel said, heading to the laptop computer he kept in the wardrobe. "I'll make sure she cannot leave town."

"Sir, do you want me to kick one of our guests out so she can have a room here?"

"No, she needs to get away from her boyfriend. Check the campground. They rarely sell out," he said, clicking buttons on the computer to tie up all of the trains and buses scheduled to leave the city for the next forty-eight hours. He would have to pay a fine for doing it but it would be worth it. "In the meantime, I'll get the dungeon ready for her, but it will take at least a day."

"Yes, sir," Antonio said, sounding relieved he had done the right thing in calling his master.

"I want you to help her today, Antonio. Help her get settled in, and keep an eye on her," Miguel said, thinking back to the way Vince had taken a liking to her. "Make sure all of my kind stay away."

"Thank you, sir," Antonio said. "Oh, I went through her backpack since she left it with me while she went to eat."

"Email me a list of what she has in there please. I need to finish my breakfast and make arrangements for the dungeon to be readied." -

Miguel hung up the phone. This was going to work perfectly, he thought. If she stayed in the dungeon he would have no excuse not to entertain her. He shook his head, why was he going out of his way to help this human? If he wanted her he should just take her. What was holding him back? Why was she so special?

Looking back to the bed he saw his breakfast waiting for him. How could he pass her up?

CHAPTER 9

The streets had begun to fill with tourists on their way to the beach, the parks, or a film. They weren't clogged but there were lots of people and I couldn't shake the feeling of being followed. I glanced around nonchalantly as often as I could without seeming suspicious, but I couldn't figure out who was following me.

Last night I was hearing voices and now I feel like I'm being followed. I needed to get a grip. There was no reason to be paranoid about traveling on my own.

When I reached the hotel, I looked through the glass doors into the lobby and front desk area to make sure there was no sign of Mark before I headed inside to see Antonio. The lobby was busy with tourists looking at maps, reading brochures on local attractions, and talking on their cell phones. The concierge desk was three people deep. I went to the front desk and asked if Antonio was still at work.

The woman behind the desk smiled and asked me to wait a moment. She turned and went into the backroom. A few minutes later Antonio came out from the room with a worried expression on his face.

"Chica, I have found a few options for you." Taking my hand, he led me to a table with two chairs and invited me to sit.

"Thank God," I said, sitting in the chair, and taking my hands back from him.

"There is nothing here in San Sebastian, but there are lots of rooms in a town about forty-five minutes away by taxi. It's inland so it will be hot, but it's very inexpensive," he said, trying to make it sound like a fun place.

"Is there anything to do there?" I asked, not liking this idea.

"Of course, many of the hotels have pools, and there is a large shopping center. I believe you call them *malls* in America."

"Is that it? Is that my only option?" I was not looking forward to a crappy little town with a crappy little pool and shopping. I didn't have room in my bag for anything except the essentials.

"Well, there is one other option, but I do not know if you are up for this kind of thing," he said, pulling a flier out of his jacket pocket, and handing it to me.

I looked at it. I couldn't read the text since it was in Spanish, but I got the idea. "Camping? Where is the campground? I don't have a tent. Do they have cabins?"

"I know it's not the best but, it's a five-minute walk to the beach and the main plaza. They don't have any cabins, but I can take you to a store to buy a tent. It's the only place I could find for you, Chica. I am sorry," he explained, and it looked like he wanted to grab my hands again.

"Ok, let me think for a minute," I said, getting up and walking slowly from one end of the lobby to another. Camping, I enjoyed camping, but would I enjoy living out of a tent? Could I make room in my pack for a tent? It may not be a bad thing to have on this trip. Who knows when it might be my only option for a roof over my head?

I walked back to Antonio and sat back down. "Does the campground have running water?"

"Yes, it is a very nice campground."

"And you wouldn't mind helping me buy a tent? Isn't it way outside of your job description?" I asked, wondering why he was doing this.

"Of course, but I have been off the clock since ten this morning I was just waiting for you to come back. Mark is dog shit. Please excuse my language, but I want to help you."

I didn't know if I could trust this guy or not, but I had pepper spray and a multi-tool with a large knife in my daypack. What other choice did I have but to trust him? "Ok, thank you so much, Antonio. Let me get my backpack and we can go."

"I'll go get it. You wait here." Antonio turned and went back through the door behind the front desk.

While I waited I opened my daypack, fished to the bottom of it, found my can of pepper spray and my multi-tool. Then I put them in the pocket of my jean shorts.

Antonio returned with my backpack and motioned toward the back of the hotel. "My car is parked in the back," he said, taking a step in toward the back of the hotel.

"Here we go," I said, mostly to myself and got up to follow him to the back lot.

Antonio drove an older Peugeot hatchback that my backpack barely fit into but it was better than walking. I got into the passenger side while he held the door for me and slammed it closed. As he walked around to the driver side, feeling paranoid I tried to open it from the inside and it did not budge. He opened his door and saw me struggling with the door.

"I am sorry the door was bent a few years ago in an unfortunate gas station incident by my brother. I can only open it from the outside now," he said, putting his seatbelt on.

I followed suit, attaching my seatbelt and rolling the window down. The warm day had already made the inside of the car too warm, or maybe, it was my growing anxiety over this outing with a man I barely knew. The window stuck for a moment but when I put some more brawn behind the lever it opened. Worst case scenario I could crawl out the window if Antonio ended up being a serial killer.

"The sporting goods store is only fifteen minutes from here. Once we get you a tent I'll give you a ride to the camp ground. It's at the base of Mount Urgull," he said, smiling and not taking his eyes off the road.

"Hum, okay let's just start with finding a tent," I said, trying to pay attention to where we were going in case something happened and I had to find my way back on my own.

A few minutes later, Antonio pulled into a shopping center. It looked like any strip mall in America except the signs were in Spanish instead of English.

"Here we are," he said, parking in a space close to the front doors of what looked like a sporting goods store. He got out, shut his door, and came around to try and open my door. After a few minutes of pulling on his side and pushing on my side, the door finally opened. We made sure to lock the doors since all of my possessions were in the back of the car and walked into the store.

Antonio was a great help translating between me and the salesman. I settled on a small lightweight three-person tent. From the sporting goods store we began to make our way toward the campground and Antonio seemed to grow more nervous with every mile.

"Hey, what's going on, Antonio?" I asked, since he was starting to make me nervous too.

"Oh, nothing, Chica. I have a lot to do today is all," he said, giving me a sideways glance before concentrating on the road again. "Most of my family is in town for the film festival and they are all staying at my apartment. They are waiting for me to get home so I can spend some time with them," he said, looking over at me.

"Jeez, Antonio, I'm sorry. Why didn't you tell me you have things to do?" I asked, feeling guilty for taking up so much of his time.

"It is no problem. I'm glad I was able to help you find a place to stay, but I feel like I am leaving you on your own when you need more help."

"What do you mean? I'm not afraid of staying in a tent. I've been camping many times."

"It's not that. There are some in the city who would take advantage of a single women traveling on her own is all," he said, clearing his throat, and wiping the sweat off his forehead.

I stared at him and tried to figure out what he was saying. "Are you one of those people, Antonio?" I asked, gripping my daypack, and looking for a safe place to jump out the window.

"No, I just ask that you be careful while you are here," he said, slowing the car and turning into a driveway with a sign that said *El Campamento de Mount Urgull.*

I looked out the window of the car and saw lots of campers and a few tents scattered on the side of the mountain. It was green and clean. I could see small buildings scattered around that I guessed were bathrooms, and a large building in the middle, was the main office.

Antonio stopped the car and quickly got out to work on the passenger door until it opened. I got out as he went to the rear of the car and opened the hatch. Following him I pulled out my backpack, put it on and grabbed the tent box. "Hey, if you need to get back to your family, please go I can handle everything from here."

He looked at his watch then at the doors leading into the main office. "No the owners do not speak very much English. Let me help you get your spot then I will leave you," he said, heading up to the door and opening it for me.

I watched as Antonio negotiated with the owners for what hopefully would be the nicest tent spot on the grounds. When they were done, I gave them my credit card and paid for three nights up front with the disclaimer that if I found another place to stay they would refund my money.

With a map of the campground in my hand, Antonio and I walked out of the main building and towards his car. "Thank you so much for your help today Antonio. I don't know what I would have done without you," I said, sticking my hand out to shake his hand.

"It was my pleasure," he said, taking my hand. "I am sorry I have to leave you to set up camp on your own," he said, pulling a card from his back pocket. "I really have to get home to see my family. Here is my phone number though. If you need anything, please call me," he said and turned toward his car.

"I will. Thank you again," I said as he got in and started up the engine. I watched him pull out of his parking space, honk the horn, and head down the road

I turned and walked along the path toward my tent space. It really was a nice campground. There was a lot of room between each individual space, and it was cleaner and in better repair than most of the commercial campgrounds I had visited with my family. I found my space, took my pack off, and looked around. It was right at the edge of the hill and it opened to a steep side of the mountain overlooking the Bay of Biscay. It was quite the view. I turned and noticed my neighbors were a good twenty-five yards away, and the bathhouse was only about twenty past them. This wouldn't be so bad.

I set to work setting up my new tent which was much easier than I thought it would be. There were only three poles including the rain fly. When the tent was set up, I unpacked and organized my very small living space.

When I was done, I looked at my watch. It was well past lunchtime as my belly had been trying to tell me for quite some time. I pulled my traveling lunch out: an apple and some hard cheese. After lunch I thought about what I really wanted to see in San Sebastian. I looked up at Mount Urgull. I wanted to hike up to the remains of the fort but it was a long hike and I wanted to spend more than a few minutes there. I looked down to the beach and at Santa Clara Island, my decision was made.

CHAPTER 10

Vince was mad, he had lost her when she and Antonio had taken off in his car. He wondered where they were going and if Miguel had anything to do with it.

Vince turned Antonio into his slave years before only because of the way Miguel was treating the poor boy. Of course Miguel had no idea that Antonio was no longer his since Vince gave him instructions to do everything Miguel told him and report it to Vince.

The system had worked well, the text message he received that morning from Antonio made him worry for the human though. Why was Miguel so enamored with her? He was never one to keep a mistress, especially since he had not tasted her yet.

Vince was glad Miguel had given him this assignment because he thought there was something more to this girl than her ice-blue eyes and curvy figure. He wanted to find out what it was before Miguel could sink his fangs into her.

Vince was loyal to Miguel, had sworn fidelity to him when he first came to the city over a hundred years ago. Most of the time being his second was a good place to be, but it felt like things were changing. He wanted to make sure he was on the right side of the change; he needed to look out for himself before anyone else.

He was standing on the top floor of one of Miguel's buildings. It had been fitted with UV protected glass so he could safely look out across the beach. It was too late in the day for the human to do anything else. It was crowded with people and he searched for more than an hour thinking she had to be down there somewhere. He was missing her somehow.

He was about to turn away when he found her walking toward the point where swimmers begin their swim across the channel to the island. Was she going to swim the whole way? He hoped she was a strong swimmer. He watched her take off her shirt, shorts, and sandals before stuffing them into a bag. She was tanned, but not overly so. He watched her turn reach her arms over her head and he saw it. He was not sure what it was, he was too far away to get a good look, but something inside told him he needed to get a closer look before anyone else saw it.

He watched for a few more minutes to make sure she was indeed swimming across the channel to the island. Once he was sure, he moved quickly down the stairs and into the basement. He wondered how long it had been since anyone used the tunnel that went under the channel to the island, it had probably been decades. He hoped it was still open.

It was, and he raced to beat her there. There was not much on the island, but he had set up a safe place to watch the beach years ago. He was happy to find it was still in good shape. She was just coming out of the water when he settled himself down to watch her.

CHAPTER 11

It was an easy swim, I thought as I walked up the beach smiling at the people who had been my temporary companions. There were a lot less people here than there were on the mainland beach. I found a clear spot a little away from the other beach goers and lay out on the sand to dry out and catch my breath.

I was dozing off when I heard it. *Eres mucha bella*, it was the whisper from behind me. I sat up, turned, and looked around. No one was near enough to whisper in my ear.

Escucha me? The voice asked no longer in a whisper and I realized he was not talking, he was thinking to me.

Yes, I thought back, still looking around. The closest person to me had to be at least ten yards away and looked asleep lying on his stomach. There was no way he was trying to speak to me. *Where are you?* I thought trying to project my thoughts to whoever was in my head, or at least tried to.

"Where are you?" I asked aloud this time.

Not far, the voice said switching to English. Thank God. There was only so much Spanish I could understand.

Feeling like a complete idiot for talking to myself I pulled my phone out of my waterproof pack and pretended to talk to someone on the other end instead of someone in my head. "Who are you? Why can I hear you in my head?" I asked into the phone.

You can call me Vince, and I have no idea why you can hear me in your head, he thought sounding both concerned and excited at the same time. *Am I the first person you have heard in your head?*

"Yes," I said quickly but then I remembered the voice in the bar the night before. "Wait, I'm not sure. I heard a different voice last night in the bar, but it could have been a real voice not one in my head. Do you know what I mean? And then out on the street last night. Was it you?" I asked, rambling.

You heard me last night as well? What did I say?

"Good evening," I said.

Yes, it was me, he thought sounding pleased I heard him. *But I do not know who you are talking about in the bar.*

What in the hell was going on? Was I dreaming? Was I losing my mind? There had to be some explanation for this. Why was I hearing voices? "Can you show yourself to me?" I asked, hoping that seeing him face to face would help me believe what was happening.

Not at the present time, he thought sounding annoyed.

"Can I come to you?" I knew asking was risky but I needed to know what was happening.

Unfortunately, no but I would like to meet with you soon.

"Okay, when?"

Perhaps later tonight, but it will depend on my schedule.

Where are you staying?

"At the campground at the base of the mountain," I said, not believing I was telling this man, well voice, where he could find me.

If I can, I will come to you, he paused as if thinking hard about something. *Is that a tattoo on your side or a birthmark?*

I looked down at the bird on my side. "A tattoo. Why do you ask?"

It reminds of something very important, but I am not sure if I am remembering it correctly or not. I will explain more later if I can.

"That's all you can tell me now?" I asked, thinking this guy was nuts.

Let me confirm my thinking then I will tell you all I can. I could tell he wanted to tell me more but something was stopping him.

"Okay, well I am going to take off then. I think I'd better get to a hospital and see what is wrong with me," I said, putting my phone back into my waterproof pouch and heading towards the water.

You are not insane. I promise. I will prove it to you as soon as I can, he thought, starting to sound far away as I moved into the water. *Please be careful. There are those who would try and take advantage of your gift,* he thought as I dove into the water and out of range.

During the swim back to the mainland, I thought about what Vince said. Antonio had said something similar to me earlier in the day, but he had no way of knowing about this gift. I wasn't convinced it was a gift but some psychotic problem.

How could I explain that I had gone twenty-three years and never heard a voice in my head other than my own? This was big. I needed someone to talk to about it, but Mark was out, and it was the middle of the night back home. Besides the last thing my parents or my friends needed was me waking them up in the middle of the night, and going on about how I could suddenly hear voices in my head.

I came to the shore of the mainland and lay on the wet beach for a few minutes catching my breath and clearing my head. I didn't have any answers for the questions that were pouring into my mind but I thought Vince might. I hoped he would visit me tonight.

I put my shorts and t-shirt back on and walked along the shore towards the campground when a familiar face ducked behind a beach umbrella. I moved quickly backward to get a look at the man who looked like Antonio.

"Antonio?" I called out to his back as he made his way to the stairs leading up to the street.

He turned around looking defeated and walked down to me. "Are you here with your family?" I asked and it dawned on me. He didn't really want to talk to me. I was work for him, not a friend.

"Hum . . ." He trailed off, looking down at the sand.

"You know what, never mind, it's none of my business," I said, continuing down the shoreline. "Thanks again for your help today I'll never forget it."

"Wait, Katie, did you swim out to the island?" he asked, catching up with me and matching my stride.

"Yes, why?" I asked, trying to sound excited and not terrified about what had happened on the island.

"It's dangerous. You should not have gone on your own."

"Thanks, but I was hardly alone there were a lot of people going back and forth the whole time. I'm a strong swimmer."

"I know but there are other things that may hurt you on the island. Promise me that you will not go back out there," he said, stopping and placing his hand on my shoulder.

"I'm a big girl, Antonio," I said but the look in his eyes made me want to believe him. "But now that I have been there I can't think of a reason to go back. Besides there are tons of other sights I want to see while I'm here," I said, giving into his puppy dog eyes.

"Good. I have to get back. I'll see you later alright?"

"Have a good evening," I said as he turned and walked toward town.

As I made my way back to the campground, I began to plan. I needed to come up with a new itinerary for my trip. I never really cared where I went, I just wanted to see the world and everything in it. It had been easy for me to acquiesce to what Mark wanted to do because I wanted to see it all. Now that I was on my own, I was going to have to figure out what I wanted to see. I needed to let everyone back home know that Mark and I had broken up. My parents were going to try and make me come home. They didn't think I would be able to survive this trip without a man to take care of me. If they only knew I was the one who had been taking care of Mark this whole time. I was my own person and now was the time to figure out who that was.

Tomorrow, I thought, I would plan my new trip and go up to the fort. Maybe I would just camp while I was here. My spot was great after all.

I stopped at a grocery store and picked up some chips, some hamburgers and a six pack of the local beer. There was a communal grill at the campground and I could use some real American food for a change. After taking a shower and eating my dinner I sat at the picnic table that was part of my camp space. I drank my beer and tried to draw the sun setting on the ocean. I wasn't an artist but I enjoyed trying to draw. I took a few photos too, so I could look back and see what I had tried to draw. Before the last rays of light faded to black, I made a small campfire with the wood provided by the campground and stared into the flames for a long time.

CHAPTER 12

"Thank you for the update, Antonio, you did well today," Miguel said into his phone as a knock sounded on the door.

"Yes, I will need you to go and see her tomorrow to see if she wants to stay in the dungeon, I mean cottage, it should be ready by late morning," he said, happy that his crew was able to take the boards off the windows, and get rid of the donors inside so quickly. The new furniture and linens would arrive in the morning and he would be sending Juan out to stock the pantry as soon as the markets opened. "I will call you when everything is ready," he said, then ended the call. "Come," he said to whoever was waiting on the other side of the door.

Juan opened the door and allowed Vince to enter the room. He walked to the front of the desk and genuflected. "Master."

"Vince, good to see you. Rise," Miguel said unable to keep the grin from his lips. He was excited about Katie. "What can I do for you?"

"My report on the human," Vince said, surprised Miguel had not already gotten to the point.

"Yes, yes," Miguel said, standing, and going over to look out the window where he could see the outline of the cottage.

"It appears she left the man she was traveling with. Antonio took her somewhere in his car today and I lost them for a few hours. I caught up with her on Santa Clara Island, she swam out and back. It does not appear she knows anyone else in town. She is staying at the campground now," Vince said, trying to avoid any personal observations.

"What did you think of her?" Miguel asked, turning, and looking at Vince.

"She smells good," Vince said, trying to think of mundane things to say about her. "She is athletic, and daring. Easy on the eyes but not model material."

"Vince, you need to get laid once in a while. Did you notice anything else that stood out?"

"Not really, she seemed depressed but that is a given I would think since she left her boyfriend, and she is all alone in the middle of Europe," Vince said, walking over to the copy of the tapestry hanging on the wall.

He carefully looked at the quail portrayed there. It was an exact copy of what Katie had tattooed on her side. But a tattoo? The prophecy said marked, not tattooed. She could hear his thoughts though and it had to mean something. Schooling his features, he turned to Miguel.

"Did you talk to Lolita about the rumors on the Ivory Coast?" Vince asked, trying to move his thoughts away from Katie. He did not want Miguel to know what he suspected.

"Yes, they were rumors. According to Lolita a slave said they saw it in an attempt to get her master to change her," Miguel said blandly.

"Well that is good, you are in the right location after all."

"I believe so, but my patience is waning. I hope it comes true soon," Miguel said, his voice drifting away as he envisioned his future with his sister and his queen at his side.

"Is there anything else, Master?" Vince asked, trying to pull him back into the conversation.

"Yes, I am going to be having company beginning tomorrow," Miguel said with his business voice. "I expect you and everyone else to be on their best behavior. Can you please spread the word around?"

"Yes, Master." Vince turned, and walked to the door.

CHAPTER 13

I wasn't paying attention to my surroundings as I watched the campfire. I don't even remember what I was thinking about. I was staring into the flames and the next thing I knew there was a man standing on the other side of the fire. I jumped to my feet with a start.

"What do you want?" I asked, balling my hands into fists. I could scream, there were lots of other campfires going around me. Someone would hear me and come to help. The man said nothing, he stood there with his arms at his side and stared at me.

Hola, I am Vince, he finally thought to me.

I relaxed a fraction and took in one of the men who invaded my thoughts. He was tall at least six feet five, his hair was long, hanging loose around his shoulders. I couldn't quite make out its true color by the light of the fire but I thought it must be a shade of brown. His face was oval with a sharp nose and large eyes. He was big, he had a long sleeve shirt on but there was nothing but muscle under it. His chest tapered down to the perfect V. His skin was a light bronze color like he spent most of his time in the sun.

"I'm Katie," I said, realizing I had been staring at him too long. Not sure what else to do I sat back down on the edge of the picnic table bench. "Would you like a beer? I have a few left that are kind of cold."

"No, thank you," he said with a laugh. "Are you satisfied that you are not going insane now?" he asked, walking over to my side of the fire.

"Not really, maybe this is a dream," I said, thinking this man was a god. I wiped my hand over my chin just to make sure I wasn't drooling.

"I am real," he said, taking a seat next to me and looking into the fire. "My question is, are you?"

"Is that a pick up line?" I asked not sure if it was how he meant it.

"No, not at all," he said, stretching his legs out in front of him and clasping his hands together in his lap. *Will you tell me about the tattoo on your side?*

My brows drew together, why was he changing the subject? "Why?"

"I believe it is a powerful symbol."

"A powerful symbol? I found it in my mother's sketchbook. I had it tattooed because I thought it would make me feel closer to her," I said, then added. "How did you see it on the island?"

"I have my ways. You should not show it off, it might bring you trouble."

"How would a tattoo bring me trouble?" I asked, self-consciously tracing the outline with my hand through my shirt.

"A long time ago a prophecy was made by an oracle on a Greek island. It refers to a mark that matches your tattoo. The woman with the mark would be 'The One'," he said, putting emphasis on the last two words.

"It's just a tattoo a guy in Denver did. I doubt there's any magic in it," I said, laughing at Vince. "Why would I of all people be 'The One'? There's nothing special about me."

"I thought at first that there was some mistake since you had it tattooed on, but you can hear us in your mind. Your ability is part of the prophecy." He got up and stood near the fire.

"What else does the prophecy say?" I asked, starting to worry.

"There is not enough time to get into it now. I cannot be seen talking to you and he knows where you are staying. He may come to check on you."

"Who is going to come and check on me?" I asked, starting to worry. "You can't just stop by my camp to tell me I'm 'The One,' that someone may be watching me and leave. Give me something please," I said, floundering. I don't know why I trusted him but I did. Something told me I needed his help to stay safe.

"I do not want to leave you on your own but he would find out if I moved you. I will try and come up with a plan to keep you safe. I do not trust him," he said mostly to himself I think.

"Who should I not trust?" I asked.

"What?" he said, looking at me like he forgot I was there. "I am rambling. Make sure you do not let anyone else see your tattoo. Can you do that?"

"If it will keep me safe until I leave this city, yes," I said, making sure my shirt was pulled down, but I wasn't sure why. This guy had me thoroughly freaked out.

"I need you to do one more thing," he said, turning, and

crouching down so we were eye to eye.

"What?"

"Do not tell anyone that we have met. I am going to try to help you but if they find out we have met I will be forced to leave, and likely without you," he said, leveling a stare on me showing me he was dead serious.

"I think I can manage that." It wasn't an unreasonable request; it wasn't like he was asking me to smuggle drugs for him.

"I must go," he said, pulling a card out of his back pocket.

"Save this number in your phone then burn the card," he said, handing it to me.

"Alright," I said, looking at it. All it had was a phone number. No name or address.

"I will be in touch when I have a plan," he said, bowing to me, and leaving.

I tried to remain calm and enjoy sitting by the fire but Vince had freaked me out. I saved his number in my phone and burn the card but, every pop of the fire or rustle of grass had me jumping. I finally gave up. I put the fire out, locked myself in my tent and willed myself to sleep.

I looked around from atop the fort watching the town below me burning. Flames sprouted up from the buildings far below. I heard an explosion and watched the cathedral splinter then fall to ruin. Gasping I turned away and looked at the fort.

"Mom?" I asked, hoping this would be like the dream I had the night before. I waited but there was no answer. I was alone, and I knew the destruction going on below was my fault.

"Why would your mother be here?" A women's voice asked from beyond the smoky dark night.

"Who're you?" I asked, looking into the darkness trying to find the woman who was speaking to me.

"Your new master," she said with a laugh. She stepped out of the smoke and darkness as it seemed swirl around her.

She was short, had a slight figure with barely a hint of curves at her breasts and bottom. Her hair was white, long and flowed over her shoulders. She looked like she was wearing a toga with a gold belt around her waist.

"Why would I call you master?"

"You did this to my city. Now you will be my slave or you will cease to be," she said, coming at me with a knife in her hand.

"How could I have done all this from up here on the mountain?" I asked, stepping to the side as she ran toward me with her arm cocked back, ready to stab me.

"You made my brother crazy, and now you have to pay," she said, turning quickly, and coming back at me.

I tried to sidestep again but she tripped me and I fell to my knees. She pushed me down onto my back and straddled me. I grabbed her arms and pushed with all my might to keep the knife from coming down on my throat. I had no idea what this woman was talking about; I didn't know her brother. I just wanted to live. *Mom*, I called out mentally into the night as my strength gave out and I watched in slow motion as the knife came down towards me. Before it reached me, a bright white light flashed before my eyes and I was again standing on the edge of the cliff with my mother holding my hand.

"Mom, what was that?" I asked, without looking at her but

squeezing her hand.

"A dream," she said, squeezing my hand back. "A dream of what may come."

"How can I stop it?" My eyes began to burn with unshed tears.

"Like I said before, be strong and brave. You must look beyond what is on the surface and into the depths to find the truth and honesty you will need to survive."

"I love you mom," I said, not really understanding what she was saying.

"I will always love you Katie. Remember what I have said," she said and disappeared.

I wiped the tears from my eyes and looked around again. "Mom?" I called. "Why do you always leave when I have more questions than answers?" I called out to the deserted fort.

Katie, you must wake up, a voice said in my mind.

"Who's there?" I asked, looking around the fort.

Katie, wake up, the voice said again.

I jolted awake forgetting where I was for a moment. It was dark and I could hear the thumps of rain falling on the tent. That's right, I thought to myself, I'm camping in San Sebastian. I sat up and looked at my watch pushing the button for the light. Three in the morning. I lay back down and pulled my fleece blanket over me.

I am glad you are awake, Vince thought. *It sounded like you were having a nightmare.*

"I wouldn't call it a nightmare but it was not full of rainbows and unicorns," I said, staring at the ceiling of my tent. "Are you standing out in the rain Vince?"

No I am sheltered from the rain, he said chuckling. *Tell me about your nightmare.*

"The city was burning, and it was my fault. There was a woman there and she tried to kill me. Then my mom showed up and we talked," I said, feeling vulnerable sharing my dream with him.

Why was the city burning your fault?

"The woman who tried to kill me said so." I closed my eyes trying to remember every detail of the dream.

Do you remember what she looked like?

"Yes, I'll never forget her," I said, closing my eyes, and remembering. "She was short and thin like a bean stock. She was pale. Her skin looked hardened like ivory or marble. She had white long, almost glowing hair." Vince was quiet for so long I thought he had left. "Vince?"

I am still here. Just thinking over what you have told me of your dream. Do you have dreams like this often?

"No, never this dark. I've never had dreams where people are trying to kill me before. When I was little I would dream of my mom, but it's been years since I dreamed of her. Do you know what it means?" I asked, not really expecting an answer but giving it a shot anyway.

No, I am sorry, he thought to me. *I would not dismiss it though. If you are 'The One' there is a good chance they are foretelling of the future.*

"Just what I want to hear," I said, pulling the blanket over my head. How was it going to be my fault the city burns? "What are you doing out there in the rain anyway? I thought you were afraid to be seen with me."

I am, but watching from a distance should be okay. He thought sounding nervous. *Is your tent dry? It is really coming down out here.*

"Yes, I'm dry for the most part," I said, feeling the floor of the tent. "No leaks, thank God."

Good, go back to sleep, Vince thought and I could feel him moving away. *I will be in touch with you soon.*

"I'll try," I said, shaking off a sudden chill. "Thanks for checking on me."

Anything for you, he thought moving further and further away. Then he was gone.

How had I done that? I wondered, I had never *felt* anyone leave before. These changes were really starting to scare me. What would be next? Shooting laser beams from my eyes? Maybe that's how the city catches fire.

CHAPTER 14

I went back to sleep and woke up to the rain still coming down on the tent. It was a nice sound until I thought about my bathroom needs and making my way to the bathroom in the campground would mean getting wet even with my umbrella.

After using the facilities, I returned to the tent wet and cold only to sit there and listen to the rain, now coming down in sheets. I decided while camping could be fun, it had its drawbacks. My tent was too small for me to stand up in, and there was nothing to look at since the rain was coming from the same direction as the door. A hike up to the fort was out of the question. I pulled out my phone and caught up on some emails. I changed my relationship status to single on my social media, and posted that Mark and I were over. It was too early to call anyone and my battery was dying. Another drawback of camping. I picked up my book and tried not to let the rain get to me.

"Hello, Katie?" A muffled male voice asked, shaking my tent. "Are you here?"

"Antonio?" I asked, moving over to the zipper in the door and pulling it down to look outside.

"Yes," he said, smiling from under an umbrella. "How are you enjoying our lovely weather today?"

"Well, it could be better," I said, pulling out my umbrella and stepping out of the tent.

"I have some wonderful news for you then," he said, turning, and looking out at the cove. "A rental cottage has become available. The people who were going to rent it had to cancel their plans."

"It sounds kind of expensive," I said, thinking about funding this trip all on my own. "I'm on a very tight budget."

"I have spoken to the owner and he would rather have it occupied, even if it is for very little then have it sit empty this weekend. It's a little bit out of town but it was stocked with everything you should need before they canceled, so you will not have to worry about food."

This seemed perfect, but it also sounded like the beginning of a horror movie. I looked at the sky, the weather report said the rain was not going to let up until the next day. I looked at my tent, it was completely wet, thankfully only on the outside, and I crumbled. "Well it won't hurt to at least look at it," I said, beginning to formulate a plan of how I was going to do this. "I can take a cab to look at it. If it will work I can come back and pack all of my stuff up and take a cab back out to the cottage," I said, more to myself than to Antonio.

"Katie, I do not have to be at work until late this afternoon. I can take you out there."

"Oh, thanks Antonio, but I'm sure you have a lot going on with your family in town and everything. I can just take a cab," I said, thinking Antonio was being too helpful about this whole thing. "What's in it for you?"

"Right now they are all crammed in my apartment because of the rain. Believe me I would rather be anywhere then in my one-bedroom, one-bathroom apartment with ten members of my family," he said, grimacing at the thought. "Any excuse to stay away makes it worth it. Even if I am having an overly long conversation in the rain."

"Okay, fine," I said, chuckling to myself. "Let me just grab my daypack and we can go," I said, heading back into the dank, dark tent. For some reason I still didn't trust Antonio completely, but a warm dry cottage sounded better than a tent.

The drive to the rental house was quiet except for the rain beating on the roof and the constant *whap whap* of the windshield wipers. The property was not far from old town but it wasn't walking distance either. I was glad I had already seen most of the major attractions. Cabbing it back forth was going to be expensive.

"It is a little far out from the tourist district, but I think you will love the cottage," Antonio said as if he was reading my mind. "We are almost there." He turned in front of a large black rock wall and an impressive black iron gate. There was a call box with a video screen like a bank drive-through.

"Who owns this place?" I asked, looking beyond the gate at the expertly groomed lawn and trees. I shook with a sudden chill; I didn't know where it came from but it wasn't from the cold. It felt like someone was watching me, I couldn't see anyone but a presence was definitely there. Maybe it was Vince.

"A very old family who has been in residence for longer than most people know. They are known as the patrons of San Sebastian," he said, before pushing the button on the call box.

"Why are they renting out their cottage if they are so

established? It doesn't look like they need the money."

Antonio turned and looked at me for a moment, trying to find the right words. He opened his mouth to speak when a voice from the call box said, "Bueno?"

He turned back to the call box and began to speak in rapid Spanish that I couldn't follow. After a few back and forths, the gate opened and Antonio put the car into first gear to move through it.

"When there is a big festival in town they open up their cottage for people to rent," he said, answering my question while being careful not to hit the gate. "They normally donate the money they bring in from the rentals for community projects."

"Okay," I said, thinking this seemed very odd. Something about this whole situation was not sitting well with me. I looked out the window as we drove down the cobblestone driveway. The grass was green and trimmed and large mature trees dotted the property. We passed by the main house but house was the wrong word. A classic Spanish villa was more appropriate. It was two stories and the stucco walls were covered in ivy and other flowering creepers. We veered away from the house and I turned to see a small one-story cottage standing about two hundred yards from the villa. "Is that it?"

"That is it," Antonio, said grinning in my direction. "What do you think?"

"It's amazing from the outside," I said, admiring the tiled roof and small windows divided by square panes. We pulled around to the front door that was made of a heavy, hardwood. Antonio stopped the car and came over to let me out since the door handle was still broken. He led me up to the door, opened it and we walked inside.

It was cozy. There was a small living area open to a basic

kitchen, with only a refrigerator, microwave, and a cooktop. The living room had two overstuffed loveseats in a tan color sitting at ninety degrees to each other with a glass coffee table in between. Both sofas faced a window with different views.

"Wow, this is perfect," I said, turning in a circle, and noticing a short hallway. Down it I found a door on the left leading to a linen closet stocked with towels, blankets, pillows and the like. I closed the door and proceeded to the door at the end of the hall. I opened it to find a bedroom. There was a queen size bed with a white iron frame covered in a white and puffy down comforter and pillows. On the other side of the room, there was a lightly stained dresser and two doors. There was a large picture window with a view of the ocean; the sunsets from in here would be amazing. I walked across the room to the doors. One was a smallish walk in closet. The other lead to a small, European bathroom, with a pedestal sink, a small mirror with a shelf, a stacked washer and dryer, a half bathtub, and a handheld shower wand.

I slowly walked down the hall back to the living room looking at the artwork on the walls. This place was too good to be true. I was sure the nightly rate was going to be way out of my price range.

"This is a great little cottage," I said, joining Antonio at the table. "How much are they charging for rent?"

"How long are you going to stay?" he asked, looking back at a piece of paper.

"I was able to get reservations to go to Madrid the day after tomorrow. So I would need this for two nights."

"According to this note left by the owner, he is willing to let you rent this for twenty-five euros a night."

"You're kidding." I said, disbelieving the low price. "Why

would he want to rent it out for so little?" I asked, unable to help smiling and walking over to the kitchen window. Something was not sitting well with me. I was still being watched. It didn't feel malevolent but it did not feel friendly either. This had to be safer than the tent though. I could actually lock the doors here not just put a crappy padlock on the zipper that wouldn't keep the honest thieves out. Was being dry and warm worth the feeling of being watched?

The past two days of my life had me wishing to be home, somewhere comfortable and away from the voices, and the people who I had been forced to interact with. Maybe being out of the city would give me the peace I needed to get a grip on everything going on.

The rain was still coming down and visibility was not the greatest, but I had a feeling that on a clear day I would be able to see the ocean. This would be much better than a tent, especially given the weather. "I'll take it," I said, decision made and going over to my pack and pulling my wallet out. "Do I pay you or who?"

"I'm not sure. Let me call up to the villa and find out," Antonio said, pulling out his phone.

I wandered over to the kitchen to see what kind of food was on hand and to see if there was anything else I would need for the next few days. The fridge contained milk, eggs, cheese, salami, and juice. In the cabinets, there was bread, butter, and some canned food. There was a wine rack with a few bottles of red and white.

"Okay, Katie you can pay me the money and I will give it to the caretaker. Do you want to go and get the rest of your luggage now?" Antonio asked, looking toward the door.

"That sounds like a plan," I said, taking a fifty-euro note from my wallet and handing it to him.

After a dash to the car through the rain we headed back to town. As soon as we left the gates behind us it felt like the presence who had been with me since we had entered left and I gave myself a shake.

"Are you okay?" Antonio asked.

"Just a chill," I said, turning, and looking out the window.

"Let me turn the heat on." Antonio reached over, and adjusted the knobs for the heat settings. "The heater is one of the few things that work in this car."

"Thanks," I said, rubbing my arms, and looking out the window. "If you want I can pack my things and take a cab back over to the estate."

"No, I can help you. It is really no problem," Antonio said, sounding frustrated.

"Sorry, I just feel bad making you help me in the rain when you could be out doing something fun," I said as we approached the campground.

"It's fine really. I do not mind helping you," he said, pulling up in front of my tent.

"So, here is the plan," I said, turning to him before he stepped out in the rain. "You stay here while I pack everything inside the tent. Then you can help me take the tent down. If it is okay with you, I will just put it in the back not in the bag. It's soaked and I'll to let it dry out before I bag it up."

"Can I help you pack your bag?"

"There's not enough room for both of us in the tent, but thanks for the offer."

He got out and opened my door, and I dashed to the tent unlocked it and jumped inside. It didn't take me long to pack everything up. I wasn't worried about weight distribution since I wasn't going to be packing it around on my back. Besides everything felt damp, it would need to be taken back out to dry. Once I finished packing, I stepped out of the tent and pulled my backpack out. I moved as quickly as I could to the car as Antonio jumped out and opened the hatch back. I threw my bag in the back and while under the cover of the hatch I asked, "are you ready?"

"Yes, I will go to the far side, you go to this side then pull the stakes and the poles on your side and I will pull them on mine," he said.

I ran to my side of the tent and Antonio started to pull the stakes out of the ground on his side. I followed unclipping the rain fly and he did the same on his side. I took my side in both hands, and before I even thought about what would happen, I shook it soaking Antonio with water in the process.

"Oh, I am so sorry," I almost yelled. Embarrassed from soaking a nice man who was so much help to me. He stood there in shock looking down at his wet clothes.

"Aun no consigo, obtener incluso," he said in Spanish while giving me an evil grin. "Take it back to the car and I will start pulling the tent poles."

I took the rainfly and ran it back to the car. I crumpled it up and put it on the rubber mat in the back, then headed back out to help pull the other pole.

"Here you put these in the bag and I will get the tent," he said, handing me the long poles.

I broke the poles down as quickly as I could. With one down, I shoved it in the bag and started on the next pole when a cold splash landed on me. Now I was just as wet as Antonio was. I looked up to see him standing a few feet away with one corner of the tent in his hands smiling and laughing.

"Don't get mad, get even," he said as he began rolling up the tent.

"Is that what you said in Spanish that I couldn't understand?" I asked and he nodded; I could not help but to laugh with him.

We quickly finished putting the tent in the car, got in, cranked up the heater and headed back to the cottage.

As soon as we went through the gates of the villa, the same feeling came back, I was being watched. I looked through the windows of the car but they were so wet and the rain was coming down so hard I could not see if there was anyone out on the grounds watching me.

There was an enclosed porch at the back of the cottage and Antonio helped me set the tent out to dry and take my pack inside. It was a little damp so I left it on the porch with the tent.

"I'm all set. Thank you so much for all of your help," I said, walking Antonio to the front door.

"It was my pleasure," he said, turning to face me. "If you need anything give me a call. Please be careful even here."

"I'll call you if anything comes up," I said, giving him a quick hug, and pulling away.

He looked startled and scared that I hugged him. I felt my face redden at my faux-paus. "Sorry, it's just that I don't know what I would have done if you had not helped me out."

"I think you would have been fine," he said and turned to

leave. "Enjoy yourself."

After he left I returned to the porch and went through my bag. What I really wanted was a hot shower and some dry clothes. Everything in my bag felt damp, and I wished I had hit a laundromat before heading out. Then I remembered the small washer and dryer in the bathroom. I took an armload of clothes and headed to the bathroom. I wondered if there was any detergent on hand. If nothing else, I could just run them on a rinse cycle. I wouldn't be picky today. Looking in the cabinets next to the washer, I found a box of detergent and started the washer. I looked longingly at the shower, but I wanted dry clothes to put on afterward. The shower could wait. I went into the kitchen cooked up some scrambled eggs and made some toast on the stove.

I had never been much of a cook but after weeks of not having a kitchen I was more than willing to make something. I ate at the table and thought about calling my parents to give them a heads up that I was continuing on alone. I pulled my phone out of my pocket and nothing but a blank screen greeted me. I hoped the battery had only died and that the rain had not killed it. Leaving my food, I went to my bag in search of my charger. I wiped off the moisture that had accumulated, plugged it into the wall and plugged my phone into it crossing my fingers that the battery was just dead.

I pulled my book out of my daypack and read while finishing my lunch. It was still there, while I read, the feeling that someone was watching me. I looked around the room looking for cameras or some other spying device and found nothing. What was it with this place? My phone chimed alerting me to a new message so I stood in the kitchen and pulled up my message screen. There were ten new messages on my phone. One from my parents and nine from Mark.

I looked at my watch; it would be around eight in the morning at home. I should be able to touch base with them. I pushed the call button and waited for the phone on the other end to ring.

"Katie, is that you? What is wrong?" My adopted mother asked before I could say hello.

"Nothing is wrong Mom; I just got your message. I have been camping with no way to charge my phone," I said, already feeling like everything was my fault.

"What happened with you and Mark?" she asked. I could hear her walking around. Likely looking for my dad so he could listen in.

"Mark and I are done." I really did not want to get into why we were done if I did not have to.

"He called here yesterday wondering if we had heard from you." I could tell she was motioning to my father to pay attention. "You had us really scared sweetie, why were you camping?"

"Mom, I sent you an email. I'm fine. I was camping because of this stupid film festival. I couldn't find anywhere to stay and I couldn't leave town because all the trains and busses were booked. I bought a tent, found a really nice campground, and tented it last night." I was wishing I could pace while I talked but I was tethered to the charger. How did people talk on the phone before cordless or cell phones?

"What are you going to do with the tent now?" Mom asked, sounding concerned that I would throw it out and waste money.

"I bought a superlight packable one I can take with me. You never know when camping may be the only way you can have to have a roof over your head. Besides, I found a cottage to rent so it was only for one night."

"So now you are renting a cottage? How much is it costing you? How long are you going to stay?"

"Two more nights then I'm heading to Madrid. I somehow got a great deal on this place so stop worrying about money, I have enough to get through this trip," I said, looking forward to leaving this place behind.

"I'm just worried honey. Is there any chance that you and Mark will get back together? I would feel much better if you were not on your own over there." I could hear the concern in her voice.

"Mom, he's been cheating on me for months. I caught him practically having sex on the dance floor of a club while I was in the bathroom. All he's wanted to do on this trip is go bar hopping," I said, unloading on her. "I know you and Dad are worried, but believe me I'm safer without him."

"Alright, be careful. Your dad wants to talk to you. I love you."

"I love you too, Mom."

"Here's your dad."

"Katie, what's this I hear about Mark cheating on you?" he asked in his deep gruff voice. "I will kill him myself."

"Dad, he's not worth you going to prison over. I'm just glad I figured out who he really was before I invested any more time into the relationship." I smiled, thinking of my dad hitting Mark with a baseball bat repeatedly.

"I should have known about him," he said, berating himself. "Are you sure you want to continue on your own?"

"Actually I feel better about this trip now than when Mark and

I left the states." Realizing it was true after the words left my mouth. Even with all of the drama over the past few days, I was happier than I had been with Mark.

"Do you need anything? Money?" he asked, my dad the protector.

"No Dad, I'm fine I have reevaluated my budget and I can still see everything I want with what I have with me especially since I will not be spending so much time in bars."

"Okay, well keep us updated. I love you sweetie."

"Love you too Dad," I said and hit end on my phone.

I smiled to myself and heard the washing machine click off. I moved the wash to the dryer and started another load. It was going to be so nice to have freshly laundered clothes again.

I picked up my phone and scrolled through the text messages Mark had sent me. They ranged from *I am sorry. Please come back.* To, *where the fuck are you?* To, *I can't find my socks.*

I wanted to throw my phone across the room. He made me so mad, I started to text him back about what an ass he was but I stopped myself. There was no point replying to his messages, he would just keep texting me. It was time for a clean break.

Frustrated I walked down the hallway to the bedroom and snooped around. The dresser was empty but the closet had one of those super thick terry cloth robes found in nice hotels. Decision made, I headed to the bathroom for a hot shower.

It helped. I was able to let go of the anger I was feeling about the text messages from Mark. He always overreacted. If I didn't pick up the phone when he called or was late getting home, he always seemed to turn it around on me. Like it was my fault I wasn't at his beck and call twenty-four-seven.

I stared at myself in the mirror, the realization dawning on me for the first time. If one of my friends had told me about a relationship they had with similar complaints, I would have told them that they were in an abusive relationship. Not your classic physically abusive relationship but mentally. How in the hell had I not seen this before? I had always thought of myself as a tough woman who would not put up with that type of man. I felt stupid; it had taken breaking up with him to realize what I had allowed to happen to me. I was mad. Mad at Mark for being a controlling ass and I was mad at myself for not seeing what was going on sooner.

The more I thought about it the more I realized he had been slowly alienating me from my friends. Over the past six months they had stopped inviting me places because they didn't think I could go, and they didn't like Mark. God, I was an idiot. I promised myself to never let a man have that kind of power over me ever again.

After my epiphany, and a few tears at my stupidity, I cuddled up on the sofa in the robe. I read and watched the rain fall outside. At twilight, the rain finally stopped and I could see the sun setting on the ocean. The dryer had finished a few minutes before and I went to put on a pair of yoga pants, bra, and a t-shirt before heading outside for a better look at the sky.

CHAPTER 15

"Sir, Katie is getting settled into the cottage as we speak," Antonio said after genuflecting in front of Miguel's chair.

"Good," Miguel said, getting up and looking out the window towards the cottage. "Do you think she suspects anything?"

"She might, but the cottage is much nicer than the wet tent she was staying in," Antonio said, shoving his hands into his pockets. "Sire, if I may ask. What are you going to do with her?"

Miguel turned, surprised by the question. His slave should know better than to question his reasoning. "Why is it any concern of yours?"

Antonio shuddered for a moment. "She is a nice girl and I don't want anything bad to happen to her," he managed to say before doubling over in pain.

"What I do with her is no concern of yours. You will make sure not to question my motives ever again." Miguel walked over to him, and leaned to see Antonio's face. "Do you understand?"

"Yes, sir," Antonio whispered between his teeth through the pain.

"Very well then," Miguel said, releasing him from the pain. "I want you to go back to your daily routine. Your help is no longer needed here."

Antonio stood, gasping for breath. "As you wish, Sire." He turned and left the room slowly trying to recover from the pain.

Miguel went back to his chair behind the desk and sat down hard. He did not understand why everyone, himself included, wanted to fall all over themselves for this average, pretty woman. Had everyone lost their minds? Thinking back, it seemed like Vince was the only person who could care less about her. Or was he lying? Picking up the phone on his desk he called Vince.

"Yes Miguel," Vince answered on the second ring, sounding distracted.

"Vince, what are you up to this rainy afternoon?" he asked trying to sound happy.

"Moving some of my investments around . . ." he said, trailing off. "I received a tip that things were going to be changing and I want to be prepared."

"That sounds like a very boring way to spend the day," Miguel said, looking at his manicure.

"Well, business is business. What can I do for you, Master?"

"I wanted to talk to you more about this human, Katie." He paused for a moment, swiveling his chair around for a better view of the cottage. "Everyone who comes in contact with her is enamored with her except for you. Why?"

"I do not know. From what I saw there was nothing overly special about her." He sounded like he was only half-paying attention.

"You have not spoken to her though, correct?"

"What? No, you told me to follow her and that is all I have done." Vince was paying more attention now.

"Maybe that is the key," Miguel said, more to himself then to Vince. "I need to talk with her."

"Why?" Vince asked, fully alert now. "Just slake your thirst and be done with her."

"Why do you care so much Vince?"

"I do not care except you are spending a lot of time thinking about this human when there are other concerns you could be thinking of."

"What I do with my time Vince, is none of your concern," Miguel said, his anger rising.

"I do not mean to anger you, Sire." Vince chose his words carefully. "I have never seen you so distracted by a human before."

"I know," Miguel said quietly. "I need to take care of this problem, and I will as soon as the sun goes down."

"That sounds like the best course of action, Sire."

"Have a good evening, Vince," Miguel said, and without waiting for a response he ended the call.

He leaned back in his chair and stared at the ceiling. He would go over to the cottage at dusk and drain this woman. He had to. She was already monopolizing too much of his time as it was.

He looked back at his compute, forcing himself to stop thinking about her and looked for the tip Vince had talked about. He wanted to make sure his fortune was secure.

CHAPTER 16

I pushed the button on my camera for the tenth time. It seemed like every second the sunset became better than the moment before. The sky was alight with pinks, oranges, grays, and purples. The reflection from the far off ocean made it even more enchanting. I was content again. I had left the memory of Mark behind me. I was in the moment, but not so much that I didn't feel someone approach.

"Who's there?" I asked aloud and turned in the direction where the feeling was coming from to see who the incoming mind belonged to. Wait, I knew they were coming because I could sense their mind? I had never sensed Antonio's mind before. What in the hell was going on? I turned and walked quickly back to the cottage. Relieved that I only wandered a short distance from the back door. I didn't see anyone. The incoming person had stopped when I asked, but they had not identified themselves either. I made it to the door of the porch before they said something.

"Katie, please do not go," the voice said from behind a bush.

"Show yourself," I said, keeping my eye on the bush and reaching behind my back trying to find the door handle. A man stepped out from behind the bush and took a few steps toward me before stopping.

"Who are you?" I asked. He was tallish, not super tall, but not short maybe five-ten, five-eleven. He had dark brown hair pulled back into a low ponytail. He was far enough away that I couldn't make out all of the features of his face, but I could see he was very pale.

"My name is Miguel, Katie."

"How do you know my name?" I was starting to feel creeped out. Where had I put my pepper spray? I wondered, remembering it was back in my daypack; just my luck.

"A mutual acquaintance told me. How are you feeling after the fight in the bar?"

"You saw me at the bar? What did you see?"

"I saw your boyfriend, making out with a woman who was not you on the dance floor. Then he proceeded to lie to you about who started the make out session," he said, sounding unsympathetic.

"So it was you who told me he was lying?"

You heard me last night? He thought, sounding astounded.

"Yes, you said 'he is lying to you'."

How long have you been able to read people's minds?

"I can't read people's minds, I can only hear them when they project to me." I relaxed a hair.

"May I come closer?" he asked taking a tentative step closer.

"Please do." I needed to see what this man was, and try to figure out how he was able to speak to me in my mind.

He moved slowly and fluidly as if he was trying not to scare me. Based on the feeling I had a few moments ago, when I felt him coming towards me, he could move much faster than he was now.

He stopped a few feet in front of me and bowed at the waist. "Señorita, it is a pleasure to meet you." He stood up straight and met my eyes.

"It's nice to meet you too, Miguel." I studied his features: his eyes were a dark mocha brown, his nose was slim and sharp, and his face was heart shaped. "What are you doing here?" So much for getting away from all the crazy, I thought.

"This is my estate. I knew you needed a warm and dry place to stay, I made it happen," He looked around as if admiring the cottage for the first time.

"How did you know I needed a place to stay?" I was not liking where this was going. Did I have another stalker? I wondered, thinking of Vince, something about Miguel reminded me of him.

"The same acquaintance told me." He obviously did not want to give me either Antonio or Vince's name. Those were the only two people who we could both know.

"Do you know why can I hear you speak to my mind?" I did not know what else to say.

"I have no idea, but I will look into it." He put his hands behind his back and began to pace back and forth in front of me. "Is this new? Have you always been able to hear people thinking to you?"

"Never until you." I thought about Vince. I was going to have to be very careful with my words to make sure I didn't bring Vince up with Miguel. I was never a good liar, and I had a feeling this guy would be able to tell if I was lying better than most people. "I can't read everything you're thinking. Only when you are thinking at me. Does that make sense?"

"Yes. Is that your camping gear on the porch?" He just then

registered that there was a tent stretched out.

"Yes, everything was soaked when I got here." I turned and wished it would have already been dried. "I want to make sure it is dry before I put it away."

"I see. He turned to continue pacing. He was a man of few words, and he didn't seem to be in a very good mood. "Can we go inside and continue this conversation?"

"I think it's best if we talk out here for now." I needed to protect myself until I knew this guy better. Remembering he owned the house I said, "But if you own the house I can't keep you from coming in."

"Nonsense, you are staying here and you deserve your privacy." He turned again. "I'm sorry I am not in the best of moods this evening. It has been a trying day. Would you give me another chance?"

"Sure, I have had a few rough days of my own lately." I could feel his guilt over his actions.

"Will you have dinner with me tomorrow night?" He stopped, and turned to me. "I will see if I can find any more information on why you can hear my thoughts."

"Sure. What time?" If he could come up with an answer for me on why this was happening I could suffer through a dinner with him.

"Come up to the house around eight thirty." He finally gave me a genuine smile. "In the meantime you are free to use the pool and anything else on the grounds."

"That sounds good, and thank you for the pool. The ocean is too far to walk to from here, and I love to swim," I said, feeling a little more comfortable with him now.

"I'm sorry but I need to attend to some business. I will see you tomorrow night." He turned to leave.

"Goodnight," I said, smiling.

"Goodnight," he said, making his way slowly back toward the house.

I turned and walked inside. As soon as I was through the door I felt him take off in my mind and he was gone. I made a sandwich for dinner and opened a bottle of wine from the rack. After I ate, I did my dishes and realized it had been a very long day and bed, a soft bed, sounded amazing.

CHAPTER 17

Vince watched the scene play out between Miguel and Katie from the bushes. He wondered when Miguel had turned his donor's dungeon into a cottage. When Antonio had told him Katie was staying there he almost blew a gasket. The dungeon had been a dark desolate place with no sunlight so Miguel could have a sip whenever he wanted. There were no comforts in those rooms beyond cots and a bathroom.

How had Miguel changed it so quickly? It looked nothing like it did the night before. He must have had people working around the clock to make it look like a cottage and not a dungeon.

Things were changing too quickly. The plans Miguel had in mind when he found 'The One' were abominable. Vince could not let it happen. He only stayed in San Sebastian as long as he did to keep an eye on Miguel and make sure if he found 'The One' that none of his plans would come to fruition. Since he knew who Katie was it was time to leave town, he just had to convince her to come with him.

He needed to come up with a plan to get Katie out of Miguel's domain before he figured out what she was. It was going to be hard meeting with her while she was staying on the property and it was going to be even harder to convince her to trust him and not Miguel.

CHAPTER 18

I slept like the dead, no nightmares, no one waking me up and the bed was soft and warm. When I woke up I forgot where I was for a moment but then it all came back. There was something very odd going on. I could hear people talking to me in my mind, because of this I had a patron who gave me his cottage to rent when there was nowhere else in the city to stay.

Another man wanted to help me, but didn't want me to tell anyone about him. Then there was the strange concierge who was following me and helping me get things done for no apparent reason. On top of everything else, there was the revelation that I had been mentally abused by Mark. I had a feeling Miguel wanted more than just a friendship with me, but I was not ready for anything like that with anyone. I should have made my intentions clear last night. I was not looking for a new man. I wanted to cancel my date with him but I didn't want to be rude. He had helped me find a nice place to stay.

Then there was Vince. I didn't think he was romantically interested in me. He was obsessed with my tattoo and what it meant, and for some reason he wanted to protect me, but from what?

I looked out the window and saw the sun was out and there were almost no clouds in the sky. It was going to be a beautiful day. It looked like a good morning for a run. I got up did my morning bathroom routine and dressed in my running shorts and sports bra. I walked out of the bedroom and toward the kitchen before remembering what Vince said about not showing off my tattoo. I turned around and went back into the bedroom for a tank top that covered my side.

After a banana and some stretching, I plugged my ear buds into my ears and headed out. I was not sure how big the compound was but I thought I would start with a run around the perimeter and head out of the gates from there.

The grounds were spectacular. High up on the mountain with panoramic views of the ocean on three sides. There was a steep cliff on one side that fell to the ocean. It was too bad there was no access to the waves. After I ran along the west perimeter I headed back up the other side which went by the villa.

The villa was beautiful, more gothic looking than you typically see in Spain. The brick was gray, almost black and the windows were all so darkly tinted that you would not be able to see inside if you stood in front of it and cupped your hands around your face to try and block out the glare.

When I got to the front gate, it opened automatically for me. There must have been a pressure switch that triggered it from the driveway. I ran through the gate and took off down the road since the road dead ended just past the gate. Once the gate was closed behind me I felt the presence that was with me while on the grounds leave. It was like I was going out of range of it. I wondered if who or whatever the presence was felt me too.

As I ran down the road following the switchbacks off the mountain I knew the run back up was going to kick my ass but it would give my mind an escape from everything weighing me down. At the bottom of the hill, I turned to head back up when I felt him with my mind.

"Who's there?" I asked quietly, trying not to draw attention to myself. I didn't see anyone around but you never knew who lurked in the shadows.

Why are you staying on his estate? I explained to you that you could not trust him. Vince said, sounding angry.

I started to walk back toward the estate. "Are you talking about Miguel? You never told me who not to trust."

I am sorry, you are right. How did you end up staying in his cottage? Vince asked trying to calm down.

"Antonio said he had found this place for me. The tent was wet, cold and boring," I said, defending myself. "I didn't know it was his estate until last night, and as you know there aren't very many places to stay in the city."

Antonio. Of course, he thought and I could feel him sigh in frustration. *I am sorry I was short with you. This is not your fault. I understand wanting to stay in a dry and warm place. I am just worried about you, and I do not know how well I will be able to protect you while you are staying there.*

"Why do you think I need protection?" I asked, continuing to move up the hill. He was nearby and moving with me, even if I could not see him.

Because you are 'The One,' as I told you the night we met, he thought in a tone that said I should already know this.

"I know you think I'm 'The One,' but I have no idea what I am supposed to do as, 'The One'" I said, not buying it for a moment. "Shouldn't I know what is expected of me if I'm 'The One'?"

I thought you would but the goddess will work in mysterious ways. All that is important for now is that you are kept safe until you are ready. I worry that if what Miguel believes is true and he finds out about your tattoo he will take advantage of you.

"What Goddess? I don't have anywhere else to go unless you know of a place. I wasn't able to get a train ticket out of here for two more days. I'm not going back to the tent now." I wanted to believe everything he said but I was having a hard time with it.

I would ask you to stay with me, but Miguel would find out and until my preparations to keep you safe are ready we cannot risk his anger. I do not want him to know we have met.

"When are you going to have everything ready?" I asked, wanting to trust him.

It is taking more time than I thought because I am working behind Miguel's back. I should have everything ready in a day or two. For now, you need to go back and pretend you just had a good run.

"How do I know you're not trying to do the same thing that you say Miguel is doing?" I was getting tired of being dependent on men. I had to have some reason to believe Vince.

You must look beneath the surface and into the depths to find truth and honesty. I cannot say anything that will make you trust me at this point. However, I hope in time I will be able to show you, he thought, and was gone.

Wasn't that what my mom had said? I thought to myself as I

began a slow jog back up the hill to the villa. To look beneath the surface to find what I was looking for. I tried to let go of everything Vince said, but of course, I kept turning it over and over. Why did I want to believe him? When he thought to my mind it came through as frank and honest. I didn't get the same feeling from Miguel. From Miguel I got a feeling of entitlement and self-assuredness. It was honesty in a way that he believed to be the truth, but I had a feeling it was twisted by what he wanted to believe.

I wanted to go home at that moment, sleep in the room I grew up in, hug my parents, and pretend this was all a bad dream, but I had to face this. I needed to look at this as a life changing adventure. It was hard to have a positive attitude when I wasn't sure if I was going to like the person who I became at the end of this.

The incline increased and I was finally able to let go of everything in my head and concentrate on putting one foot in front of the other to get myself back up the hill. When I reached the gate, I stopped and gasped for breath for a few minutes before hitting the call button.

"Si?" an irritated voice asked before his faced popped on the small screen. He looked like a butler you would see in a Victorian era movie. He had dishwater blond hair, combed neatly to one side; his skin was pale, as if he was stuck inside for most of the day. He had bushy eyebrows and beady eyes. He was wearing a very starched shirt with a shoestring bowtie.

I relayed in broken Spanish that I was the guest staying in the cottage, and I needed to get back in the gate. He finally got the idea and opened the gate for me. I headed back to the cottage to shower and eat some breakfast.

After eating and showering, I went to the pool. Luckily, I had more than one bathing suit since Vince didn't want me showing my tattoo to anyone. I put on my tankini and some shorts. I grabbed my book, music player, and sunscreen then made my way to the pool.

It wasn't a large pool but not a plunge pool either. It was kidney shaped and I found out after I dove in it was unheated. I gasped. When I reached the surface I could feel someone laughing at me. I turned toward the villa but I couldn't tell if someone was watching me or not. I felt the goose bumps pucker on my skin and looked down at my breasts to make sure I was not giving anyone a show of my very hard nipples. My top had a little bit of padding and, from what I could see it wasn't enough. The laughing stopped and a lustful feeling entered my mind. I spun around to face the lawn instead of the house.

Someone had been watching me. I not only could I hear people in my mind, but I could sense their feelings. I didn't think their feeling had influenced me, beyond embarrassment yet.

I swam around for a while enjoying the cool water before my run caught up with me. Exhausted I headed for a lounge chair in the sun. I popped my earplugs in and grabbed my book. This was the down time I had needed for a very long time.

The last time I had been at a pool, Mark had been drinking heavily and joined a pool volleyball game. I had to watch to make sure he didn't drown or start a fight. So laying there by the pool, with my tunes and my book, felt like heaven. Except for the feeling of being watched. Well, at least I knew I had a peeping tom and I would be able feel him coming if he had plans to attack me later.

I flipped over onto my stomach and put my head on the small pillow built-in to the lounger. I drifted in and out of sleep and wakefulness for the next little while. I could not remember the last time I felt more at ease. As soon as I felt it I chastised myself.

There were a lot of things I needed to be on guard about. I ran my hands down my side to make sure my top was covering the tattoo. It was, thankfully, I turned over again and looked at my phone finding it was already six o'clock. Thinking about the time made me realize how long it had been since I had eaten. Dinner was not until eight so I gathered up my things and went back to the cottage.

On the way back I tried to pinpoint the moment when the mind I had been sensing left. It never did, which told me I had a range of at least two hundred yards. The question that ate at me now was, could they sense me? It could be a huge disadvantage to this power. Was it a power? Like a super power? Was I becoming a super hero like Ironman or Hulk? I really hoped I was not becoming the Hulk. Imagine the number of clothes I would go through if I changed into a super-human amazon.

After grabbing a light snack, I pulled the email up on my phone to see what else was going on in the world. Before I could even look at my email, I found twenty text messages from Mark. I didn't bother reading any of them I just sent one back that said, "STOP. We are over I'm blocking your number." I hit send and blocked his number.

There was nothing too interesting on my email but, when I got to my social media account I gasped at the number of instant messages I had. I looked at the first few which were to the chime of: *How could you leave him? You were meant to be,* and *what did he ever do to you.* Luckily, a few said: *It's about damn time,* and *He had always been a jerk.* I looked at Mark's status updates and I understood what was going on. The day I left him said the following: *Katie, I'm so sorry will you please come back? I don't know what I would do without you.* The next day said: *Really Katie, don't be a pain in the ass. Just come back.* And the coup de grâce, *Katie, you are a slut and a doormat. I will have a better time without you.*

Without hesitation I unfriended Mark then checked in with a few friends and let them know what really went down with Mark. I wasn't one of those people who aired their dirty laundry on social media for everyone to see. I looked at the clock and saw it was time for me to start to get ready for my date. With the horrible things Mark had said, I was ready to go out and have a good time.

It dawned on me that I forgot to tell Vince I was going to join Miguel for dinner. I didn't know Vince very well, but I was positive he was going to be mad. I thought about everything he said about what Miguel would do if he found out I was 'The One'. I picked up my phone and sent Vince a text message letting him know what my plans were and I would let him know when I got back from the date. At least he would know where I was if something bad happened.

After showering, putting on some makeup and arranging my short hair in an Audrey Hepburn, *Sabrina* style, I went to the closet where I had put away my clean clothes and pulled out the one, kind of nice, dress I had and put it on. It was a flowery, spaghetti strap, princess cut and fell a few inches above my knees. The flowers were outlined in bright blue while the rest of the dress was an off white. I put on the one pair of dressy sandals I had with me and I was ready to go.

I gave myself a look in the full-length mirror on the inside of the closet door and blew out a breath. I stood up straight and sucked in my stomach. It would have to work, I thought to myself.

I went to my daypack and pulled out the small clutch I brought with me to go out at night with. I made sure my pepper spray, my phone, and some money were inside. I slung it across my body and left. The walk to the front of the villa took longer than I thought because I kept stopping to look at a flower or a tree. The grounds were so beautiful.

When I made it to the front door, I took a deep breath and smoothed down the front and back of my dress. I pushed the button for the doorbell and waited.

"Si," the same man from the video screen at the gate asked after opening the door a crack. He stood very straight and had one arm behind his back. He looked upset that I had interrupted whatever he had been doing.

"I'm Katie, I am meeting Miguel for dinner," I said, reminding myself not to let this man cow me. I held my head up high and waited to be invited in.

"Please, follow me." He turned to allow me entrance to the foyer then closed the door behind me.

The interior of the villa was the opposite of the exterior. Where the exterior was dark, the interior was light. The floors were a pale polished marble. The walls were bright stark white with what I guessed were priceless paintings and artwork dotting the walls. This was the most lavish home I had ever been inside of.

I followed the man through a doorway leading into a sitting room. I wasn't sure if it was the correct word for the room but it sounded good to me. It was large with at least three different seating arrangements. It reminded me of a Jane Austen movie with the antique settees and straight-backed chairs. I didn't think anyone would want to sit in there for long, nothing looked comfortable to sit on. I already felt like I was going to break everything I touched.

In front of a lit fireplace, Miguel stood with his back to me. "Señor, Katie has arrived," the man said, using English for my benefit no doubt.

"Thank you, Juan," Miguel said, turning around, and smiling at me. "Please inform us when dinner is ready to be served." He dismissed Juan who turned and left.

"Buenos noches," I said, slowly walking toward Miguel. He looked handsome in a lightweight beige suit with a navy-blue button up shirt. The beige jacket set off the brown in his hair.

"Good evening," he said. While I couldn't hear what he was thinking, I could see it in his eyes and body language. It was the universal signs of a male checking out and sizing up the opposite sex when they liked what they saw. "Please come and sit down. Can I get you a drink?" he asked indicating one of the two chairs near the fireplace.

"Vodka on the rocks. If you have it," I added as I took a seat in the straight-backed chair. Just as I thought, like the hard, wooden bench outside the principal's office, very uncomfortable.

"Interesting choice." He walked to the corner of the room where a bar was located. I watched him place ice and vodka in the glass and bring it back to me.

"Aren't you having anything to drink?" I asked, feeling odd being the only one with a drink in my hand.

"I already had mine, but I will have wine with dinner."

I took a sip of the vodka; smooth as silk, I had never had

anything so elegant before. "This is amazing. What kind of vodka is it?" I asked as he sat in the chair closest to me.

"It is from a very small distillery in Russia. A friend of mine gets it for me since they do not export it," he said clearly happy I was enjoying it.

"Cool." I looked around the room for something to talk about. I didn't want to talk about the whole mind reading thing yet. I was nervous, and I could tell he was too. "Antonio told me this villa has been around for a very long time with the same family living here. Did you grow up here?"

He looked shocked at my question, but recovered quickly. "I have spent most of my life here, but I have visited quite a few places in Europe as well." It felt like he had deflected my question. Hey, if he didn't want to talk about it there was no reason to push it.

"It's very beautiful," I said, looking around. "The inside is such a contrast to the outside." His face looked upset again. "But that makes it very unique and altogether different than other villas."

"Yes, we renovated the interior just recently," he said, looking around and I could feel his pride. "But I cannot bring myself to change the outside while it is still in good repair. It reminds me of where I came from."

Juan appeared at that moment to tell us dinner was served. We both rose to follow him into the dining room. The room was open to the sitting room and was long and narrow. It worked perfectly with the dark, thick, long table centered in the room. There were two place settings in the middle, on the long sides of the table. That was good, when I first walked in I thought we would be placed on opposite ends and have to yell to hear each other. I followed Juan around one side and Miguel went to the other.

"Please sit down," Juan, said holding the chair out for me. I sat down as he pushed the chair in and he left the room. The table was set with china and crystal. I was going to have to be careful not to break anything.

"How was your day?" Miguel asked taking the bottle of wine from the table and pouring it into my glass then his own.

"It was nice." I watched while he took a small flask out of his breast pocket and added a few drops of red liquid to his glass. Watching him, I flinched. Was he trying to use a date rape drug on me? "Is that the antidote?" I, tried to make it sound like a joke but my voice was too hard.

He looked at me puzzled. "What do you mean?" he asked picking up the glass and swirling the liquid in it.

"Do the drops you added to your glass neutralize the drug in the wine?" I elaborated, keeping my hands in my lap.

Recognition finally replaced the puzzled look on his face, then it turned into a knowing smile. "Why yes it does," he replied and added a few drops of the liquid to my glass as well. "Now neither of us will be played the fool by the 'drug' in the wine." He smiled and a low bemused laugh bubbled out. He picked up his wine glass and motioned me to do the same.

Convinced he wasn't trying to drug me I picked up my glass and held it up next to his.

"Saluda, to new friends," he said, and took a sip of wine. I followed him and let the sharp flavors burn my tongue and the back of my mouth before swallowing.

"All joking aside. What did you put in my wine glass besides the wine?”

“For me it is a cure.” He sat silently for a moment as though framing his next words carefully. “You see, I have a great passion for wine, but my stomach does not. The liquid will save me from hours of despair later while you will most likely not even notice that I added it to your wine.” He almost sounded jealous of me.

“It’s too bad to have such an ill effect toward something you love.” I thought about coffee. How could I live without it?

“Yes, well I can only be happy there’s a way around it.” He took another sip. He seemed almost to be fidgeting. Could he be nervous too?

“This is a very nice Bordeaux,” I commented, even though I knew next to nothing about wine.

“Are you a connoisseur?” He again, looked pleased with himself.

I felt my cheeks begin to turn red. “No, I just read the label. All I know is that red wine is for red meat and white is for chicken and fish.” I wished the blush would go away. “But I never figured where pork falls in that?” I concentrated on my breathing hoping the makeup I applied camouflaged the fire in my cheeks.

He smiled. “Pork is always the hard one.” He stuck his nose in the wine glass and took a deep breath. “What it really comes down to is drink what you like and to hell with what everyone else thinks.” He looked past me out the window and across the grounds.

Juan came out just then with the main course. It was a small steak with rice and a thick gravy. I had not realized how hungry I was until I began to eat. The food was divine along with the wine. We didn’t speak while we ate but when I finally had enough, I looked up to see him staring at me. *You look amazing*, he thought and I could not help but smile.

"Thank you." I smiled but could tell he had not meant for me to hear him that time. "Have you been able to find out why I can hear your thoughts?"

"I have searched through everything I can get my hands on and I have come up with more questions than answers." He folded his hands and placed them in his lap. "I have a call in to my sister, she enjoys oddities like this. I am hoping she will have some ideas."

"Does she live here?"

"No she is a constant traveler. I never know where she will be from one day to the next. You said you have never heard anyone else's thoughts before the night in the bar?"

"Never." It was hard to pay attention to what he was saying when his emotions were banging around all over the place. One moment he seemed excited and happy then next he was angry and irritated. Something about him was putting me off.

"Well, I hope you will allow me to assist you in figuring out what is going on."

"I don't think I have a choice." I hoped he could come up with an answer better than some ancient prophecy. "What are you though?"

"What do you mean? I am a man," he said and although his face didn't change I could feel his uneasiness.

"Yes, I can see that but what else? Why can I hear only you in my mind?" I asked, even though I didn't think he knew the answer. "I can't hear Antonio, and I couldn't hear Mark, otherwise, I would have ditched him long ago." I looked anywhere but at him. Realizing I was making him uncomfortable, I met his eyes. "I'm sorry. I know you don't have all the answers. I was just thinking out loud."

I watched his hand reach out across the table then his index finger was under my chin and pulling it up forcing me to meet his eyes. He tilted his head to one side and thought; *I wish I could answer these questions for you. Right now, I have no idea why you can hear me.*

I sucked in a deep breath at the contact between his fingers and my chin. It wasn't the shock you get from static electricity, but it definitely made me feel something deep in my belly. He was holding himself back from succumbing to a desire I could not name and I tensed.

"Do you think I will hurt you?" he asked still not letting go of my chin.

"I don't think you want to hurt me," I said, choosing my words carefully and forcing myself to look into his eyes. "But I get the feeling that you don't trust yourself."

He let go of my chin and got up from his chair. *How is it that you know me so well?*

"I wish I knew." I followed him and watched his body stiffen as he listened to my response. "You didn't mean for me to hear that did you?" I stopped next to him.

"No, to be honest this is very new to me. I have never been able to communicate with someone through my thoughts before." He placed a hand at the small of my back; *let's go back into the sitting room.*

I nodded and allowed him to lead me back between the opening of the dining room and the sitting room. I sat on the settee while he went to stand by the window and look out.

"I think it's interesting that I can hear your thoughts but you can't hear mine."

"You have tried?" he asked, looking out the window. He was becoming distracted.

I almost said yes, on the island, but I remembered just in time that it had been Vince I had tried it with and not Miguel. "Yes, last night after I heard your thoughts." I got up and joined him at the window.

"Very interesting," he agreed, not taking his eyes off the window.

"Are you okay?" I was suddenly uncomfortable.

"Yes, just thinking," he said finally, turning away from the window, and locking eyes with me. "I feel more comfortable with you then I thought I would." He took my hand and led me away from the window and towards the settee. He sat down and pulled me down next to him. "It's been a long time since I felt anything for anyone other than myself. It feels oddly good."

"Well, that's good." I found it odd that he would admit to something like that. "What's changed?"

"You." He slid closer to me. "I don't know why or how but for some reason I think our connection is more than a chance meeting. Whatever force brought you to my attention has a meaning behind it." He tucked a stray piece of hair behind my ear. *Were you sent here to save me?*

"And what would I be saving you from?" I reached for his free hand. He winced but allowed me to take it "Was that thought not meant for me?" I gave his hand a squeeze. His mind was feeling very conflicted; it almost felt like he was trying to make himself believe what he was saying.

"No, it was not." He squeezed my hand back and gave me a sheepish smile. "But it is good. I want to be honest with you about everything." He said, then seemed to lose himself in his own thoughts. While I couldn't hear them I could feel them and they were still in turmoil.

I yawned involuntarily let go of his hand and stretched. "It has been a long day," I said, giving him back my hand.

"Oh, my dear, look at the time. I should let you get to bed," he said, after looking at his watch. He got up but kept my hand. "May I walk you home?"

"Sure." I stood up and felt a jolt of emotions from him. I was going to have to practice schooling my body language. Sometime over the course of the evening I had decided not to tell Vince or Miguel about my new feelings detector, but it was going to be a challenge to keep it from them.

"It should be a good night to look at the stars," Miguel said as we walked to the front door. I went to reach for the handle, but Miguel beat me there and held it open for me. After we were through the door, we walked slowly toward the cottage.

"Do the stars look different here then they do where you are from?" he asked looking up at the starry night.

I looked up and studied the stars. The moon had not risen yet and there were no clouds to distort the sky. The stars winked at me and I smiled recognizing a few constellations. "They look pretty much the same here as they do in Colorado." I remembered all of the times I had driven into the mountains to get a better view of them. "There is more atmospheric interference here because Colorado is at a higher altitude, but the constellations are the same."

"You are from Colorado?" He smiling to himself. He didn't feel surprised only smug, like he somehow already knew.

"Yes, born and raised, I love it there." I felt a tiny bit homesick.

"I have never been that far west in the States. I have only been to Miami and New York City."

"You will have to visit at some point. We have everything but an ocean."

"What will you do now that you and your boyfriend have parted ways?"

"I am going to continue on my own. I have changed all my reservations, I leave in two days." I felt his mood darkened after I spoke.

"What if we have not figured out why you can hear me?"

"I will have to let it go as one of nature's oddities," I said, thinking of Vince. He would probably follow me wherever I went, would Miguel too? "I'm not going to let this little thing ruin my trip."

"Are you sure you want to continue on your own though? There are bad people everywhere. I would hate for you to become a victim," he said as we moved closer to the cottage.

"Thanks for the concern, but I don't need a man to travel with," I said defensively. "I can take care of myself most of the time."

"I'm sorry if I offended you." His anger bubbling to the surface. "I do not want anything bad to happen to you."

"I'm sorry," I said as we reached the front door to the cottage. "Since I left Mark all of my friends and family are worried about me traveling alone. Mark always wanted everything his way." I realized I was not making a lot of sense. "What I mean is, I'm tired of people telling me what I can and can't do. I'm making my own decisions from here on out."

You are a wild one, he thought to me smiling. "I understand; I am sorry you feel you must do this on your own. I would think it would get lonely."

"I guess it will be something for me to find out." I looked at the door. "Look I know I just bit your head off and I'm sorry. Can I make it up to you by offering you a night cap?"

Are you sure about that? I don't know if. . . He caught himself before finishing the thought and sighed.

"Don't feel like you have to." I squared my shoulders, and lifted my chin. I could be a big girl damn it. "You just seemed like you wanted our walk to last a little longer," I said in a small voice.

Mi amor, you are feeling vulnerable because of your break up with Mark. I do not want you to do anything you would regret in the morning, he thought turning toward the door again.

"I did not intend to Miguel." I felt hurt and angry at being called a slut in not so many words. "I wasn't asking you to fuck my brains out. I was asking if you wanted a drink. Last I checked the two are mutually exclusive."

"I am sorry." I felt the regret he had for making an assumption. "I was told that an invitation of a night cap means that you want to have sex." I think he tried to blush but it did not really work, he just looked cowed.

I wasn't sure how to respond. I wasn't going to apologize for standing up for myself. That was what Mark would have demanded, I thought and I was not going to be that woman any more. "Just keep it in mind."

I understand. He turned to face me, took his free hand, and cupped my face. We gazed into each other's eyes. "Perhaps another night Katie, but know I will be with you here." He placed our held hands over my heart. He leaned in and I closed my eyes as he slowly touched his lips to mine. *Buenas noches me amo, hasta mananna,* he thought to me. When I opened my eyes a moment later, he was gone.

CHAPTER 19

Miguel's trip back to the villa was much quicker than his trip to the cottage with Katie. There was something about this woman that was going to be the death of him. He needed to figure out why she was making him lose sight of his goals. It was interesting how she could hear his thoughts, even a few he didn't want her to hear, but why was he going to such extreme lengths to make this female comfortable and happy?

He entered his office and found Vince admiring the copy of the tapestry on the wall. "Vince." He moved to stand next to him, and take in the faded beauty. "What brings you here this evening?"

Vince turned and looked at Miguel with the same schooled features he always had when dealing with the ruler of the kingdom. He bowed from the waist, waited a moment, then rose back to full height. "The company of a friend. Do I need to have an excuse to call on you?"

"Of course not. Since you are here though, I will need one more ticket for my party, I am sure it will not be a problem." Miguel moved to sit at the chair behind his desk.

"It will not be problem, Sire." Vince move to stand at the desk with his hands behind his back. "Is there anything else you require of me?"

"No, not at this time," Miguel said, while glancing at the tapestry. "Do you think the prophecy will be confirmed in our lifetime Vince?" he asked with a faraway voice. All thoughts of Katie left him when he looked at the quail on the tapestry.

"I am sure it will if we live long enough." Vince glanced at the tapestry again.

"I feel like I have been waiting forever already. I wish we had more accurate information to study. I have gone over it many times but it feels like there is some piece I am missing. Do you remember anything else about the signs of the coming?"

"'Those of my begotten who have forgotten me will be made to heal by a woman bearing my mark. She will be found on the east shores of the great ocean beyond the Pillars of Hercules, in a protected bay.' That is all I have ever read about the coming of her. It would help if we could find someone who could read the original prophecy, but the longer we search the less likely we are to find someone who can translate it. And the translations we have are so inconsistent and contradictory I fear there is no way of knowing what will happen when the time comes."

"Well, I will have to continue to be patient." Miguel turned away from the tapestry, and faced Vince. "That will be all Vince have a good evening."

"Master." Vince bowed, and left the room.

Miguel pulled up the email program on his computer and caught up on the events of the day. His daytime servants were required to send him a report of the day's happenings each evening. The reports were long tonight, which was no surprise; this was one of the biggest tourism weeks of the year for San Sebastian. The film festival always brought lots of movie stars and stargazers to the city.

He was about half way through the reports when his phone rang. He picked it up off the desk and saw it was Lolita. He tapped the answer button. "Sister, how are you this evening?" he closed his laptop to give her all of his attention.

"The world continues and so must I," Lolita said, sounding sad.

"What is wrong?" Miguel turned to look out the window behind his desk and look over the grounds.

"I just finished a wild goose chase concerning the prophecy and came up empty handed." He heard her blow out a long breath. "I had a really good feeling about this one, but it was wrong."

"Where are you?" Miguel asked knowing she rarely spent more than one night in the same city. She was constantly looking for any information on the prophecy. Following the smallest of leads and she always came up with nothing.

"Paris," she said in a loathing voice. "Charles, one of Paris's masters, said they heard a report of a sketch book with the bird in it. They said a woman had it at a café. However, the café did not have any security cameras and the witness could not remember what the woman looked like only the image of the quail. To be honest I do not even know if we can trust that. How could the human know what the bird looks like? Charles claims he embedded the image into all of his human's minds, but I think the human mind lacks the detail that we have."

"I agree. I don't think we could trust what a human saw. Especially if it was in a book."

"It does not match anything in the translation." Miguel could hear her begin to pace. "I need a break from all of this prophecy business anyway which was why I was calling. Would you mind brother, if I came for a visit?"

"Of course not, I was going to call and beg you to come. I have a unique situation I think you will enjoy."

"Really?" she asked smiling into the phone. "What have you done Miguel?"

"It is not about something I have done." Miguel tried to find the words to explain. "There is a woman who can hear my thoughts. Have you ever heard of such a thing?"

"Can she hear the thoughts of humans as well?" Lolita sounded interested.

"She says she never has until she met me."

"Has she met any other vampires that you know of?"

"Vince was sniffing around her, but I called him off. I don't think she has been around any others and I would like to keep it that way." Miguel hoped Vince left straightaway and didn't take a walk around the grounds as he sometimes did.

"Have you had her blood yet?"

"No, the woman is nothing special except for her smell and her gift. For some reason I am not inclined toward her blood." he thought it was strange, he had never come across someone whose blood did not entice him.

"I will be there tomorrow. We will see what we can do from there," Lolita said.

"Until then," he said and hit the end button on his phone.

CHAPTER 20

After Miguel left I sent Vince telling him I was home, changed into a t-shirt and boxer shorts, went into the living room, and poured another glass of wine. Vince had not replied to either of my messages. I wondered if I put his number in my phone wrong, or if he simply didn't care.

I thought back to what I said to Miguel about not needing a man to keep me safe. Was I already starting to depend on men for the answers I needed? No, I wasn't. I was using these men to find out why I was able to hear them in my head. When I left this town would more men find me because I could read their minds? I hoped not, I was tired of men telling me how to live my life.

A soft knock at the backdoor brought me out of my thoughts. I rose and slowly walked to it. I peeked out the window from the edge so whoever was there would not know I was checking to see who was there. The problem was I couldn't make out any features in the dark other than he was big.

"Who's there?" I asked softly.

Vince. Can you come outside? He thought feeling agitated.

I slid into the flip-flops I had left by the door. I was glad Vince had stopped by, but he did not seem happy about it. I went out the door and closed it softly behind me.

"What's up?" I asked, crossing my arms over my chest, I had taken off my bra.

Why did you go to dinner with Miguel? He thought putting a hand on my shoulder and moving us to the far side of the cottage, I guessed so no one in the villa would see us.

"Because he asked." I blew out a breath. "He is giving me a great deal on staying here and I was hoping he would have a different explanation about why I can hear both of you in my mind."

What did he tell you? Vince started pacing back and forth the length of the cottage.

"Why aren't you talking?" there was no reason why he could not talk to me right now.

Voice's carry and Miguel knows mine very well. I do not want him to know we are acquainted. What did he tell you? Vince ran both of his hands through his hair.

"He told me he couldn't come up with an explanation, but his sister might." I did not understand why he was so worried. "He is going to ask her to come and see."

"Lolita is coming here?" Vince stood stock still as if in shock.

"Miguel said he was going to ask her to come." I could feel his terror. "Why is that a bad thing?"

She is a sociopath, she is going to hate you because you have a gift she does not have, he said resuming his pacing. *If she finds out you are 'The One', she is going to try to kill you or make you her slave.*

"What are you talking about Vince? How is she going to make

me her slave?" I was not following where he was headed with this.

When can you be ready to leave?

"I'm leaving in two days. I already have my train ticket to Madrid." I still was not understanding the fear he was feeling. "It is the soonest I can leave the city."

Would you be willing to leave with me? I have a car and we could be gone tonight, Vince thought hopefully.

I could tell he was scared, and he didn't come across as someone who scared easily. Could I trust him? There were too many things happening for me to think clearly about any of this. I want to leave town but did I want to leave with this guy who I barely knew and was not up front when answering questions about himself? "Vince, I can tell you're scared for me and I appreciate it, but I need some time to think. I don't know you from Adam and I'm not comfortable taking off in a car with a man who dodges personal questions."

What do you want to know? he asked, locking his hands behind his back.

"Right now I need some sleep." I was not thinking clearly. "Let's talk tomorrow and we'll see. Okay?" I turned and began moving toward the back door.

Be careful. Lolita will do whatever it takes to keep the power she has gained. She will not take kindly to a woman competing for her brother's affection. Will you call me tomorrow?

"Yes, I will," I turned, and went back inside.

Good night, Vince thought as I closed the door behind me.

I looked at my almost full glass of wine sitting on the coffee table then glanced towards the bedroom. I poured the wine down the drain in the kitchen, locked the doors and went to bed. I didn't want to think anymore that night.

CHAPTER 21

Miguel slid the hidden door in the linen closet open and listened for any movement nearby. It was quiet but her smell, that lilac, woman smell had permeated the cottage. He took a deep breath and willed the smell into his pores so he could have her smell with him the next day. He shook himself, what was he thinking? She smelled good but it should not have affected him like this.

He opened the door to the hall and silently went in to Katie's bedroom. For a moment, he thought she was awake. She was thrashing around on the bed with her eyes closed. She was asleep. He made himself take a deep breath and not run to comfort her from the bad dream. He walked over to the bed instead and watched her.

Her legs moved as though she was running and he could hear her heart race. He finally forced himself to sit down with his back against the side of the bed and listen with horror as she flung herself about. He didn't want to risk waking her to find him in her room. After the way their evening ended, his presence may not be welcome.

Suddenly she stopped thrashing and one hand reached over the bed right next to him. He thought she was looking for something or someone to grab. Unable to keep his distance any longer, he took her hand gently and hoped it would not wake her. She squeezed it tightly and seemed to relax somewhat. She was still dreaming. He could feel the muscles in her hand spasm oddly in his hand. She began mumbling the same thing over and over again. Every time she said the words they became more and more recognizable. Listening hard he was able make out what she was saying: "I have to save him."

Who do you have to save? He thought to her without thinking twice that doing so might wake her up.

"You," she answered in a very quiet whisper. Her dream must have ended because gradually her heartbeat slowed, and the twitching in her hands stopped, but she didn't let go of his hand.

What did she mean? She had to save him? From what? It was just a dream he reminded himself as he settled in to stay as long as she held his hand. He listened to her heartbeat; let his entire mind thinking of nothing but the slow steady beat of the heart inside her breast. There was something about this female that was making him crazy. Why couldn't he get her out of his mind? Why did he even come back over here? He thought while lightly rubbing his thumb across the edge of her palm.

She was average, nothing more beyond her gift. He wondered if she could hear the thoughts of other vampires. It would be a handy tool if she could. He wanted to keep her and make her his, but then when he looked into her eyes there was something there that made him want to give her whatever she wanted. Why could she do this to him?

He could not let this female have power over him when he had none. He pulled a small pocketknife out of his pants and stood gently prying her fingers away from his. She was laying on her back with her mouth open just a little.

He used the knife to cut into his wrist. He quickly held it over her mouth and let a few drops of blood fall through her lips. His skin healed too quickly for him to get any more blood into her, but it would be enough. Guilt, a feeling he had not experienced since he was human, poured through him. He hated the feeling but it was done. Now he could be sure that she never went far from him.

He wanted to take some blood from her as well to solidify the bond but there was no he could do it without her noticing it. He would have to live with it. A time would come when she would ask for it, he thought as a plan began to develop in his mind.

He sat back down on the floor and took her hand again listening to her deep breathing and the thump-thump of her heart. He let his mind wonder and relax. He did something he had not done in over a hundred years, he fell asleep sitting there against her bed with one hand in hers and the other over his unmoving heart.

CHAPTER 22

I woke up slowly not sure, when I regained consciousness but I was finally awake. The dreams the night before still had my stomach in knots, though I could hardly remember them. If I could put off moving or opening my eyes, I might be able to remember.

I had been standing on the sand on a bright and sunny day. I wasn't sure where I was going or where I was coming from, but something had made me stop and look around. Then Mom was standing in front of me.

"You have to save him," she said.

She meant Miguel, and I took off running toward the villa. I made myself run harder and faster. "I have to save him," I kept saying to myself. When I reached the gate of the villa, it was closed and locked. I pulled on it trying to force it open just enough for me to squeeze through.

Frustrated I closed my eyes for a moment and heard Miguel ask, "Who are you trying to save?"

Finally registering that it was his voice I opened my eyes and said, "You." Then I held my hand out to him and he took it from the other side of the gate.

I tried to remember what happened after that but there was nothing but darkness. Frustrated that I couldn't remember anymore I rolled over in my bed and felt my hand let go of something. I quickly rolled to see Miguel's eyes spring open.

"Am I still dreaming?" I made sure I was covered since I didn't have any clothes on, and turned slightly red at the thought of being nearly naked with a strange man in my room. Vince's warning about showing Miguel my tattoo sprung into my mind. Had he seen it? I froze and tried to get a reading on his feelings. He was embarrassed.

"No, I don't think so," he said, standing up and turning his back to me. "I'm so sorry to intrude on your privacy." He sounded embarrassed. "I came to check on you last night. You seemed to be having a nightmare when I arrived and it seemed to end when I took your hand." He brought his hand up to his face. "I guess I fell asleep too, and here we are."

"Miguel, it's okay. I remember that part of the dream. I was trying to find you, but I was stuck outside the gate of the villa. Then you were there and the dream ended." I was trying to understand what it all meant. It felt odd not touching him after holding hands for most of the night. I fought the desire to reach out to him only because I was hiding my body in the blankets of the bed. "If you would give me a few minutes to get dressed I would like to talk about why you felt the need to come and check on me." I tried to sound positive but he was freaking me out.

"Yes, of course." He walked over to the door. "I will wait for you in the kitchen." He opened the door to the rest of the cottage he began to walk out of the door and stopped. He let out a deep breath then calmly closed the door again. "I'm sorry Katie, but I am unable to leave this room at the moment." He turned around to face me. "I will explain everything as soon as you are decent." I felt the disgust he was having with himself. "Is there anything I can do to assist you?"

"Well, since you can't leave, could you throw me the robe hanging in the closet?" I made sure I was still all tucked in and wondering how in the hell I had attracted another crazy man.

He walked over to the closet keeping his eyes straight ahead, opened the door, grabbed the robe, and threw it on the bed. "I will just go in the closet while you put it on." He stepped into the closet, and closed the door behind him.

I jumped up and flung on the robe. I looked in the mirror and tried to flatten the mohawk that blossomed on my head in my sleep to no avail. Giving up I walked over to the closet and opened the door. "You can come out now," I said with a small smile then retreated to the bed. I sat down and looked him over. "Are you super hungover or something? Can't stand the bright lights yet?" Great a stalker and a drinker, I thought to myself. Wow. I can really pick them.

"I only wish that was the case." He strode silently out of the closet. "May I sit next to you?"

"Sure." I scooted back, turned and pulled my legs behind me.

He moved to the bed then sat down with plenty of space between us. He pulled one leg onto the bed bending it at the knee so we could be face to face. His rich brown eyes held mine for a long time before he said anything. Not being very good at sitting still, I began squirming waiting for him to start talking.

"What would you say if I told you I couldn't leave this room because none of the shades are drawn on any of the other windows in this place?" He looked away now almost ashamed.

I pulled my brows together. "And that would be because of what?" I felt myself grow hard as I braced myself for the lie he would answer me with.

Looking up he locked his eyes with mine again. "Because." He paused as if it wasn't easy for him to get the truth out. "Because I am a vampire."

"You don't seem like the 'Goth' type," I said, trying to curb the giggles escaping my mouth. "They must do things different on this side of the world."

"What do you mean by 'Goth' type?" He seemed genuinely confused. "Why are you laughing?"

I watched his face as everything I said fell into place. His expression changed from disbelief to frustration. "You think I'm lying."

I thought for a moment reading his feelings. He was being as honest as he could be. "No, I think you truly believe that you're a vampire."

"I guess I will have to prove it to you," he said more to himself then to me. "But how? I could walk into the sun and you could watch me burn. I could bite you, but that may not turn out well," he continued to himself. "Well how about this for a start?"

He leaned back and gave me a smiled an ear-to-ear smile. I didn't realize I had never seen him smile that big. His jaw was locked too tight and his teeth fit together so perfectly that I couldn't see what he was trying to show me. "Are you trying to show me your teeth? They look very white."

He rolled his eyes and opened his mouth. I moved closer to inspect them. They seemed normal until I got to the canines. They looked like fangs all right. "Whoever did this did a great job." I leaned away from him.

He grabbed my wrist and I winced at the force behind it. It was not painful but I wouldn't be able to break his hold without a machete. I watched as he brought my wrist to his nose and took a deep breath leaving his mouth open. I blinked and I shook my head in disbelief. His canines grew as he inhaled. Shit maybe he is a vampire, I thought and I tried to pull away from him but he would not let me move.

"Miguel, please. Let me go." My voice cracked with fear as I begged.

After one last breath, he let go and I shrank away from him to the furthest corner of the bed. I was out of breath and my heart pounded in my ears. My fight or flight instinct kicked in and I thought about ways to escape. I could jump off the other side of the bed, but I was positive he would beat me to the door. The sunlight. He had already admitted to being sensitive to it. I could get to the curtains before he could, maybe.

I'm sorry. I did not mean to frighten you, he thought. *But I had to make you understand that I was telling you the truth.*

"Just give me a minute," I replied, thinking it through and calming down.

I do not want to be a monster anymore. He thought to himself, I think. Well he has not hurt me yet or even tried, but why did he come here last night? So could he fool me into becoming his slave? I had so many questions I needed answered. He seemed to be ready to answer them, but could I handle the answers?

"First let's get out of here," I said, getting up and moving toward the door. "I will go and make sure all the shades are down. Will it be enough for you to be able to come out?" I asked with my hand on the doorknob.

"Yes, it should be plenty. I can skirt around any cracks of sunlight." He looked nervous. *Thank you for trusting me.* He thought as I opened the door, ran out, and slammed it behind me.

"You never know, I could have just used that as a ploy to get away from you." I smiled to myself outside the door. Maybe it wasn't a bad idea, I thought remembering everything Vince had told me the night before. "For all you know I could run off right now to find a stake or something to kill you with." I giggled and began closing the drapes one by one, thinking I wouldn't run until I got some answers.

I trust you, he thought to me. *Even more after hearing your dream last night.*

"I can hear you," I said, making my way through the small living room and continuing into the kitchen. "But can you still hear me?"

Yes, we have excellent hearing, he thought and I could feel him smiling.

"You can come out now." I went to the coffee pot and began filling the decanter with water. "What are you smiling about?" I turned the faucet off and turned to the coffee maker to pour the water in.

"I'm glad I can trust you," he said into my ear. "You could have just pretended to close all the blinds and lured me out here to kill me in the light."

I whirled around at the sound of his too close voice. The shock must have shown on my face because he cautiously backed away from me to give me space. "If only I would've thought of that," I said, regaining my control. "Could you please give me a little space for the time being?" I returned to my task of making coffee. "I'm a little freaked out right now and I need to brush my teeth." I dumped the last scoop of coffee in and turning the machine on. "I'm going to wash up. Can you wait here while I do?" I turned to face him for a second before heading towards the bathroom.

"Of course, take your time." He sat down at the small table, folded his fingers together and rested them in his lap.

I almost ran to my room. I closed, then locked the door, took out a pair of shorts, some underwear, a black tank top and bra. I went into the bathroom, shut and locked it too, just to be on the safe side, again remembering what Vince had said about showing the tattoo to Miguel.

I brushed my teeth, wet my hair, so it would stay down, washed my face, and used the facilities. After getting dressed, I went back into the kitchen ready for my coffee and some answers.

"Will you answer some questions for me?" I asked, going to the cabinet, and pulling out a coffee mug.

"I will do my best." He pulled out one of the chairs at the table and sat down. "Will you join me?" He motioning to the chair opposite of him.

"As soon as I get a cup of coffee. Would you like some? Sorry dumb question I am guessing you don't drink coffee."

"No, thank you," Miguel said, smiling at me.

"So obviously you can be awake during the day but you can't go out in the sunlight?" I picked up my mug, and walked over to the table.

"Yes, our kind does not have to sleep away the day, and if it is really cloudy we can go outside for a short time. Most of us don't risk it though; you never know when there will be a break in the clouds. Not very many things are painful to my kind but burning flesh is the worst and is known to be fatal," he said casually and honestly from what I could tell.

"So you're super-fast too I see, and silent, and I'm guessing strong just like most of the vampire stories out there. How often do you have to eat...? I mean drink?" I stuttered not sure what verbiage to use. Would he call me dinner?

"I only have to eat a few times a month, but normally I have at least a snack once a week or so. It depends on what is happening around me. Young vampires must drink almost nightly to be able to think straight."

I picked up my coffee cup and swallowed the last bit before framing my next question. I could tell he did not like this subject but I had to continue. "Are you going to drink my blood?" I noticed my hands were shaking as I put the coffee cup down.

Allow me, he thought and went to the coffee pot to fill up my mug again. "No, I do not wish to at this point." He gave me the mug and slowly sat back down. This was only a half-truth from what I was picking up from his feelings and I wondered what that meant.

"'At this point'? Does that mean you may change your mind and suck me dry?" I was trying to get an answer without giving away that I could feel his emotions.

"That is precisely what I do not want to do," he said, gripping the edge of the table. It was the truth. He didn't want to kill me. *I cannot find the words to explain this yet but as soon as I do, I will tell you.*

"Ok moving on. How did you become a vampire?" I asked, drinking more of my coffee.

"It's a long story but one worth telling I think," he said, pausing like he was trying to find the best place to begin. "One afternoon when I was around ten, I was running from a farmer; he was chasing me with a pitch fork through a field of grain. When I made it to the edge of the field, I knew I was home free. I jogged through the brush bordering it, even though I lost him I didn't stop jogging, instead, I zigzagged through the brush on some invisible trail I found.

"When I came upon a cluster of Almond trees, I stopped my jog and walked over to the trunk of a big tree. I sat down and emptied my pockets. I had stolen two apples and a small loaf of bread. I couldn't remember the last time I had eaten so I tore into the bread, barely taking the time to chew it. When it was gone, I devoured the apples, core and all. Then leaning back against the tree, too bloated to move, I let my eyes close and fell asleep.

"When I opened my eyes night had fallen. It was dangerous to be out alone at night. There were things that would kill you. I got up and looked around suspiciously. There was nothing to see except the dark shadows of the trees and the glow of the full moon through the open patches in the canopy.

"As quietly as I could, I walked out of the grove. Once I had cleared the trees, there were fewer shadows to play mind games with me, and I began to move quicker through the brush not being as quiet as before.

"I made my way around a tall bush anxious to reach the field again. It would be harder for someone to sneak up on me in the field. I froze as a woman dressed in all black approached me. Her head tilted up to the moon as if she was basking in its light. I had never seen a more beautiful woman in my entire life. Her hair looked white in the light and her skin was very pale for this part of the world. She looked down and made eye contact with me.

"I knew I should run. Every nerve in my body was itching for the command to make a break for it, but she mesmerized me. She advanced and I found myself unable to move. I wanted to reach out and touch her but I knew she could be nothing but evil. I suddenly thought about how Eve must have felt about the apple in the Garden of Eden. The temptation was too great.

"'My poor boy,' she said lightly placing one of her hands on my cheek. It felt cool, not frozen but not normal either. 'Are you hungry?' She asked locking her eyes with mine.

"The fear finally overcame my hypnotic state and I was able to back up a step knowing I needed to get away from her. 'No,' I said softly scared to say anything more.

"'Do you have anywhere to go?' she asked, taking another step toward me to close the distance.

"I felt my heart jump into my throat and pound so hard it hurt. 'Yes, I . . . I have to get home now.' I knew I was not doing a very good job of lying. 'My brothers will be out looking for me.' I tried to make the lie sound more believable.

"'You are a bad liar.' Was her only response.

"That is how I came to know the vampire who became my sister," Miguel said, resting his ankle on his thigh. "I was around ten when Lolita took me in. My parents were peasants who worked in the fields, owned by a nobleman near here. They had gotten sick the winter before and died. I was on my own and lucky to have been able to steal enough food to keep myself alive. I slept in barns when I could, but I didn't know how much longer I would have lasted if Lolita had not taken me when she did. I would have starved or been beaten to death for stealing eventually.

"Lolita took me to her, 'father,' or maker. He went by the name of Phillip although we always called him Father. Lolita had been 'made' by him over a hundred years before I joined them. They had recently lost their houseboy in a carriage accident. I think their need for a human was the only reason why I didn't die the night she found me. I realized quickly she wasn't evil but a loving caring person. I didn't find out what they were until much later.

"They schooled me in the disciplines all boys of my age would have learned, growing up in a privileged family. I worked for my keep though, and worked hard for them. I felt like I could never do enough to thank them for taking me in and giving purpose to my life.

"They hid their true identity well. Always with some excuse to why they could not go outside during the day. Why the few windows there were in the house were always bolted shut and blacked out. They went out almost every night and I thought that was what the nobility did. After eight years I became their head butler. I made sure the house ran smoothly. It was a good life. They treated me fairly and never beat me too badly.

"I don't remember why I needed to speak to Father that night but I thought it was vitally important. I walked into his room without knocking. The room was lit with torches and when I looked around, I gasped. It looked like something out a Dionysus myth. There were naked bodies everywhere some moving in pornographic ways some lying still like they were on acid just staring at the torches or the ceiling.

"When I finally found my father, it looked as if he was kissing the neck of a naked woman. When he felt my eyes on him, he let go of the woman and looked up to meet my gaze. Blood covered his mouth. The woman under him had a constant trickle of blood flowing down her neck, over her shoulder, and between her small breasts. After a moment, he went back to the woman's neck and I ran as fast as I could out of there.

"I didn't know what to do as I ran through the streets of the city. Was my father really a monster? Who should I go to? The constable? The church? What would I tell them? Would they believe me? What would happen to me if I turned my father in to them? Would I end up on the streets again? I would not be able to get another job as a butler anywhere if I turned in my current employer for witchcraft or was it devil worshiping? I didn't know what they were at that point. I decided to go home and not tell anyone what I saw. They were my family and I couldn't bear being alone again.

"When I returned home they were waiting for me. 'Miguel, can you please come in here?' Lolita called.

"I walked into the parlor with my eyes down feeling ashamed, and ready to take any punishment they gave me as long as it was not to throw me back out on the streets. 'Miguel, please close the door.' Father said from his position on a settee.

"Doing as I was told, I walked over to him, and with tears running down my cheeks I lowered myself to my knees. 'I'm so sorry Father I should have knocked,' I said in a raspy voice.

"'Who have you told my son?' Father asked pulling my chin up to look me in the eye.

"'No one, Master. I could not. I love you both as though you are my real family, and I can't bear losing you.'

"'He's telling the truth, Father,' Lolita said placing a hand on my shoulder and squeezing it lightly.

"I looked into my father's eyes for what seemed like an eternity. I was beginning to imagine that my punishment might very well be worse than being thrown out of the house. Finally, his eyes switched to Lolita. 'Lolo, how would you feel about having a brother?' he asked, looking back at me with a small curve to his lips.

"'That's why I brought him home in the first place,' Lolita said, smiling brightly and putting her arms around my shoulders.

"'This will be painful for a moment, Miguel.' Father said then he was biting my neck.

"His teeth were so sharp it didn't hurt right away, similar to when you cut yourself with a sharp knife. There is nothing first, but then it seems to be much more painful. I could feel him sucking the blood as it came to the surface of my skin I faded away then into nothingness for a long time.

"'Miguelito, my son you must drink from me now or you will go to meet your maker,' Father whispered in my ear holding his bleeding wrist to my mouth.

"I don't know if I wanted to die or become what he was. I was so distraught that when he put his wrist to my mouth sucking seemed to be the only option there was. After drinking from him for what seemed like hours I passed out and woke starving three nights later."

"Are you going to run away screaming now?" he asked,

folding his arms across his chest defensively.

"No, I'm . . ." I hesitated, trying to find the right words. "I'm still processing everything I think."

"Well, I'm sure you have a whole new round of questions for me now." He slumped in the chair. "Let me first say I would never do that to you unless you were able to make a well-informed decision about it," he said, unfolding his arms, and placing them on the table, stretching his long pale fingers as far apart as he could. "I don't want you to be my human servant as I was for years either. I just need to be near you and I cannot understand why."

"The villa is where you lived when you were changed?" I asked, beginning with the simplest question in my mind.

"Yes, it has been my home for the past two hundred and fifty years or so." He looked surprised that it had been such a simple question.

"Well, that explains part of my dream," I said, mostly to myself. "I couldn't figure out why I would come here to save you." I continued my thought. "Why did you bring me here? Why tell me all this?" I pushed my coffee cup away.

"I wish I knew. I am drawn to you, Katie, and I have no idea why. It's not only because I can speak to your mind. I was drawn to you before I knew you had this gift. I have been driving myself up the wall trying to figure out why I need you. I wish I knew. I enjoyed your company at dinner last night, and holding your hand while you slept. Last night was the first time in over a hundred years I slept. You have no idea how hard it has been for me this morning to not touch you every second," he said shyly looking at his hands again.

I knew what he meant, because I had been fighting the same

urges to touch him. "What did you put in my wine last night?" I remembered him adding a few drops of something to it. I had a good idea now but I needed to hear it from him.

"The only way I can drink wine or anything for that matter is if it is mixed with blood." He didn't like telling me the truth but he did. "It was from a blood bank that does a very thorough job of testing. As I said last night, it will do you no harm but it helps me a great deal." He looked like he wanted to reach out to comfort me but he did not act on the impulse.

I should have felt disgusted that I drank blood last night, but with everything I just learned it seemed like a small thing to complain about. "That's what I thought."

"Do you have any other questions for me right now?"

Sitting at the table, I looked at the clock. Had we really been talking for three hours? I was in mental overload. I had so many more questions, but I didn't know if I had the room in my head to make sense of the answers. "Please don't take this the wrong way, but we have been talking for hours now, and I need some time to think all this through and try to understand it." I looked into his eyes and smiled. "I need to go outside for a while, get some air."

"Yes, I understand. I have a few things to take care of as well." He looked at the clock.

"Aren't you stuck here until the sun goes down?" I gave him a puzzled look.

"Um, no there is a tunnel between this cottage and the villa." He sounded shy again. "Come, I'll show it to you." He got up and offered me his hand. I took it, stood up, and interlaced my fingers with his.

We moved out of the kitchen and back down the hall toward the bedroom. He stopped at the linen closet and opened the door. We stood on either side of the door and I watched as he pushed the back of the top shelf. There was a click and the whole shelving unit slid forward to reveal a stairway leading down.

"Secret passage? How cool." I leaned in to take a look better look. "So that's how you got back in. I was pretty sure I locked all the doors last night."

"I missed you, what can I say?" He brought our locked hands up to his lips and gently pressed them to the back of my hand. "Will you stay on the grounds today?" he asked giving my hand a small squeeze before continuing. "And will you not talk to anyone who may not seem one hundred percent human? We can walk in the shadows during the day, and there may be some who would hurt you to get to me."

"Why do you want me to stay on the grounds?" I felt a little irked, he didn't have the right to ask me that.

"I'm only concerned for your safety." He held his hand up in an, 'I mean no harm,' sort of way. "There are other vampires in the city and your smell may entice them as it did me."

I wanted to say, 'tell me something I don't already know,' but instead I said, "I appreciate that you want to protect me. I'll take your requests into consideration." I took a step backwards and started to pull my hand out of his.

"May I call on you at dusk?" he asked not allowing me to have my hand back but not being forceful about it.

"I don't see why not." I looked down at our hands. Didn't I try to let go a moment ago? Now it was the last thing I wanted to do and it gave me yet another reason to get away from him and think.

"I will see you then." He smiled and backed toward the open passageway until he hit the top of the stairs. He pulled on a rope and the door closed.

Even though I could no longer see him, I could still feel his presence. I wondered if he was waiting on the other side of the door for me to leave before he did. "Have a good day," I whispered, closing the door.

You too, mi amor. He thought to me and his presence began to fade.

CHAPTER 23

I went back to the kitchen and made some eggs, sausage, and toast for breakfast. I took my plate to the patio through the kitchen door and sat at the table to eat and think. There was a lot to think about.

Why was I so attracted to Miguel? He was handsome and polite, but when I really thought about it I didn't know him well enough to be feeling like this for him. His story about how he became a vampire touched me though. He had already been saved once, which begged the question, why did I need to save him? What did he need to be saved from?

He was a vampire. Was Vince a vampire too? Is that why I could only hear them in my mind and not regular people?

I looked over the manicured lawns while I finished eating and pondered everything I learned from Miguel. In many ways it was more than I had gotten out of Vince so far. Miguel didn't know about my tattoo though. What would he do if he saw it? Without any answers to my questions I went back into the house and did the dishes.

While washing the coffee pot I thought about the next question. What was with the connection I felt with Miguel and he felt for me? I couldn't be completely comfortable around him unless we were touching. Even now, I thought, if I tried to relax I would be able to, to a point, but to get to a completely contented state, he would have to not only be near me but be touching me. It seemed similar to the feeling I had when I was little and my parents would leave me with a new babysitter for a night. It wasn't bad but I never really felt okay or slept well until I could feel them tucking me in when they got home.

It was the feeling of security, I concluded. I felt very safe when I was with him. It seemed like the stupidest thing I could do. After all he was a bloodsucking vampire. I must be pretty messed up to think I would be safe with him. But, when I looked deep down inside me, where there should have been fear, there was only a calmness.

When I was done with clean up I looked at the time; it was already mid-afternoon. Part of me wanted to take a cab to town just because I was a free woman, but the other part of me thought staying on Miguel's good side was important. I needed to get all the information I could from him.

It was too warm to run and running around the compound sounded boring. Pool it was. I went into the bathroom where I had hung my tankini up to dry the day before and put it on. I really wanted to wear my normal bikini top, but I wanted to follow Vince's advice until I could learn more about what was going on.

I put a towel and book into my beach bag and went into the kitchen to find my phone. It was on the charger where I had left it. I unplugged it and hit the button to wake it up. I had two missed calls and a voicemail. I unlocked it and called my voicemail.

"Katie, please call me," Vince said in a short, clipped tone.

I hit the re-dial button and called the number back. "Hello?" Vince answered like he didn't know who was calling him.

"Ah, it's Katie," I said, trying to be polite.

"Katie?" The voice asked. "Are you alone?"

"Yes in the cottage."

"Please do not say my name out loud," he said very quietly.

"I figured. Why not?" I put my bag down, went into the living room and sat on the sofa.

"Can you go outside to the back of the house to talk?" he sounded paranoid. "Maybe pretend I am a friend from home or one of your parents."

"Becky, where are you? This isn't the number I have for you in my phone." I played along while towards the back door. "I haven't heard from you in forever, what's going on?" I left through the back door, and closed it behind me.

"Okay, I'm outside," I looked down at my bare feet.

"We should be okay now, I do not know if he bugged your cottage or not," Vince said, speaking a little louder.

"Why would he bug my cottage?" I was astonished that Miguel would do such a thing.

"Because he does not understand why he is so enamored with you, and he wants to find out why. Have you thought about leaving with me?"

"So much has happened since our conversation last night I haven't had a chance yet," I said, examining my toenail polish, I needed to redo it soon.

"What are you talking about?" His voice sounded worried.

"Are you a vampire?" There was silence on the other end of

the line.

"Why would you think that?" he finally asked.

"Because Miguel is one and the two of you are the only people I can hear in my mind. If you are, it would answer a lot of questions." My voice was just above a whisper.

"How do you know Miguel is a vampire?" he asked in one of those voices where he's pretending not to care what the answer is, but if I answered it wrong he was going to blow up.

"He showed me his fangs. At first I didn't buy it but he smelled me, and I watched his fangs grow." I sounded a little giddy, even to my own ears. "It was kind of creepy."

"Did he bite you?" he asked in the same voice only slightly hopeful.

"No, he said he wouldn't."

"When did this happen? Why didn't you tell me about it last night?"

"Because it happened this morning. When I woke up he was in my room, and he couldn't leave because all of the blinds were up. He was pretty much forced to tell me." Just like I was forcing Vince to tell me.

"Yes, I am a vampire." He sounded relieved. I wasn't sure if he sounded that way because Miguel didn't bite me or because he could tell me the truth. "He spent the night in your room? Did you check yourself to make sure he did not bite you?"

"Thanks for being honest. Don't worry I won't tell anyone. Yes, I checked before I changed into my bathing suit. And don't worry he has not seen my tattoo either."

"Thank the Goddess for small favors," he said dryly. "Will

you please leave with me?"

"I know what you said last night about his sister, but I don't think Miguel will let her hurt me. My dreams all said I need to save him, and save the city. Not that I think my dreams are going to come true or anything. Believe me I want to leave but I feel like I need to stay."

"You had another dream?"

"Yes, the city was on fire again. I had to find Miguel and save him."

"I do not know what your dreams mean. If they are just dreams or if they are predictions of what may come to be," he said, sounding thoughtful. "I think you are right, we should err on the side of caution, and assume they are an omen of what may happen."

"So what should I do about them?" I sat down on the table, and swung my legs back and forth.

"I think you should. . ." he paused as if he did not like what he was about to say. "I think, at this point, if you trust him, and you are comfortable staying there; you should stay where you are and learn as much as you can."

"Well, I'm glad we are on the same page," I said, staring at my crossed legs. "I'm not sure why but I trust you more than I trust anyone else."

"I will always be honest with you Katie," he said, sounding resolved. "What are you doing today?"

"Miguel doesn't want me to leave the grounds. He said there are vampires who may try to use me to get to him or some such." I wondered if Miguel wanted me to stay away from Vince. "Is he talking about you?"

"Most likely. I am the strongest vampire in San Sebastian after him, and I think he wants to keep you to himself. He does not want anyone else to know you can hear us in your mind. It is an unheard of gift that can be used to make us more powerful."

"What about the prophecy? Do you think he knows about the tattoo? What do I do about it?"

"I know you are trying to hide it, but I do not know how much longer you will be able to," Vince said, sounding unhappy. "When it happens just go with the flow like you have no idea what he is talking about if you can. I have not told you very much about it on purpose, but I hope that will change soon."

"Do you want me to keep you updated?" I wanted to have a way to call him if I needed him.

"Yes, this is a burner phone so even if he looks at the number there is no way to trace it back to me," he said, pausing for a moment. "You must be careful if you call me. Make sure you are out of Miguel's range and any humans who work for him."

"I will."

"There is one more thing I wanted to talk to you about. It is very likely Miguel will introduce us at some point. We both need to pretend that we have never met."

"I thought it was a given," I said, smiling.

"Good, have a fun day and try to stay out of trouble."

Lying on the lounge chair letting the sun dry my skin I

finally was able to relax and empty my mind. *You look amazing right now with the water glistening off your wet skin.* A thought whispered in my mind.

I was too comfortable to move. "Where are you?" I asked, not looking around. I was facing away from the main house and I would have to move to try to guess where he was.

In the house I have UV protected windows; they allow me to look out but the sun cannot come in. I am sorry to intrude on your alone time, but I could not resist watching you when you were so close and easy to watch.

"That's okay, I was wondering why I was able to relax more now." I felt odd talking to myself. "I've come up with a bunch of questions for you." I smiled to myself thinking of one specifically, but I wasn't sure how to phrase it and it wasn't a question I could ask Vince.

Do you want me to answer them tonight when I come over? He thought and I could feel him smile.

"Yes." I rolled over onto my stomach in order to look up at the windows on the house and try and guess which one he was standing at. "But this is nice too, if you aren't busy."

No everything I needed to get done has been completed. I am going to be having a guest later this evening and I needed to make sure her rooms were ready.

"Oh? Is she a . . ." I asked, trailing off not sure how to phrase the question, "vampire or human?"

Lolita is coming. Does that answer your question? He sounded excited.

"Great," I said, suddenly nervous. Vince said she was

going to try to kill me, I couldn't wait.

What's wrong? He asked and I felt his dismay at my less than enthusiastic feelings about his sister coming.

"I'm just nervous to meet another vampire," I was struggling for a reason to be happy. "I hope she can explain what's going on."

I hope so too. This attraction we have for each other is very odd. I feel like I need to touch you constantly. Even now I would give everything I have to sit next to you in the sun just to hold your hand.

"I wouldn't mind either," I said, feeling my body twinge in lust. "Have you ever heard of a bond, I guess that's what you would call it, like this before?" I was trying to ignore the warm smoldering feeling washing over me.

No, I have not and I think it's something much more than a bond. Which is why I called Lolita and asked her to come. She has traveled the world and spent time with many different groups of our kind. I am hoping she might have learned of something like this.

"What do you need to be saved from Miguel?" I asked in a very low voice and turned my head away from the house.

That's a very good question mi amor. I have been thinking about it all day but I have not come up with an answer. I felt his attention move away from me for a moment. *I have a phone call I have to take mi amor. I will see you at dusk?*

"Yes, see you soon," I said, feeling that he already moved deeper into the villa. I jumped back into the pool and forced myself to swim laps for an hour. I felt like all I had been doing was laying or sitting around. When I gave up on my exercise, I went back to house to get ready for Miguel to come over.

CHAPTER 24

Miguel smiled to himself as he went back to his desk. His plan was going smoothly. She believed the feelings she was having were due to some magic. It was magic, he thought to himself, just not the kind of magic she thought it was.

He blew out a breath; there was something about her he could not resist. Lolita would help him figure things out to a point, but she could be jealous. He was going to have to play them both at the same time. He loved a challenge.

He wasn't sure about making her his slave, guilt had crept back into his mind. He wasn't sure why though, as he had told himself time and time again she was just a woman with a gift. A gift he planned to use to help him take over the world, if 'The One' ever showed up. He could do what he planned without 'The One', but this human made him dream of how easy it will be.

She was going to be hard to break. She had a temper, and a will of her own but his digging into her past had given him a clue. She submitted to that asshole Mark. Now she would submit to him. He would try to treat her better than Mark she was special after all.

He needed to give her more of his blood without her knowing it; he would have to wait until tonight as she slept. It would be so much easier if she would just move in with him. He would have to work that angle tonight, he thought.

CHAPTER 25

I showered again, put on some makeup, and put on my nicest shorts and blouse. I wasn't sure if he was bringing dinner with him tonight or not. Erring on the side of caution, I made a sandwich and watched the clock tick by slowly. I picked up my book and waited for the sun to set, trying not to think about how much I needed to be close to Miguel. The book was helping, but I felt my eyes grow heavy and I drifted to sleep.

I felt someone caressing my cheek when I awoke, and I somehow knew it was Miguel. I opened my eyes and smiled up at him.

"I must have fallen asleep," I said, stretching my body for a moment before relaxing into the sofa again.

"You were talking in your sleep." He leaned back into the other sofa.

"I want to know what I said, but I need to use the bathroom first." I sat up and got to my feet. Miguel took my hand and stood up with me. "Why don't you open a bottle of wine?" I asked, letting go and hurrying down the hall to the bathroom.

Okay, but please do not be too long. I feel like we have been apart for years instead of hours, he thought and I noticed every step I took away from him was harder to take then the last. I made myself do it. I didn't want Miguel going to the bathroom with me. That was just gross and I hoped this bond between us would not get any stronger.

I finished up in the bathroom, checked my face, it still looked good, even though I had slept on half of it for a few hours. I walked back out to the living room and seeing Miguel come into view I ran. I couldn't help myself. He opened his arms to me. I jumped into them wrapping my arms around his neck and my legs around his waist. A feeling of contentment and warmth flooded me when we made contact.

This is so much better. He thought squeezing me to him.

"I know," I brought my nose to his neck, and inhaled deeply. "What are we going to do if the bond keeps getting stronger?"

"I do not know my sweet, but I can't remember ever feeling happier." He was telling a partial truth, and I could not figure out why.

It was okay though because I had some reservations too. "I know what you mean. I have a ticket to Madrid for tomorrow morning." I wasn't looking forward to leaving. There were too many things happening here, and with the way I was feeling toward Miguel I didn't know if I would be able to leave.

"Why are you going to Madrid?"

"After I broke everything off with Mark, I changed my itinerary. Mark didn't want to go to Madrid because it is just another big city and it takes a long time to get there by train. I wanted to go because there is a ton of history and culture there I would like to see." Miguel put me down and we moved together into the kitchen where an open bottle of wine waited.

"You will like Madrid very much. Maybe you would like a new traveling companion?" he asked handing me a glass of wine, taking my hand and leading the way to the patio.

"How can you leave all of this though?" I gestured at the grounds with my wine glass.

"I don't think I will have a choice with the way this bond is behaving." He kissed our interlocked hands. "But I need to stay here until the end of the festival which is the day after tomorrow and I may need a few more days to set things up for my absence. Do you think you could stay here for a few more days?"

"I think I can delay for a few days if it means you are going to come with me." I took a sip of my wine, and looked up at the stars.

"I don't know how I could be apart from you." His voice came out husky and he brought his head down to kiss my lips lightly. Electricity zinged through my body when our lips met. He deepened the kiss, opening his mouth, and probing my lips with his tongue, requesting admittance. I opened them allowing it, and he gently rolled his tongue over mine. I followed his lead and did the same to him.

His hands roamed my back, rubbing lightly up and down as if he was afraid I would disappear. *I have never felt anything like this before*, he thought to me.

I pulled away and looked at him in the eyes. "I know what you mean. This is the most intense feeling I have ever had." He moved back, smiling with his elongated canines and I jumped back. Fear coursed through me one second, only replaced by loneliness in the next. My head was beginning to throb in pain.

What is it? Miguel asked with his arms stretched out, looking completely shocked that I had moved away from him.

I pointed at his teeth. "Were you going to bite me?" I wanted to move further away, but the bond wasn't allowing me to move any further without my headache becoming worse.

"No, no, my love, it's what happens when vampires become aroused. It is similar to what happens to my . . ." he trailed off. I could feel him become embarrassed looking down at the straining fabric around his crotch. *We associate sex with blood. While it is very enjoyable to draw blood during sex, it's not required either. I was not going to bite you.*

I felt my face burn bright from what he just said. At least I knew he was enjoying the kiss as much as I was. I took a step forward and took his hand, my headache evaporated. I giggled, "I feel better now, but this bond is getting out of control. It is painful not touching you at this point. When we do touch, all I want to do is tear your clothes off and have my way with you," I felt a little brazen for admitting what I was feeling.

"Isn't that my line?" Miguel laughed.

"Yes, it should be," I said, still giggling. "I just can't help the way I feel towards you, but I am scared too. It seems like the closer we get the harder it is to let go."

"I agree. I am hoping Lolita will be able to help with this problem," Miguel said, looking at his watch. I thought it was strange that he wasn't scared about the pain. He was feeling more anxious than anything.

"Do you promise that you were not thinking about taking a bite out of me?" I smiled even though I was being serious.

"All I could think about was kissing you and making love to you. To me taking blood is part of making love, but I will not take your blood without your permission." He started to pull me closer to him. He was trying to be honest with me.

"And now? What do you want to do now?"

Miguel pulled me to him so our bodies were touching in every way possible with clothes on. "I want to carry you into the bedroom, tear your clothes off and have my way with you. I will not drink from you unless you ask me to."

I laughed, caught up in the moment, and maybe the bond, I nodded my head. "Okay."

Miguel lowered his lips to mine and kissed me hard forcing his tongue into my mouth. He pulled my legs up around his waist and made his way through the backdoor, down the hallway and into the bedroom. The lights were off and the shades were drawn. It was so dark I could barely see the outline of his body as he settled us down on the bed.

He ran his free hand slowly down my body starting at my cheek then down the smooth skin of my neck, over one of my breasts, across my stomach, and down the outside of my thigh. When he got to my knee, he grabbed the back of it and hitched my leg up so my thigh was resting on his. My hands stroked up and down his back slowly to a rhythm all their own.

He found the edge of my t-shirt and slowly started to move it up my body and over my head. Starting behind my ear, he kissed his way down my neck. His lips moved in between my lace covered breasts while his hands moved slowly pushing the shorts off my hips and onto the floor. Once he made it to my belly button, he worked his way back up between my breasts. Using his mouth, he moved the lace aside and found my nipple. He began to suck on it and flick his tongue making me wither with want.

He fumbled with the clasp on the back of my bra without releasing my breast. I grabbed both sides of his button-down shirt and yanked as I hard as I could. Giggling when buttons went flying all over the room.

When our bodies finally came together, skin on skin, an explosion of desire shot through me and I arched off the bed. Our lips met again, tongues going deeper with the anticipation of what was to come. His hand found its way between my legs and began to stroke me over my lace panties. I moaned and my body began to move in time with his fingers. He moved my panties to one side and ran his fingers over my warm, moist center. I cried out. I needed him inside me more than anything in the world. He thrust his finger into me and I moaned with pleasure and rocked with it, riding it. I fumbled with the button on his pants. Once I got them open I grabbed him through his boxer shorts and began to move my hand up and down his shaft in time with his finger inside of me.

He stopped, pulling himself away from me, and I let out a strangled cry. He removed his boxers and my panties. Once accomplished he crawled between my legs and positioned himself at my entrance. Thrusting forward gently he found his way inside me. I let out a breath I didn't realize I was holding. He was big, barely fit, it was perfect.

He was still for a moment as if trying to remain in control of the situation. Then he gently started to move in and out. *Is this okay?* He thought as he drove into the hilt then eased back out.

"No, it's amazing don't stop." I dug my nails into his butt. He continued at a steady pace while all I wanted him to do was speed up.

He found the spot, and his steady pace was forcing me closer and closer to the precipice I longed for.

"Almost there," I whispered. I felt him increase his speed until my muscles began to convulse around him and a bright light flashed before my eyes. I cried out in ecstasy and felt him empty himself inside me.

We were holding on so tight to each other that the pain of his fingers digging into me became pleasure. After a moment of lingering in the feeling, he collapsed on the bed next to me and pulled me into his arms.

"Wow," he said after a few minutes. "That was mind blowing."

I laughed. "Hum, yeah, definitely the best sex I've ever had." I kissed his chest. "Thanks."

No, thank you, he thought. "I don't know if I can move," He kissed the top of my head.

"Me neither. When will your sister be arriving?" I glanced at the clock.

"She should be here any time now." He was sad that he would have to move. "I guess I should get up and get dressed. If I can find my clothes." He looked around the dark room.

"No, not yet." I held him to me. "Just a few more minutes, please." I rested my head on his chest. "Do you want me to come with you?"

"Since you are the reason I asked Lolita to come you should be there," he said. *And I don't know if I could stand being that far away from you.*

"Okay." I drummed my fingers on his chest. "I know what

you mean; I don't know how long I can go without touching you either. What are we going to do?" I lifted my head to meet his eyes. "It's not that I mind spending time with you, but it would be nice if we didn't have to touch all the time." I took my hand and brushed it lightly down his cheek. While it was a great feeling, there was something not quite right about it either.

"I know what you mean. I'm wondering how we will do when we say goodnight later. You are here and me at the villa." He stilled my hand with his.

"I'm sure we'll work something out." I was trying not to sound worried. "Well, we had better get ready to go." I sat up and looked around.

"No, love, we have lots of time." He sat up with me, wrapped his arms around me and pulled me back down with him. *Lolita can wait. We will get up when are good and ready.*

"When was the last time you saw her?"

"It's been around a hundred years. Give or take," he said, thinking back. *I asked her here to help us figure out the bond and to help me change you.*

"Why do you think I would want to be like you?" I asked, tensing.

"I don't know what I was thinking when I talked to her about it. I know now it's not what you want. All I want is to be with you, get to know you, and spend time with you. If a time comes you want me to change you then we can talk about it, but I won't change you unless you want it. The bond has made me realize, if I ever want you to love me, changing you into a vampire will have to be your decision. I think it needs to be an informed one." He believed what he was saying for the most part. "I wish I could hear your thoughts as you can hear mine right now."

"I'm not so sure about that," I said but not pulling away. "Thank you for your honesty and for not draining me or changing me without asking. I don't know what I want right now. Except you, any way that I can have you." I brought our locked hands to my lips and kissed his hand. I let our hands drop, leaned into him, and kissed his lips softly. The kiss grew and I felt the hunger for his body rise in me again. I moved closer and deepened the kiss while he began to stroke me from hip to breast.

Lost in the moment it took both of us a second to hear the phone ringing. Miguel rolled onto his other side and reached for the phone on the bedside table. "Yes?" He listened to the voice on the other end of the line for a moment. "We are on the way," he said and hung up the phone. "Lolita just went through the gate. I would be a horrible host if I did not try to meet her at the front door. Can we continue this later?" He turned back to face me.

"I guess," I said with a sheepish grin. "Time to meet the sister." I climbed out of bed, and turning on the light. My nerves were beginning to hum. I wasn't looking forward to meeting Lolita thanks to Vince. Maybe she would be nice and nothing like he indicated. I was thinking of all of this while looking on the floor for my clothes. It took me a second to notice Miguel standing frozen in place staring at me.

"Miguel, is everything okay?" I asked, feeling exposed.

"Where did you get that tattoo?" I noticed his feelings were going from elation to fear and suspicion within seconds.

"Oh? Do you like it?" I thoughtlessly asked, twisting to look at it. "It was a drawing my mother did. I was so in love with it that I had it tattooed for my twenty-first birthday." I opened the door to the closet and walked in.

I fell to my knees as soon as I left Miguel's sight. The pain in my head felt like an ice pick going in one eye and out the other side. I closed my eyes and somehow it made the pain worse. I opened them and tried to crawl out of the closet. Every muscle twitch hurt, but I forced myself to keep moving. Once I cleared the door and saw Miguel the pain eased a small amount. He was on his knees trying to move toward me. After what felt like hours, our fingertips touched and the pain vanished. I let my legs give out and lay with my face on the floor. Anger was all I could feel from Miguel.

I almost commented on it but remembered I was keeping that ability to myself. "That sucked," I said instead and pulled myself up to a sitting position, but still touching him.

"Are you all right?" he rubbed my hand with his thumb.

"I am now." I closed my eyes, relieved there was no pain in the action. "I guess we should stay within sight of each other now."

"It would appear that way." He got to his feet, and offered me his hand to help me up from the floor. "Let's hurry, but also be careful not to leave each other's line of sight." He kissed me briefly before turning and looking for his clothes.

We dressed and left without any more painful experiences although the bathroom break was interesting. Something had changed with him, but I couldn't put my finger on what. I was glad I didn't have to explain anything else about the tattoo. I wished I could have felt more of his reaction to it, but the pain blinded me so quickly I couldn't think for myself let alone evaluate his feelings.

We entered the house through the pool entrance and walked quickly toward the main door. Miguel didn't let go of my hand until we walked around the last corner before the front door where a woman stood. I assumed it was Lolita.

She looked like the women who tried to kill me in my dream. I dropped Miguel's hand. Her almost white hair seemed to glow and her skin was porcelain. Almost like, she had a light bulb on the inside of her and the light from it was trying to find a way out. She looked sixteen, was tall, thin, and beautiful.

"Miguelito," she called as soon as she saw us. Dropping the bag in her hands she opened her arms to him.

Not sparing me a glance Miguel ran to his sister. I smiled for a moment watching the two of them have their reunion until the pain came back.

I put my hands on the side of my head, leaned against the wall and tried to breathe through it. I could not make a sound. Looking at Miguel, he turned very slowly and made his way back to me. The closer he came to me the more the pain ebbed. By the time he made it, I was standing on my own with a clear head. Miguel took my hand. *This is going to be difficult,* he thought as we headed back to his sister.

"Brother?" Lolita asked. "What's going on?"

"I will explain everything Lolo. Let's go sit down." He reached out with his free hand to take Lolita's. He led us into the parlor where he indicated Lolita sit on one settee while Miguel and I sat on the other one facing her.

"Lolita, this is Katie, the one I told you about." He pulled me in and kissed me on the cheek. "Katie this is my sister, Lolita."

"It's nice to meet you. Miguel has told me so much about you." I offered my hand to her.

"It is nice to meet the woman who made my brother call me home." Lolita reached across the distance, and shook my hand. Her hand was hard and even colder than Miguel's. She was feeling very excited, but I don't think it was from meeting me. "Do I know you from somewhere?" she asked as though touching me made her remember.

"No, I'm sure I would remember you." I flashed back to the knife coming down towards me.

"Now that you are here I am hoping you can help us with this bond." He squeezed my hand and he felt like he needed to choose his words very carefully.

"I can see it is causing you both some discomfort," Lolita said, scrutinizing me as she spoke. "And you have not tasted her yet either?"

"No, sister not yet. I'm going to let her make up her own mind on whether or not she wants to change. I have no desire to even taste her blood." He put an emphasis on the last word.

She nodded in acknowledgement and smiled. "My little brother has finally found love after all these years. How wonderful." She looked genuinely happy for me, but her feelings were darker. "What is going on with the touching? When you let go of her and came to me it appeared you were both in pain until you were touching again. Is the bond doing this?"

"That Lolo, is why I seek your knowledge of the world." He looked from me to Lolita. "Let me tell you everything that has happened since I met Katie." He barreled through the story of how we met and ended with what happened in the front hall. He kindly omitted that we had made love earlier in the evening.

"The connection is very interesting. It seems like something I heard of a long time ago," Lolita said, looking at me now. "I will have to look into it, make some calls." She got up, walking over to the wine bar on the far side of the room. "Miguelito, may I?" she pulled out a bottle of red wine.

"Of course. What a horrible host I am. Let me do that sister," he said, standing up. I stood up as well; I didn't need another headache, ever.

"Let's be a little bit more careful. I'll go with you," I said, squeezing his hand.

"That is a good idea, love." He squeezed back and we walked the short distance to join Lolita.

Lolita retreated from behind the bar, sat on one of the stools, crossed her legs, and watched us approach. "How long has this been going on?" she looked from Miguel to me then back at Miguel.

Let's see if we can do a few feet without too much discomfort. Miguel thought to me. *Sit down next to Lolo and I will go behind the bar and serve the wine. It's just a few feet.*

I nodded and he released my hand then I took a seat at the bar. "The first time I heard his voice in my mind was four nights ago. "Why do you ask?"

Miguel moved behind the bar and I felt pressure, but it was tolerable at this distance. *Let me know if you cannot handle it.* He thought and watched me for any sign of pain. He touched my hand for a moment, smiled, and ducked under the bar to retrieve three wine glasses. The slight pressure was gone when we touched and was back as soon as our connection broke.

"Watching you two move together you would think this had been going on for years if not decades." Lolita watched Miguel pour the wine into three glasses and placed a flask on the bar motioning for Lolita to take some of the blood first.

"Hearing the thoughts he directs at me helps a lot." I picked up my glass and stared at the dark red liquid. "Just now he told me to let him know if the pain got too bad. He's so thoughtful."

After Lolita had added a few drops of blood to her glass, she pushed it towards Miguel who put a few drops in his, and held his glass up in salute. "To the return of my sister. Home at last. Hopefully she will stay awhile this time." He wiggled his eyebrows at her. We all took obliging sips of wine and smiled at each other.

"Tell me what it is like to hear his thoughts," Lolita said, getting back to the subject at hand.

It was hard to explain. I had to think it through before replying. "The first night I heard him it sounded like someone was behind me whispering in my ear. When I turned around, I saw no one of course. Where were you anyway?"

"I was upstairs in the VIP section watching the crowd, Love."

"Oh," I said, shrugging my shoulders. "But now that I know what's going on. It's him talking without moving his lips. It's really hard not to respond out loud sometimes."

Lolita laughed and sipped her wine. "How do you both feel right now?" She looked from me to Miguel then back again.

"I feel like there is a vise between my temples and the further apart we are the more it squeezes." I paused to take a sip of wine. "Right now it's almost tolerable."

"And you Miguelito?" Lolita sipped her wine.

"You know we do not have to breathe but it is more comfortable to. I would describe it as a hole in my chest. It is not very deep at the moment just a small indentation the size of a tennis ball, but when I ran to hug you earlier it morphed into the size of a soccer ball. When I did breathe, it was like breathing in hot ash. Every breath burned my lungs and the pressure was all but unbearable." He grabbed at his chest with one hand while reaching out and taking my hand with his other hand.

"The change that occurs when you touch is astonishing," Lolita said, fingering her glass. "It's like the whole room breathed and relaxed with you. I have never seen anything like this before; I hope we can find out what is going on. Let's go and sit on the settees where you two can cuddle and relax. Katie, you look dead on your feet." Lolita refilled all of the wine glasses to empty the bottle and got up.

Miguel came around the bar without letting go of my hand and I rose. We walked hand in hand over to the settee where we were sitting before, with our wine glasses in our free hands. "Between the bond and my dreams it has been a trying few days," I admitted, settling myself against Miguel's shoulder with his arm around me.

"You have been having bad dreams?" she looked concerned.

Not yet my love if you can help it, he thought giving me a squeeze.

"Yes, they're foggy, but they aren't pleasant." I yawned and settled myself against Miguel's chest.

"Hum, I wonder if it has anything to do with the bond," Lolita said speculatively.

"I have been wondering it myself." Miguel kissed the top of my head. "As soon as I touch her while she is sleeping she goes from her dream into a dreamless state."

"Well, that may have something to do with it or, your touch wakes her just enough to end the dream. How often have you been with her when this has happened?"

I closed my eyes and let my mind drift. I felt safe leaning against Miguel while they continued their conversation.

"Only last night and this afternoon when she was taking a siesta," he said, sounding worried.

CHAPTER 26

"She's asleep," Miguel said in Spanish, pushing some of Katie's hair back away from her face. "Let's continue in Spanish, she barely understands it."

"You began the process," Lolita giggled. "Why are you carrying on about this bond nonsense? There is nothing special about her."

"I gave her a few drops last night while she slept." He crossed one leg over the other. "At the time I was not sure why I did it. I realized, as well, that she was average in looks, intelligence and spirit, but there was something about her that made me want her." He paused and waited for Lolita to look up from admiring her manicure.

"I'm listening." She folded her hands and rested them on her lap.

"Earlier tonight after we fucked for the first time. She turned on the light, and I saw the most beautiful thing in the world." He carefully pulled up the side of Katie's t-shirt.

Lolita leaned forward and looked at the partially exposed tattoo on Katie's side. "What are you saying Miguel?"

"That she is 'The One', and I have ruined my chances with her." Miguel buried his face in his free hand and let the shirt settle back in place. "I was so drawn to her, and it infuriated me that some average human had power over me. I took matters into my own hands before I knew. Now all is lost and I don't know what to do."

"How is everything lost?" Lolita reached out and took his hand away from his face. "You have begun the process of making her your slave. Follow through with it and the world will be ours for the taking with her as our figure head."

"You know that is not what the prophecy says." Miguel pulled his hand out of Lolita's.

"Says who? The prophecy has been translated a hundred different ways. I read a few that say the one who enslaves her will control her." Lolita wished her romantic brother would be practical for a change.

"That's not how I wanted it to happen. I have been waiting for centuries. I was going to woo her, treat her like the queen she is. I was going to make her fall in love with me. I wanted to be her equal, her king, now my only option is to enslave her and control her. I do not like this at all."

"This will be better and deep down you know it. You will answer to no one now. She will have to go along with what you decree; you will be the supreme leader of the vampires and the world. You will be God." Lolita clapped her hands together.

Miguel tensed as Katie stirred but didn't wake. He raised one eyebrow to her in warning. "Do you think it will work?"

"There is no reason why it shouldn't as long as you finish the slave process." Lolita got up and took the wine glasses back to the bar.

"You will have to change her to gain her power though. She will only be so strong as a human slave. All of the translations say that she will come into her power when she is turned." Lolita returned to her seat on the settee. "You will need to brainwash her first, so she knows you will always be her lord. That she must come to you in all things. It will take time."

"We can stretch out this bond nonsense for a while, then she won't be able leave my side," he said but he regretted it. He needed some alone time too. He was going to have to make some changes.

"You know this will work," Lolita said, leaning close to Miguel. "Here is what we are going to do."

CHAPTER 27

I rolled onto my side and felt the cool skin of the vampire lying next to me on the bed. This wasn't a dream, but I had no idea where I was. I opened my eyes and saw nothing but blackness. This was not the bed where I had spent the last two nights. It was bigger and there were no windows in this room. I had a feeling the sun was up but I could see no evidence of it.

Are you awake? Miguel asked in my mind.

"Yes, where are we?" I answered, running my hand through his long hair.

"In my room in the villa. Here, let me turn on a light." I felt him shift to get to the light switch. The white light made me blink blindly until my eyes adjusted to the brightness. "You slept for a long time." He turned back to me and leaned on his elbow.

"What time is it?" I asked, looking around the room for a clock. It looked like a room from a medieval museum. Everything was made of distressed wood that was probably a hundred or more years old.

We were in a huge four-poster bed with a white canopy and a

white down comforter on top of us. There was a massive wardrobe against the wall across from us, and a dressing table to my left. I noticed my backpack leaning against the other wall and it looked empty.

"Around noon," Miguel said and leaned down to kiss my exposed shoulder. "You slept so well last night. What did you dream of?"

"We were leaving town. It wasn't a bad dream; it was kind of good. You were with me and that was all that mattered." I smiled at him and leaned in for another kiss. He kissed me then pulled back, cocked his head, and looked at me. "How did you sleep?"

"I slept very well," he said, coming back for another kiss. This time I could feel intention behind it and I felt my body convulse as I reciprocated the kiss.

"I'm glad," I said in between the kisses.

Me too, he thought to me while grabbing my ear in his mouth sucking and nibbling on it.

"Watch your teeth," I said, enjoying the nibbling but unable to not worry about it. He broke off then and sat bolt upright.

"You are right. It's been too long since I have eaten," he said, not letting go of my hand.

"Are you hungry?" I could almost feel the hunger or maybe it was just me. I hadn't eaten in over twelve hours.

"I am, but not overly," he said, turning, and looking down at me. "You have nothing to worry about."

"I know, but I don't want you going hungry." I knew how men get when they need to eat.

"You are the one who is most likely hungry. When was the

last time you ate?"

"Before I fell asleep on the sofa yesterday afternoon."

He rolled without letting go of my hand and picked up the phone. *What would you like?* He asked while he waited for the phone to be picked up on the other end.

"Whatever is easy." I didn't want to be a nuisance. "Toast would be fine."

"Juan, Katie would like some breakfast," Miguel said into the phone. "No just something simple she does not want to be a nuisance. Toast or something," he paused while Juan talked. "Sounds good we will be up in a little while."

"How did you know what I was thinking?" I asked as soon as he hung up the phone.

"What do you mean?" he asked turning back to me and pulling me into his arms.

"I was just thinking that I didn't want to be a nuisance, and you said the same thing to Juan." I wondered if he could hear my thoughts now.

"I didn't hear you. I'm just getting to know you I promise." He gave me a quick kiss. "Should we get up?"

"I guess so. Who brought my backpack over?" I sat up, wondering how bad it would hurt when I let go of his hand to go to the bathroom.

"I had Juan bring over all of your things last night. It is safer for us both if we stay here," Miguel said kissing my cheek. *Are you afraid to let go?*

"Yes, I am. I don't want to deal with the pain anymore."

"Nor do I. Why don't we try it in stages for now? First let's stop touching but stay close." He let go of my hand but did not move away from me.

I took a deep breath, so far there was nothing. "That's okay," I said and slowly moved to the edge of the bed. As I stood at my side of the bed a tiny prickle of a headache started but it was bearable. I pulled my arms over my head and stretched, "I can deal with this. How about you?" I looked over at him and saw his creased forehead. I jumped back on the bed and crawled to his side as fast as I could.

"I'm sorry. I should have checked with you before I got off the bed." I rested the back of my hand on his cheek.

He started to laugh and put his arms around me. "I wasn't in pain; I was just thinking about how badly I wanted to touch you. Thank you for coming to my rescue though," he said, kissing me.

"Anytime." I was happy, laying there in his arms. "As much as I would love to spend the day in bed with you, we have to figure out how to get rid of this bond."

"Really? Are you tired of me already?"

"No, but if we don't fix it, there are things we are going to have to learn to do together that we may not like." There were a million things running through my mind I wanted to do without him. "Like you need to eat, and my bladder is full."

"Yes, I was thinking of a few things as well. We will have to be very tolerant for a while I think," he said, letting go of me. "Let's take one thing at a time, and it sounds like that would be the bathroom currently."

"What's next?" he asked while I washed my hands.

I looked at the tub and realized how grimy I was feeling. "I could use a shower.”

So could I, he thought to me. “How about a bath?” He motioned to the tub that was the size of a hot tub.

“That sounds so nice.”

He slowly moved away from me to turn on the nozzle and stopped up the drain. The water poured out like a fire hose. It would take very little time to fill up. *I’m going to go in the bedroom for just a moment if you think you can handle it,* he thought while taking both my hands in his.

“Go ahead, just hurry.” I tried not to let the panic of the coming pain take over.

And he was gone. *We are really going to have to work on this problem,* he thought to me. I jumped when he was back at my side rubbing my arms. He wasn’t gone long enough for the pressure to register.

“Wow, that was fast.” I had never seen anyone move that fast before. He was in front of me one moment, gone the next and then back again. “How did you do that?”

“Vampires are very fast, my love. Since I knew exactly what I was going to do I was able to do it as quickly as possible. My speed will come in handy as long as I’m not caught off guard like last night. We are beginning to figure out our limitations. If we are careful we should not put each other in much more pain,” he said, beginning to pull at the bottom of my t-shirt.

“Yes, it’s already helping.” I looked down at his fumbling hands. “Do you want me to take it off?”

No, I want to take it off for you, he thought and began to pull it up in earnest while waiting for my response.

"Please," I said and smiled at him. He pulled the shirt over my head and dropped it on the floor. He grabbed the drawstring on my pants, pulled the bow apart and let them fall from my hips as I went for his and did the same. He turned and shut the water off to the tub.

"It's ready," he said, turning back to me sticking his pointer fingers in between my panties and my hips. He smiled and pulled them down until gravity took over. He took my hand then and helped me step into the hot water.

He followed and went to a shelf that held an assortment of soaps, shampoos, and conditioners on it. He picked up a pink bar of soap and glided through the water towards me. *Turn around*, he thought. I obeyed placing my hands on the edge of the tub. I heard him lathering the soap for a moment before his hands were on my back rubbing in a circular motion over my shoulder blades and working his way down to my bottom. Still rubbing in circles, he squeezed each cheek then moved to my arms. He lifted each one in turn and lathered them all the way to the tips of my fingers then dipped them into the water to rinse them and place them back where they started.

I concentrated on the feel of him touching me in such a gentle and caring way. I tried not to think of how he was making my insides tighten and surge with every caress.

Turn around, he thought, placing a hand on my shoulder to turn me to face him. *Lay back and relax.* He placed a hand on my leg and followed it to my feet. With the soap, he washed one foot then moved up my leg with long firm strokes. He began on the inside of my leg moving the soap in circles up to my inner thigh and continued back down on the outside of my leg.

After repeating this with the other leg, he spread them and

moved in-between them. Starting at my collarbone, he made small circles across my chest slowly. Too slowly, he made it to my breasts making circle after circle around my nipples, which were standing at attention.

He moved to my side and washed the tattoo over and over again before finishing with my stomach. He placed the soap into its dish on the other side of the tub and took my hand to help me rinse off the soap. When he was done, he took me in his arms and kissed me so deeply that I lost myself for a second.

Finally, able to pull away I went to the soap dish and picked up a green bar of soap. "Your turn," I said and he turned around obediently. I started with his arms soaping them up and messaging them as I went along. When I finished with his arms, I moved to his neck and shoulders then moved down his chest. His stomach was so hard, flat, and rigid that it gave me a new definition for washboard abs as I ran the soap over them.

I passed by his rock hard, long, thick cock, moved on to his legs, and rubbed them down as I did his arms. After I finished with his front, I turned him around, started on his back, and spent some major time on his butt digging my fingers into his cheeks, enjoying it. When I finished, I put the soap back in its dish and turned to find him less than an inch from me. He tilted his head down to meet my lips and we locked in a kiss that grew until I wanted him inside me more than I wanted my next breath.

He sat down bringing me down onto his lap and I wrapped my legs around him. We continued kissing and his hands caressed my body relentlessly. I pulled back from the kiss to straighten my neck out from bending over him and he latched onto my nipple stroking and sucking it until I felt a twinge of pain. A moment later, he had pushed me to the other side of the tub so hard my head bounced off the porcelain edge.

"What's wrong?" I cried out, trying to focus on his face to see if I could read anything from it. His eyes were bulging and bright. His mouth was open and his fangs elongated. He looked as though he was panting, breathing deeply and quickly with his tongue hanging out. Then I felt it, hunger. A hunger so intense it was making me hungry.

Get out now and stop the bleeding, he thought to me.

I looked down and saw a small trail of blood from just above my nipple trailing down my stomach into the water. I leaped out and lunged for a towel. I got it pressed to my chest just before the vise on my head began to squeeze. The pain was so intense my brain was having trouble telling my lungs what to do. I tried to breathe but my lungs would not fill up with air. I forced my shaky legs to move toward the tub and the vampire in the throes of blood lust, while trying to fill my lungs. Finally, I was close enough to allow a small breath of air to reach my lungs. Moving closer I could think again.

He bit me. I thought pushing the white towel against my breast and fighting back tears. He promised he wouldn't. "How could you?" I choked out. "You promised."

I didn't mean to. It was an accident. I could felt the sincerity in his thoughts. *Have you stopped bleeding? We have to get out of here before I lose control.*

I looked down at my breast; I was pretty sure the bleeding had stopped. "I'm not bleeding anymore," I said, keeping my eyes on him for any sudden moves in my direction.

I'm going to get out. I need you to throw the bloody towel as far away as possible and grab a clean one, then I'm going to get us out of here, he thought already half-way out of the tub. I threw the towel to the other end of the bathroom, reached for a new towel, and threw another one to Miguel. He caught it, grabbed my arm, and drug me quickly into the bedroom slamming the door behind him. He picked me up and threw me onto the bed. *Please pick up the phone and tell Juan that Lolita must come here now*, he thought grinding his teeth with his back to me.

I scrambled over to the phone and picked it up. It rang twice before a voice came through on the other end. "Yes, Master?" he asked with a thick accent.

"Hum, this is Katie. Miguel needs Lolita right now," I said with a trembling voice.

"Yes, Mistress. I will send her down right away."

I put the handset back on the receiver and huddled under the blankets with my back to Miguel. *I'm so sorry my love. I'm fighting the blood lust as best as I can right now, but since we can't be more than a few feet from each other I'm not sure what to do. Lolita will at least be able to hold me back until we can figure something out.*

"Can I get some clothes?" I asked, inching toward my backpack.

Here, I will get them for you; don't move. He thought racing around the room and depositing my clothes in front of me. I pulled them on trying to move as little as possible. There was a knock at the door and Miguel was there to open it as his sister glided into the room.

"What is wrong my brother?" she asked, taking his face in both of her hands, and looking in his eyes. Then she pulled up her chin and I saw she was taking a deep breath. Great, now I was in the room with two vampires instead one. How was this going to help me?

"He bit me," I said, my voice still shaking. "I don't think he meant to, but he freaked out and I don't know how to help him."

"Miguel, look at me. The only way you are going to be able to stop the blood lust is to drink. Is there a donor nearby?"

Miguel didn't speak. He looked at Lolita then back to me. *Please tell her there is no one nearby. Ask her what to do.*

"He says there is no one near. He wants to know what to do. Is there anything that can be done?"

"No, his thirst will grow until it is satisfied. He has waited too long to eat. You could help him."

NO. Miguel shouted in my head. I looked at him and felt the pain and hunger that was dominating his actions.

I wanted to help him. He had been good to me, but would I be sacrificing part of myself it I let him drink from me? What about the prophecy? I wish Vince had been able to tell me more about it. I looked into Miguel's eyes, he was going crazy with thirst. I couldn't let him suffer. "Okay, Miguel drink from me." I got off the bed and walked over to him.

"No, I will not lose you," he said finally, speaking, and backing away from me.

"Miguel, I'm here. I will not let you take more then you need to satisfy your thirst. I promise I will not fail you," Lolita said, running her hand through his hair. "Lay down on the bed Katie."

I looked at Lolita for a moment then did as she said. *I don't know if I can do this my love.*

"You have to try. I can't bear the pain you are in right now," I said in a calm and quiet voice. I was resolved to let him do this. I had to save him, and if this wasn't part of saving him then I didn't know how else to do it.

They began to move toward me very slowly and I closed my eyes. Miguel sat on the bed and pulled me into his arms. *I love you.* He brought his head down to the point where my shoulder met my neck. He gave me a light kiss then slid his fangs in.

There was no pain, only pleasure washed over me. My eyes rolled back in my head and my body arched toward him. His arms were around me keeping me in place as the lower half of my body bowed and withered with delight. Before I knew it an orgasm that put all other orgasms to shame swept over me. The bliss stuttering on and on becoming smaller with each stutter until it was gone.

I slowly floated back to earth and realized Miguel was still drinking from me. *I think you have had enough,* I thought to him and I felt him pull his fangs out and retreat.

"Thank you." He laid back on the bed.

I looked up to see Lolita hovering over the bed. "Miguel, you did it. You did not need me after all." She patted him on the leg. "When you two are ready to talk I will be upstairs." She turned and left the room.

You are the reason I was able to stop my love, he thought to me pulling me closer to him.

"How? I didn't do anything but enjoy the ride." I rested my head on his chest.

"You told me to stop." He paused looking down at me. "What do you mean? You enjoyed the ride?"

"I didn't say anything out loud, I thought to you, that you had enough." I was finding it hard to explain. "Your bite gave me an orgasm. Are you saying you heard me say 'I think you have had enough'?"

"Yes, I must have heard your thought and you stopped me from drinking more. It should have been extremely painful for you," he said, sounding confused. "Try and tell me something with your mind."

You're still naked, I thought to him running my hand down his bare chest. "Did you get that?"

"No, I didn't. Maybe it's just when I drink from you," he said, staring at the ceiling. "Words cannot convey how sorry I am. I was enjoying myself so much that I forgot I needed to be careful about the fangs." He ran his hand through my damp hair.

"I know you're sorry and I accept your apology, but please be careful in the future. Will this change anything for us? You, drinking my blood?" I was still thinking about how great it felt.

"Have you ever donated blood before?"

"Yes, I try to every six months or so." I was not following his train of thought.

"What did they tell you do after you donated?" He was mindlessly running his hand up and down my back.

"They gave me some orange juice and a cookie and had me sit down for a while," I said as the light bulb finally came on. "I see now, but you didn't take all that much did you?"

"No, I only drank from you for a few minutes and I did not take you at a vein so you lost very little. But I want you to be feeling your best." He kissed the top of my head.

"I feel great right now, but you never really answered my question. Will you have power over me now? Will I be your slave?" I pulled myself up on my elbow to look at his face.

"It does not work that way, my love. You are still your own person. The slave bond process requires you to drink from me; right now you are just a donor, as we like to say. I can't force you to do anything at the present time." He placed a hand on my shoulder and pulling me down to meet his lips in a kiss.

"I need food," I said, pulling away from the kiss. "Will you please feed me?" I moved to get off the bed.

"I guess I'll have to remember you need to eat more than I do." He got up went over to the closet in the corner and opening the door. "I'll be dressed in a flash."

I was a little lightheaded as we made our way into the dining room where Lolita sat with a laptop in front her. There was juice and a covered plate sitting in the same spot where I had eaten before. I made my way to the chair to sit down and eat. Before I could pull it out though, Miguel was there with the chair already pulled out for me. As I sat he pushed the chair in then took the seat next to me and thought, *eat.*

"Thank you for your help," he said to Lolita.

"You didn't need it." She did not bother to look up from the screen. "I have put out a few feelers to find out more about the bond you two have made."

"Nevertheless, thank you." He said placed his hand on my back and began to rub circles lightly as I ate. "Katie had an interesting experience while feeding me."

Lolita smiled, looked up from the computer, sat back in her chair and stared at us. "How did it feel Katie?"

"Amazing, there was no pain only immense pleasure," I said, lightly brushing the bite marks on my neck. They were tender but not painful.

"That's interesting. I have never heard of anyone explain being the donor as pleasurable before. It's hard to tell what has or will change. Every union is different; some couplings form bonds where the vampire can feel things about the human. While for others, nothing changes. I must say I expected something to happen since you already seem to be so bonded. How do you feel about each other?"

"I feel the same as before," Miguel said.

"So do I." I felt some relief that he didn't just want me for food.

"What about the bond? Have you experienced anything different with the proximity problem?"

"We haven't been more than a few feet apart since he fed." I said, already dreading the thought of the experiments that were coming.

"When you are ready, you should see if the distance issue has changed at all," Lolita said, and returned to her laptop. "The more information we have on this the more likely we are to figure out what is happening and if there is a way to fix it."

"Why don't we go out in the hall and see if anything has changed?" Miguel asked, getting up from his chair.

I shrugged and made a face I wasn't proud of. I was so tired of the pain. I had only been up for three hours and there had been more drama then I could handle, and there was no way this was going to end well. On the other hand, it would be nice to know if something had changed. I got up from my chair and took Miguel's hand nervously.

It will only take a moment and if the pain is too much I will race back to you as quick as I can, he thought giving me a shaky smile. We walked into the long hallway then toward the front door. Once there, we turned to face the gantlet. "I think we should start with me backing away from you. When the pain gets to be too much just let out a shout and I'll be back before you know it," he said, turning to face me and giving me a brief kiss on the mouth.

"Okay," was all I could say. I didn't like this plan but I couldn't come up with a better one either. Lolita stood beside me and took my hand in hers.

"It will be okay, Katie," she said and nodded for Miguel to begin.

For the first five feet or so it was just a pin-prick. I could handle it. My eyes locked on Miguel's as he took one step after another backward. With each step he took away from me, it felt like someone was tightening the vise around my head. It became harder and harder to fill my lungs. By the time I couldn't take it anymore I couldn't call out or even move my lips. He should be back at any moment I thought he has to be in the same amount of pain I am right? Black spots clouded my vision. I blinked, trying to chase them away but then everything went black.

CHAPTER 28

Breathe. The voice in my head was saying. I tried but my muscles had stopped doing my will and there was still a vise clamping down on my head. A moment later, the pain was replaced with a pressure on my chest and it had a rhythm: pressure, release, pressure, release, pressure, release, and then someone touched my lips and I felt the warm breath of another being forced to fill up my lungs then the pressure rhythm began again.

Realizing they were giving me CPR I concentrated on the muscles surrounding my lungs and commanded them to begin working again. Finally, they began to move properly and I inhaled a deep breath and coughed an exhale.

"Thank God," Miguel said. "She's breathing on her own again. Let's get her to the settee." He picked me up and we moved quickly to another room. He laid me on something soft then placed my head in his lap. "Why didn't you say something?" he asked his sister angrily.

"I didn't realize how bad she was until she began to fall. I'm sorry," Lolita said, sounding matter of fact. "I don't spend very much time with humans, and I forgot what normal and not normal breathing was. You really had no pain? That is astonishing," she said with an amused voice.

"Can we please wait with the twenty questions until she is conscious again?" Miguel asked and I felt his cool hands on my neck then my forehead. *Love, can you hear me? I'm so sorry I caused you pain yet again. Can you open your eyes?*

I concentrated on my eyes trying to will them open. "So you felt no pain that time? I guess feeding you my blood made you immune to the bond," I croaked out and tried to sit up but my body was not ready for it and my head began to spin. Miguel put his arms around me and pulled me back down to his lap before I face- planted into the floor.

"Shush, stay where you are for a while, love," he said, continuing to stroke my forehead and neck. "Why didn't you tell me you could not breathe?"

"It's hard to talk when there is no air in my lungs. It happened so fast. One minute I was trying to ignore the pressure and the next I could not get my lungs to work," I said, fighting back the tears pricking my eyes as I remembered the pain and the feeling of suffocation. "You didn't feel anything?" I felt a tear running down my cheek.

Miguel wiped it away. *I'm sorry*, he thought to me again. "No, I felt nothing out of the ordinary. The bond was still there I wanted to be next to you more than anything but there was no pain this time. Do you agree with what Katie said Lolo? That with her blood in my system she was still with me even though I was not with her?"

"It would make perfect sense, and it would make tracking

down what kind of bond it is much easier. I wonder if it would work both ways."

"I don't want to drink any blood." I tried again to sit up and this time succeeding without the spins hitting me. Miguel put his arm around me as I leaned against the backrest of the settee.

"But what if it meant you could go out and play in the sun?" Miguel asked. "Believe me, Love, I want to spend as much time as possible with you but do you want to spend every day inside, in the dark with me?"

"If I drink your blood what will happen to me?" I asked, tensing up. "I don't want to be your slave."

"Have you tried mind control on her Miguel?" Lolita asked.

"No, I never saw a reason for it." He brought his other arm across my chest, and locked his hands together.

"What do you mean 'mind control'? You can do that?" I asked Lolita with a sour feeling growing in my gut.

"Try it," Lolita said, without answering my question.

Relax, Love, everything will be okay just look into my eyes for a moment, Miguel thought and I complied. He gazed into my eyes but he did not stop there. It felt like he was looking at my brain by going through my eyes. He was searching for just the right spot. Then he blinked and the rich chocolate color of his eyes that I loved so much was gone.

His eyes had gone almost completely white with just the tiny dot of his pupil breaking the whiteness. I blinked and tried to pull back. His eyes were freaking me out, but I couldn't move because his arms were locked around me. *Look into my eyes Love, I will not hurt you,* he thought as his arms tightened. With no escape I did as he asked and stared into his eyes.

Why was I trusting him? I asked myself as it dawned on me that every promise he had made he broke. The broken promises were not necessarily his fault, but we still had no idea what was going on. We needed to find at least a temporary fix. It was too bad I was taking the blunt of the punishment. I was the most breakable of the three of us. How was he going to accidentally hurt me this time? I wondered.

"This isn't working," he said, sounding frustrated and blinking his eyes back to the chocolate.

"Sorry, I wasn't really paying attention. I'll try harder if you want to do it again," I said, trying to be agreeable about the whole thing.

"No," he chuckled and Lolita frowned. "If it worked it wouldn't matter if you were paying attention or not." He smiled and brought me in for a kiss.

"So this is a good thing?" I asked, looking at Lolita.

"Yes, I think so. From what I understand there are a few humans out there who are immune to us," Lolita said. "Maybe I should try it on you, and see if it is just Miguel or if it is all vampires."

"Why do we need to know?" Miguel asked, feeling very defensive. "We are only trying to see if my blood may work on her the way hers worked on me. Not to see if she can be used as a weapon."

"That is not what I am trying to do brother. You do not need to be so possessive. I am saying it would be nice to know the extent of her abilities." Lolita got up from her chair and started to pace back and forth in front of us.

"Maybe she's right. It wouldn't hurt to try." I gulped wishing I had kept my mouth shut.

"I want to see if you are the only one who cannot control her," Lolita said, looking at Miguel. "Do you trust me?"

Miguel let out a deep breath. "Of course I trust you with my existence. But I believe that my existence revolves around Katie now too," he said, looking at me. "But still. . ."

"What is the worst that could happen? You will be right here to make sure Lolita won't take advantage of me." I bit my lip regretting my own bravery. "No offense Lolita." I wanted to know if vampires could control me.

"Do I have your promise sister that if you are able to control her you will release her at once?" Miguel asked and I felt his reluctance to allow Lolita to try this.

Lolita stopped her pacing stood directly in front of Miguel and smiled. "Yes brother I promise." She held her hand out to me.

Miguel's embrace did not slacken to let me up so I kissed him lightly. "It will be fine Miguel. How could it be any worse than what has already happened today?" I asked, pulling out of his arms. "You will still stay close by though, right?" I got to my feet, remembering that I could not go very far from him.

"I'll be right behind you," he said, standing with both of his hands resting on my hips.

I took a deep breath and Lolita took both of my hands into hers. "Look into my eyes Katie." I obeyed and she blinked. Her eyes went from icy blue to the same whiteness Miguel's had. I noticed immediately that this was different. I could feel her trying to get into my head. It felt like her hand wrapped itself around the back of my brain and squeezed, trying to mold it into the shape she wanted. I took a deep breath deciding I should fight this somehow so I mentally thought about pushing back against the probing fingers. One by one I forced them out by pulling each finger away from my brain. Lolita's face was in deep concentration. I realized she was squeezing my hands so tightly that I was losing feeling in the tips of my fingers. I tried to pull my hands out of hers with no luck; I turned to look at Miguel who was smiling.

"That's enough Lolo. Are you trying to remove her fingers?" Miguel asked in a light tone.

Lolita blinked her eyes and they went back to their normal icy blue. She looked down at our hands and released mine. "I felt you pushing me out. It was amazing and frustrating at the same time." She went back over to her chair and sat down hard. "Never in my long life has there been a human I could not control to some extent. You are very strong, Katie. I would be careful if I were you. Some of us do not take kindly to humans we can't control."

"Lolo, don't scare her. What do you mean you felt her pushing you out?" Miguel asked, pulling me with him over to the settee.

"I was trying to find a hole, you understand, but everywhere I tried she pushed me back. I guess what I am trying to say is that not only did she feel me trying to get in, but she was able to keep me out altogether." Lolita didn't look happy with herself and I could feel the hate pouring off her.

Miguel chuckled. "You got further then I did. I didn't even get a chance to look for a hole; the gate was locked on the way in. She would be fine if she had my blood. What do you think Katie?" he asked turning to look at me.

I thought about it for a minute. Not being able to enjoy the sun was sounding like a major bummer. I was already wishing for the sun even though the room was full of artificial light. There was a chance I would be his slave though. Really, how was that different then where we were at now? He could leave me without feeling any pain and let me die if he wanted to. I was already at his mercy. I just hoped I could trust him with it.

"What's the worst that could happen? As we are right now, there can't be too much of a difference." I forced a smile on my lips. "Let give it a try."

Lolita smiled and got up. "You'll probably want some privacy for this," she said and glided out of the room.

"Why do we need privacy?" I asked, turning to Miguel, and searching his face.

"You said that when I drank your blood it was orgasmic?" he asked taking my hand in his.

"Oh," I said, feeling a little slow realizing what he meant. "Is it going to feel like that again?" I was beginning to look forward to it.

"Most likely." He tried to hide a smile but didn't succeed. He was looking forward to this as well.

"Ok, then how should we do this?" I wasn't sure if I should just bite him or what.

"Well, let's get comfortable," he said, kicking off his shoes and I did the same. Then he turned so his back was resting on the arm of the sofa with his legs stretched out over the seat cushions. He took my hand and guided me to sit in between his legs with my back to him.

Relax, he thought to me and pulled me so my back was resting against his chest. *I'm going to bite my wrist then give it to you so you can drink.*

I took a deep breath and nodded my head. I felt like we needed to be very quiet for some reason. I heard a crunch and his bleeding wrist was in front of my face. I wrapped my hands around each side of the tear in his arm and brought it to my mouth to drink. The blood was cool in my mouth. Definitely a few degrees cooler than it should have been, and there was a sweet metallic taste to it. I wouldn't say it tasted good but it wasn't bad either, like a penny. I swallowed and sucked and swallowed.

Gradually I felt him growing hard beneath me and I wondered why I was not feeling anything. As the blood made its way to my stomach a euphoric feeling came over me. Miguel began to thrust his hips into my back. My body responded in kind growing wet and swollen. I continued to suck and the feeling grew. I needed him, and I needed him now. I let go of his wrist and turned to face him.

Our lips met and his tongue plunged into my mouth. I moved my legs to straddle him and he continued to thrust but now he was hitting just the right spot with each upward thrust. My hands roamed over his body while his were undoing my bra from under my shirt. He moved his hands to my breasts stroking and pinching my nipples.

He broke the kiss and pulling my t-shirt up he latched on to one nipple sucking and lightly nipping it. *Please be careful,* I thought, *I don't want to have to stop in the middle again.*

Do not worry, I am. I want to be inside you right now. He thought, and without letting go of my nipple, he pulled my shirt over my head.

I was too caught up in the lust to realize I just thought something to him, and he heard it. I undid the buttons of his shirt and pulled it off his shoulders. *You are going to have to move so I can take my pants off,* he thought.

I moved to the side of him, and he took off his pants and boxers in the same movement then he did the same to me. He sat on the sofa with his feet on the floor and pulled me on top of him. He began kissing me again while one hand rubbed my nipple and the other invaded me, hitting *that* spot over and over.

Please, I thought to him and we broke off from the kiss so could he lifted me just enough to sheath himself inside of me. We both let out a cry of pleasure. He held me there for a moment just enjoying the feeling.

Slowly I began to rise and fall on him. Closing my eyes, I concentrated on nothing but the feel of him as I forced him in and out. His hands went to my hips and he found the spot that made me constrict around him. I sped up knowing each time he rubbed over that spot the closer I came to my climax. Miguel began to pull me up and slammed me back down on top of him. With one last stroke I broke and we came together. I collapsed on top of him with my whole body shaking and my breathing ragged. *Wow*, I thought, *that had to be the best I had ever had.*

Me too. He thought, bringing his arms around me, and hugging me even closer to him.

You can hear me? I thought to him and started shaking even harder but for a different reason. If he could hear me did that mean he could control me? Had we been wrong? Was I his slave now? I pulled away and got off him and scrambled to put my clothes on.

"What's wrong?" Miguel asked, coming over to me and watching as I pulled my shorts up.

"Am I your slave?" I asked, picking up my bra, pulling the straps over my arms and fastening it in the back. What was I going to do? Could I just leave? Would the pain still be there? I needed to think clearly but that wasn't happening with him standing next to me trying to find out what was going on in my head.

"Why would you think that?" he asked. *Please talk to me. What are you thinking?*

"Because you can hear my thoughts now. This whole thing is just too much for me right now." I pulled my t-shirt over my head. What do I do now? I wanted to leave; to escape from this dream that was turning into a nightmare. Fear is what kept me there. Fear that if I walked away from him I wouldn't survive it.

"What can I do?" he asked interrupting my thought process. He wanted to reach out to me but he understood my current state of mind. He did not touch me but stayed close.

"I don't know. I need to be alone, but I'm afraid of walking away from you. I'm so afraid of the pain." I rubbed my arms and felt tears run down my cheeks.

Take a deep breath love. Think about how you feel. Is there any pain? He thought, not moving from his position. *If you think you can, take a step back. If it hurts I will be next to you in a moment.*

I closed my eyes took a breath and held it for ten seconds. Was there any pain? It didn't feel like it. I took a step backward thinking it was now or never. Nothing, no pain. Another step everything was okay. I turned and walked very slowly to the door. When I got there I turned to look at him. He hadn't moved and there was still no pain. No vise around my head and, I was breathing calmly and normally.

He smiled, but didn't move from where he was. "I know you wish to leave, but I would suggest you stay indoors until we get this figured out. If you went outside and the blood wore off, you could die."

Of course. That was exactly what I wanted to do. Just sit in the sun and pretend this was all a bad dream. Maybe it was. Maybe I just needed to wake up. *Can you still hear me?* I thought to him.

Yes, what would you like to do? He asked taking a step toward me.

I would like to know if I'm your slave, but I'm so tired right now. I need to lay down by myself for a while.

Would you like to go back to my room or one of the guest rooms?

That was a loaded question, but right then I didn't really care about hurting his feelings. I just wanted to not think. *A guestroom for now*, I thought and I watched his face fall for a split second before it went blank.

"Come with me and I will show you to a room close to my office. I will be there in case the blood wears off," he said, meeting me at the doorway and walking through it without looking at me. I followed a few steps behind him to a room just down the hall from the living room and dining room. He opened the door but did not go inside. "If you need anything just pick up the phone and Juan will get it for you. If the pain comes back think to me or yell and I'll be here," he said as I walked into the room and he shut the door.

I ran to the bed and threw myself on it. I was being selfish. I could feel his pain even though he was trying to shield his thoughts from me. Everything was so out of control. Did I love him or was it just this crazy bond? I thought about the night he came for dinner and how incredible it was, and our conversation while I was at the pool. There was defiantly more than just this dumb bond. I did like him and

I was working on more, but we needed to be done with all the drama. I know, I know I was laying there creating more drama but I was scared. He never answered my question. I wondered if he did not know the answer. I just flipped out and took the chance to be by myself as soon as I could. I was the bad guy. How could I make this up to him?

Miguel, I'm sorry, I thought to him then floated into sleep.

It was cold and dank. The overpowering smell of mold and mildew almost had me gagging. I opened my eyes to see where I was but there was nothing but black. I blinked a few times to make sure I was actually opening my eyes. I had no idea where I was or why I was there. I tried to move, but I realized I was standing on the balls of my feet, and my arms were above my head, like a ballerina.

I tried to pull my arms down, but I was chained to the ceiling. I could not move my arms or flatten out my feet. I was trapped.

"Help!" I screamed and yanked on the chains as panic washed through me. I lost traction with my feet and swung around wildly until I could plant the balls of my feet on the floor again.

"Be still child," my mother's voice said out of the darkness.

"Mom?" I asked the darkness. "What is going on? Can you help me?"

"This is the path you have chosen, to be a slave to this man. You must break free of the bond," she said, coming out of the darkness to stand in front of me.

"I didn't choose this; I haven't chosen anything." My eyes filled with unshed tears.

"You exchanged blood with him, my dear, the process has begun. If you do not stop it, this is how you will live your life. Bound to him and controlled by him." She walked around me sounding disappointed. "Is that what you want?"

"No." I pulled on the chains again to no avail. "I will be no one's slave. But what about the pain? If I don't share blood with him the pain is too much."

"The pain is in your head my dear. All you have to do is remove it."

"How do I do that?"

"You must look within yourself, find where it has taken hold and pull it out by its roots." She stopped in front of me and looked into my eyes. Her eyes changed just like Miguel's and Lolita's had when they tried to command me.

I wanted to fight, but my mom was too strong. It felt like she pried my brain in half, dug her fingers in and rooted around for a while. I screamed in pain when I felt her grab onto something and pull it out.

"There it is," she said, holding a long black root with a few shoots splaying out it. "This will take away the pain he caused you," she said, flicking it away.

"Thank you, Mom," I said as the pain subsided. "What do you mean the pain he caused me? Miguel was in pain too; will his pain be gone as well?" I didn't understand what was going on.

"Sweetheart, he was never in any pain. He has been using you from the beginning." She shook her head and wiped the tears from my cheeks.

"What?" I turned my head away from her hand. "He was telling me the truth, I felt it. He told me he loves me."

"He has been manipulating you. If he is truly what you want, then I will leave you to it. But look at it from an outsider's perspective and the pieces will fall into place." She forced my head back so she could look into my eyes.

I thought about it. Miguel saw the fight in the bar. Antonio told me he would give the owner the money for the cottage. Antonio knew everything that was going on. He must have been reporting back to Miguel. Who has ever heard of all the trains and buses being booked unless there was a national emergency? Miguel was the most powerful man in the city, of course he could make sure I could not leave town. He set everything up. I wondered how Vince was involved.

"How do break the bond, Mom? How do I get away from him?" I brought my arms down and stood on the soles of my feet. My bonds broken.

"Just as I have shown you." The root looking thing magically appearing in her hand. "I cannot remove this one for you, the pain would kill you. You must look inside yourself and pull it out. It is not too deep yet but the longer you are with him the deeper it will grow."

"But how?" I asked, reaching out to her.

"Be strong my sweet, I love you," she said, before fading away into the dark.

"Mom," I called after her but received no response.

CHAPTER 29

I awoke with a start sitting straight up in bed. Had that been just a dream or had my mother warned me off Miguel? Everything she said and what I had thought had made sense. The pain of her pulling that thing out of me was real. I rubbed my temples, and ran my hands through my hair to make sure I didn't have a huge incision in my head. It all added up, why would Miguel be interested in someone like me beyond my gift? I needed to get out of here and break the bond we started when we exchanged blood.

How was I supposed to 'look inside myself' and pull it out? There was no better time than now to try since I was alone. I lay back down on the bed and closed my eyes. I pictured my brain, or what I thought my brain looked like, I kept thinking of molds people use at Halloween to make Jell-O look like brains. It was close enough. I thought about what my brain looked like, with neurons firing and moving. I looked for anything out of place. I rotated it around to get the whole three-hundred-and-sixty-degree view and everything looked normal, pink and gooey. I looked at the top, then the bottom. Nothing, it must be deeper inside. I cut it in two and looked. There it was, right in the middle. A dark, black mass, it looked different then the root like string my mom had pulled out. This was more of a ball that pulsed. I visualized taking my hand, wrapping my fingers around it and pulling. It was really stuck in there but I made it move, the pain tore through and I blinked back tears. There was no way I was going to get rid of it that way, I thought as I lay back in bed and tried to catch my breath.

I needed a new plan, but nothing came to mind. I wanted to leave, I wanted to run away and never look back. I needed someplace to go though. Vince was ready to leave. I needed to talk to Vince, maybe he could help, but I needed to go outside and get away from the prying ears of Miguel and Lolita first. I would go for a run, I decided. I could feel when I lost Miguel in my mind. I just needed to run far enough away.

I got up quietly, made my way to the door and listened for a moment. It was quiet. I opened the door a crack and looked into the hall. No one was around so I tiptoed down the hall and made my way to Miguel's bedroom where all of my stuff was.

I closed the door and looked at my empty bag. He or someone had unpacked all of my clothes. I went into the closet and looked around. There were lots of men's clothing hanging on racks. I was sure one suit alone could have funded my entire trip. The room had four rows of clothing racks, one along each long wall and two racks in the middle cut the room in half. The closet was huge, bigger then my last bedroom maybe bigger than my apartment. The far side of the closet was empty except for my things. Was he expecting me to move in? There was a built-in dresser where I found my bras, underwear, socks, and bathing suits.

I pulled my running shorts, bra and a tank top out and changed quickly. I put my phone in my MP3 player holder that fit around my bicep, and plugged my ear plugs into it. I didn't have any music on it but I didn't want anyone to get suspicious. After I put on my running shoes I went back into the bedroom and found a piece of paper and a pen on the dressing table. 'Went for a run, I will be back,' I wrote and left it on the bed where Miguel could find it.

I let myself out through the pool door and took off at an easy jog. I made myself run around the grounds first. I wanted to bolt for the front gate but doing that would look dubious and all I had with me was my phone. I was going to have to get out of here with as many of my belongings as I could. I was thinking about just going home. It sounded pretty good at that point. No vampires, no drama, just hang out with Mom and Dad, but then I thought of how easy it would be for them to follow me.

I couldn't go home yet, maybe not ever. I pushed my speed trying to hold back the panic racing through me. Miguel could find out whatever he wanted about me in minutes if he wanted to. It made me think of Vince, he has been trying to help me from the beginning. What made me think I could trust him though? He might be trying to steal me from Miguel for the same reasons. Everything was fucked up and I didn't know what I was going to do about it.

I made it to the gate with the presence, I now knew was Miguel, still with me. The gate opened thank god, I was afraid Miguel had locked me in. Once I cleared the gate I headed down the hill. It took longer for me to escape the feeling of Miguel then it had been last time I left. My mom was right about this bond, it was growing and I needed to get rid of it.

I stopped and pulled my phone out when Miguel's presence finally left. I dialed Vince and he picked up on the second ring.

"Hello?" he asked, again like he didn't recognize the number.

"Vince, its Katie can you talk?" I asked using the built-in mic on my headphones so I didn't look like I was talking on the phone. I wanted to unload everything on him but I wanted to make he had time to talk.

"Hold on one moment please," he said and I heard muffled voices. I walked down the hill waiting for him. I couldn't stand still and if Miguel sent a human out to look for me I wanted them to think I was out on a run. "Katie, are you alright?" He sounded upset. "Are you somewhere safe to talk?"

"I am out for a run; I am half way down the hill. Miguel shouldn't be able to listen in from here." I was trying to hold back tears. I was so mad and sad and lost. "I fucked up Vince, and I don't know what to do."

"What happened? Tell me everything." Vince sounded too calm.

I told him everything, the dreams, the blood, the sex, the pain. "And now I have no idea how to get rid of this bond and get away from Miguel." I was at the bottom of the hill. I needed to turn around and head back.

"Miguel is such a fool," Vince said, letting out an audible breath before continuing. "What do you want to do?"

"I want to get away from here. Far, far away, but if I go home I think he'll just follow me there and I do not want to put my family at risk." I ran out of breath as I climbed the mountain and talked at the same time.

"He would, I am sure. You need to disappear; I have been planning for this since I saw your tattoo. Did he even comment on it?"

"He wanted to know where it came from, so I told him." That was when the shit hit the fan. "The headaches started right after that, and he hasn't brought it up since."

"It was before you drank from him, right?" Vince asked.

"Yes, I didn't drink from him until this morning."

"That bastard," Vince said, there was thump like he hit something. "He must have given you blood without you realizing it, probably in your sleep."

"Why would he do that?" I was slowing down as I got closer to the spot where I had lost Miguel earlier.

"He did not know why he wanted you so badly, and he does not like it when anyone has power over him. It was his way of leveling the playing field."

"Look, I have to get back, I don't want to but all of my stuff is there. I just came out here to talk to you. Let you know what was going on."

"Here is what we are going to do," Vince said, lowering his voice, and detailing his exit strategy to me.

CHAPTER 30

Where had she gone? Miguel just went in the room she was resting in to check on her and she was gone. He looked out the windows, she was not sitting by the pool, he ran to his bedroom, she was not there either.

He went to Lolita's room and burst in. She looked up from the man she was fucking. "What's wrong Miguel?" she asked, without stopping.

"She is gone." He sat down on the sofa across from Lolita and buried his head in his hands. "I can't feel her; I can't find her. She's not on the property."

"Let me finish here and we will find the little bitch," Lolita said, clearly frustrated that her afternoon delight was going to be cut short.

"Don't call her a bitch," Miguel said and turned to leave. Lolita ignored him and sank her fangs into the man as Miguel shut the door.

"Juan!" He bellowed through the villa. "Juan, I need you now." He stomped towards his office and the butler met him at the door.

"Yes, Master?" Juan said, following him into the office.

"Did you see where Katie went?"

"Yes, Sire, the front gate opened about twenty minutes ago. I checked it and it looked like she was going for a run," he said as Miguel stepped behind his desk and glowered at the man. "Was she not to leave the grounds?"

"No, she was not," Miguel said, realizing he had not informed his butler of this. "It's not your fault, Juan, you didn't know. Go and look for her. Just to make sure she's alright."

"Yes, Master I will leave straightaway." Just as Juan turned for the door his phone went off in his pocket and he pulled it out. "Sire, someone just buzzed the front gate."

"Well, see who it is."

"Yes, Sire," he said, pushing the button that activated the camera. "Yes?"

"Juan, it's me can you buzz me back in?" Katie asked, looking into the camera.

Juan looked to Miguel, when he nodded his head Juan pushed the button that opened the gate.

"Thanks." She smiled, and jogged through the gate.

"Will there be anything else, Master?"

"No." Miguel sat in his chair and turned around to look out at the gardens.

Juan slipped out silently knowing anything he said at the moment would be taken the wrong way and may end his life.

Miguel was so mad she had been allowed to leave, hell, that she wanted to leave. She just took off without sparing him a second glance. How was he going to punish her? He could bring the pain back, but he couldn't treat her as he would his other slaves. If he broke her spirit she would be useless to him even if she was 'The One'. He needed to finish the slave binding, but he was going to have to be careful that she didn't catch on to what he was doing.

He hated that it took three times of exchanging blood to make the binding complete. He could talk her into it at least one more time before they left the city, but he was going to have to come up with a plan for anything beyond that.

He heard the door to his office open and close. "Did you find her?" Lolita asked, taking a seat at one of the chairs in front of his desk.

"Yes, she went for a run it appears." He swiveled his chair to face Lolita.

"You need to break her," Lolita said softly, trying not to further irritate him.

"What use will she be if I break her? When we turn her, what will she do to us?" Miguel answered with more questions.

"Why turn her at all?" Lolita said, growing irritated with her brother's ignorance. "We turn her and she figures out everything you did to her was a scam. How will she deal with that?" She got up and paced the room. "It would be better to break her, finish the binding and use her with the gifts she already has."

"You understand nothing." Miguel was fighting to keep himself from lashing out at Lolita. "I want her as my queen. I want the power, do not misunderstand me, but to have her love and devotion will be better than all the power in the world."

"How can you say that?" Lolita stopped in front of his desk

and using her hands for balance she leaned over the desk to get in his face. "I am the one who should be queen, she should be licking my shoes and doing my bidding. After all I have done for you, Miguel, you owe me this."

Realizing Lolita's goals were different then his, and not liking them he leaned forward. "Your help has been greatly appreciated. I would not be in this position without it. I owe you, but I am going with the prophecy on this, Lolita. You can either stand at my side or leave."

"You would kick me out of the house that I brought you into over this crying whelp? What has gotten into you?"

"Love, and the meaning of my long existence. This was Father's will too. Do not blaspheme him by changing the plans he set into motion before he was taken from us." He wanted to confront Katie as soon as she was inside. He didn't have time to fight with his sister. "Make your choice, Lolita, either stay and we do this my way or leave and do not return."

CHAPTER 31

I entered the villa through the pool entrance since it was closer to Miguel's room. I needed a shower and I wanted to get it over with before Miguel confronted me about leaving the grounds. Controlling bastard, I thought to myself. Miguel was going to be mad that I left without telling him even though I left a note.

I was almost to the bedroom door when I heard him. *Katie, where have you been?*

I turned to see him walking swiftly towards me. He was holding himself back. I knew he could move much faster if he wanted to. He was trying not to scare me, but I could feel the anger rolling off him and it was directed at me.

"I went for a run," I said, waiting for him to reach me. "Did you get the note that I left?"

"What note?" he asked as he reached me and took me into his arms to give me a bear hug.

"I left a note on the bed in your room," I said, pulling away from the hug. "You don't want to do that, I am all sticky and sweaty." I turned and opened the door to the bedroom for Miguel, allowing him to go in first.

"I checked in here but I wasn't looking for a note," he said as he passed by me and walked over to the bed. "I thought you were leaving me after what happened. I was beyond myself with worry. Didn't I ask you not to leave the grounds?"

"It's the middle of the day. I went for a run to the bottom of the hill and back. Nothing happened, I didn't see anyone. You don't get to tell me what to do. I just got out of that kind of relationship and I'm not going there with you. Can you understand that?"

"I will try, I come from a different time where women did what men told them to do. You will have to bear with me while I adjust."

"I'll try. I know you think it's dangerous but I needed to get away and clear my head."

He pulled back and his face grew dark for a split second before going blank. It looked like it was taking everything he had not to yell at me. "Next time, please let me know before you leave. I just want you to be safe, Love. Are you still angry with me?" he placed his hand on my shoulder.

"No, I had no right to be mad at you. I knew the risks going in, and none of this is your fault," I rested my hand on his cheek as he read the note. "I have some things I need to know right now though."

"I will do my best to answer any of your questions," he said, sitting on the bed, and looking at me.

"How do we find out if I am your slave?" I asked, getting to the point, and sitting in the chair in front of the dressing table facing him.

"Why does it have to matter right now? Can't we just put it on the back burner? Even if you are my slave I have no plans of ever making you do something you do not wish to," he said, forcing eye contact.

"Because I don't want to be anyone's slave, and Lolita's chomping at the bit to find out."

"This is none of her affair. We need to work on you and me right now. Since it appears we have one problem fixed at least, temporarily, if not forever we can exchange blood again if the need arises. I want to spend some time with you without being forced to."

"Miguel, until I know if I'm your slave, I'll be uneasy about this entire situation. I need to know in order to be myself or I'm going to second guess everything between us." I hoped he was buying my act.

"I want you to undo my pants and suck my cock. *Now*," he said and his eyes flared with a white glow.

I winced. He had put power behind the last word. I felt the command activate the black mass in my brain. It was trying to force me to do his bidding, but I fought it and forced it out my mind. "If that was your test you're an asshole. If you would have asked nicely I might have done it with a smile."

He forced a laugh. "That answers your question though." I was so stupid, here I was with another man who wanted to tell me what to do. "What should we do?"

"We need to leave this city and spend some time together without the drama. When do you think we can leave?"

"I want to as soon as possible, but I need to make sure I leave my city in capable hands. I have worked too hard for too long for it to crumble when I leave." He was scared, there was something else going on.

"I understand, but it's very important we get out of the city," I said, thinking I wanted to be anywhere but near him. "Let me take a shower then we can talk about this more if you want."

Can I shower with you? He asked as I headed to the bathroom.

"That sounds nice, but we need to spend some time with your sister. If you shower with me I have a feeling we won't leave this room for the rest of the night, and I'm going to need some food pretty soon."

"Your right love, I will just sit here and pretend I'm with you," he said, maneuvering himself to have the best view of the bathroom.

I faked a giggle and went into the bathroom shutting the door behind me. It took all the bravery I had not to lock the door. If I did he would know something was up.

That is so unfair, he thought. *At least give me a peep show.*

You can use your imagination, I thought turning the shower on. When the water was hot I got in and tried to cry as quietly as I could. I'd never been more scared in my life. I had a show to put on and it was a life or death situation. I could do this; I didn't have a choice.

I came out of the bathroom with a robe on to find Miguel was in the same position I had left him in but there was a neat pile of clothes laid out. *What are you doing?* I thought.

He turned toward me and smiled. "I have been thinking about how you are going to look in your new outfit." He got up from the bed.

"When did you have time to do this?" I went over to look at a white eyelet dress sitting next to a white bra and thong. It was actually something I wouldn't mind wearing.

"I had it delivered when I should have been working." He

smirked.

Thank you, I said as my stomach growled. "Sorry, I need to eat." I took the clothes and quickly put them on. Giving myself a quick once over in the full-length mirror, I smiled. The dress was perfect, if not a little on the short side.

"Let's go to the dining room then, shall we?" He offered me his arm.

I took it and smiled. *Yes, please.*

When we entered the dining room Lolita was sitting at one end clicking away at her laptop, and there was a salad sitting on the table in front of my seat. Miguel guided me to my chair and held it out for me.

"Hi," I said to Lolita who smiled tightly at me then looked back at her laptop screen.

Miguel sat down in his normal seat at the table, rested his elbows on the table and steepled his fingers together. "Lolo," he said by way of greeting.

"Miguelito, are you feeling better now?" Lolita asked, her eyes darting toward me then away.

"Yes, Katie just went for a run. She left me a note but I missed it. There was no reason to worry after all."

"And what will her punishment be?" Lolita closed the lid on her laptop and licked her lips.

"Why would there be a punishment Lolita? She is not a dog or a child, Katie can do what she wants."

"Why is it any of your business?" I asked, astonished that I would need to be punished.

"Because bad behavior needs to be punished in order for it not to happen again." Lolita folded her hands together and rested them on her computer.

"Lolita, that's enough," Miguel said slamming his fist down on the table. "Katie went for a run, she left me a note, I didn't see it until she got back. It was a misunderstanding all around. Drop it." Miguel stared down his sister.

I was surprised when she blinked first and looked away. I never expected her to be cowed by Miguel. "Well, then," she started, opening her laptop again. "The closest thing I found about your bond is a prophecy made centuries ago in Greece. There's not a lot of information but it references a woman with the Goddess Asteria's mark."

"Lolita?" Miguel said in question. He was anxious about something.

"It's all I have been able to find," she said, looking back down at her computer.

"What does the prophecy say?" I asked, hoping I might get some new information.

"There's not much, but what I have found says, the one who bears the mark will be able to hear what is in our hearts. There is more but it is in ancient Greek and I cannot find a translating program on the internet to decipher the rest of it. I sent it to a friend of mine who will be able to translate it, but he is very busy and he is not sure when he can get to it," Lolita said, her eyes darting back and forth between me and Miguel.

"Why do you think I bear the goddess's mark?" I wanted to touch my tattoo, but I kept my hands on the table.

"Katie, will you show her your tattoo? It will help us figure this out."

I wanted to roll my eyes but instead I stood and did as Miguel asked. I lifted the side of my dress and showed it to Lolita. "Is this the mark?"

"I think so. The goddess of prophecies sent it. Asteria was a Titan who escaped from Zeus by turning into a quail and diving into the sea. It is a quail correct?"

I looked over to Miguel raising my eyebrows at him. "Yes, it's a quail."

"This will give us somewhere to start," Lolita said, closing the laptop. "The question is what are we going to do next?"

"Tomorrow night is the finale for the film festival. Since I am the sponsor I need to go. Katie, it would be best if you came as my date. Lolita, do you want to make your grand entrance there or at the after party?" Miguel asked, getting up and pacing around the room.

"Movies bore me. I would much rather be seen for the first time at the club." Lolita sat back in her chair and rolled her wine glass around between her hands.

"You are right, we can make it a big surprise, even I didn't know that you were coming. Does that sound alright to you?" he asked, looking to me.

"Are you sure?" I asked, looking up from my steak and rice, that Juan had put in front of me. "Aren't you worried about my safety or something?"

"Of course. That's why you have to accompany me love. We don't know how long my blood will stay in your system or mine. I think the threat of suffocation is far worse than the vampires you will meet. What would we do if it wears off and I'm across town?"

"You're right. I didn't think of that." I turned back to my food feeling smug, he wouldn't be able to induce my headaches any more thanks to my mom, but I wished he would go without me so I could escape. "I only worry you will be so preoccupied worrying about me that you will not see the threats coming at you."

"Nonsense, everything will be fine. It will be nice to get out of the house for a while. I need to get to work now though, are you going to be alright on your own?"

"Me, yeah I am going to finish eating then settle in with my book. It's been a long day." I took another bite of food.

"I will keep her company, you go work and we will have some girl time." Lolita smiled but her feelings were anything but happy.

"I will leave you to it then." He kissed my cheek and left the room.

"How is your dinner?" Lolita asked after Miguel left.

"It's very good." I took a sip of the wine to wash it down. "Juan or whoever made this did a great job."

"Good, I will be sure to tell him." It felt like she was skirting around something she wanted to say.

"Do you have something on your mind that you would like to talk about?" I asked, finishing the last bite of food, and dabbing my lips with the napkin.

"Yes, there is." She got up and moved to stand in front of me with the table in between us. "I do not know what kind of spell you put on my brother but if you do not do exactly what he says you will have to deal with me."

"Is that a threat?" I asked, trying to be tough, but this vampire could flatten me in seconds. "I am my own person, Lolita, and I will do what I want. If what Miguel wants coincides with what I want I will do as he asks, but if I don't want to do it, I won't."

Lolita leaned over the table towards me. "I could squish you like a bug before you even know what was happening," *and it would be my pleasure,* she thought to me for the first time.

"I know, but then you would have to answer to Miguel and I don't think he would appreciate it." I pushed back from the table. "Good night, Lolita." I turned and forced myself to walk and not run out of the dining room to Miguel's room.

I pulled my phone out of my pocket and sent a text message to Vince:

'We are good to go.'

A minute later a reply came through:

'Copy that, see you tomorrow.'

I deleted both of the messages from the call history, grabbed my book and headed out to the lounge area by the pool. I turned the outdoor lights on and did my best to forget everything that was going on and get lost in the book.

A few hours later I put the book down. I'd finished it. It had been a good book; I was going to have to find something else to read. Sometimes the only way I could let go of what was going on in my life was by picking a book and letting it consume me.

With the book done, I went in search of Miguel. I listened for him outside of every door testing my abilities until I found him. Once I did, I knocked on the door.

"Come," Miguel said, and I opened the door to his office.

Hi, I thought to him. *How is the paper work going?*

"I think I can give up for the night," he said, pushing back from his desk, and coming to me. "I will get some more done while you are out in the sun tomorrow." He brought me in for a hug and a quick kiss. *You look like you are ready for bed. I am too.* We began walking out of the office and toward our bedroom.

"How did you spend your night?" he asked as we walked.

"After I finished eating I took my book out to the pool and read, it was exactly what I needed," I said, wishing I had another one to start.

"You and Lolita did not enjoy each other's company for very long." He was fishing for information.

"I don't think she likes me very much," I said in a small voice not wanting to sound bitchy.

"She is hard to get to know, but I am sure you two will get along fine before long," Miguel said as we entered the bedroom.

"I hope you're right," I said, noticing a box on the bed. "What's this?" I walked over and looked at the garment box.

"I thought you would like something a little nicer to wear to bed," Miguel said, joining me. "Open it."

I ran my fingers around the edge of the box looking for a gap. Finding one I pulled the top of the box off and set it aside. I folded the tissue paper back to find a beautiful nightgown. I picked it up by the straps. It was cream in color, silk, and long with a slit on the side that would likely reach my hip bone. "It's beautiful Miguel, thank you."

"You are very welcome." He brought me around and kissed me slowly. He parted his lips and I followed. He probed me lightly with his tongue for a moment and pulled away from the kiss. "To bed?"

"Yes, just give me a minute in the bathroom." In front of the sink I took my makeup off, brushed my teeth, and put on the nightgown.

I opened the door and left the light on for a minute so he could see how the night gown looked on me.

Wow. He thought and I felt his lust.

I hope it looks as good as you thought it would, I thought turning out the light finding my way to the bed. *Can we just sleep tonight?* I asked rolling so my head rested on his chest, and his arms went around me automatically.

"Yes, my love. It has been quite a day." He kissed the top of my head and I felt him drift to sleep.

I lay in bed for a long time staring at the ceiling with the arms of the man who wanted to make me his slave wrapped around me. I couldn't understand why I was so calm. I had to get away from him and get his blackness out of my brain so he wouldn't have power over me. I had every right to be freaking out but I wasn't. It was almost like I knew I had to beat him before I could move on.

I closed my eyes and found the place in my brain where his control was sitting, trying to take over. I pictured a pair of tweezers in my hand and gently started to pull the black mass out of my brain, each pull sent pain sizzling through my mind, but I couldn't give up. It was a meticulous undertaking but little by little I pulled it way. I stared at it in between the tweezers, small tendrils tried to escape and snake their way back to my brain. I imagined the mass catching on fire, and burning to ash in my mind. A bright spark burst caught the mass on fire. As quick as it started it was gone.

Miguel stirred in his sleep and pulled me closer. I let him, I had to. He could not know I was leaving until I was gone. I closed my eyes proud that I was able to burn out the mind control he implanted in my brain and slept.

CHAPTER 32

Vince knelt in front of the altar in the closet off his bedroom. He was not hiding the fact that he worshiped the creator of his species, but in a town like San Sebastian where Catholicism was the norm he did not want it spread around that he worshipped an ancient Titan.

He lit the candle, folded his hands, and prayed that he was worthy of protecting the Titan's prodigy. He prayed he would be able to safely remove Katie from Miguel and find a way to remove the slave control from her without turning her into his slave.

The goddess had never spoken to him directly and he was not expecting anything then, but it put his mind at ease when he knelt and prayed. He needed rest, the next few days would test him in ways he had not been tested in since he was human. "Please, Lady, give me the tools I need to accomplish your will," he said, finishing, and blowing out the candle.

Closing the door to the closet he went and lay on the bed. He quietened his mind and thought of nothing but the patterns in the texture of the drywall mud. After some time, he drifted to sleep and received his first visit from Asteria.

He found himself standing in her temple at the base of the altar. She stood behind it in a gold dress with a crown upon her head. Vince dropped to his knees at first glance and lowered his head in supplication. "My Lady, how may I serve you?" he asked in a rasping whisper.

"Vince, my loyal follower you have met my daughter, correct?" She walked around the altar to stand in front of it.

"Yes, Goddess."

"You are going to help her escape from the clutches of those who would use her for their own gains?"

"That is my wish, Lady."

"Rise and take a turn with me, Gladiator," she said, offering him her hand.

Vince rose to his feet and took the goddess's hand. They were no longer in the temple now, but walking along the sandy shores of a body of water.

"You must take her to my temple and let her look at the prophecy and the tapestry," she said as the water lapped at their feet. "She does not believe yet, and much hangs on her understanding that she is my daughter."

"Yes, Goddess," Vince looked up at her still in awe.

"You must then teach her how to fight your kind while she is still human. You will be rewarded for your help." She looked across the water as if she was seeing something completely different. A small smile played on her lips.

"Yes, Goddess, but no reward is necessary. I want to help her. I have wanted to since I first smelled her." He paused to look where she looked and saw nothing. "I fear Miguel has begun the slave binding process though, and I do not know how to reverse it. With it in place, it will be hard to keep her safe."

"There is no reason to worry." She looked down at him. "My Katie just took care of the problem."

"That will make hiding her much easier," Vince said as they continued to walk down the beach. "My only other concern is Katie's dreams, she said she needed to save Miguel. I do not know if I will be able to dissuade her from that mission."

"I will handle it, but all is not lost for him. Time will tell." She stopped walking and turned to face him. "Go back now and keep my daughter safe."

Vince awoke in his bed and sat bolt right up. Had it been just a dream or had the goddess of dreams visited him? Getting out of bed he realized it did not matter. It was all the sign he needed. He was on the right path.

I woke up the next morning feeling more peaceful then I had in ages with Miguel's arms wrapped around me and my head resting on his chest. The peaceful feeling evaporated and turned into panic when I thought about what I was going to do that night and what would happen if Vince and I failed.

What's wrong? Miguel thought as his arms tightened around me.

"I was just thinking about tonight."

"It will be interesting, and it scares me a little too." He turned his head to look at the clock. "Is there anything you need to do today?"

I thought about it for a moment. When was the last time I emailed or called anyone? "I need to check in with the real world. You know check my email maybe call my parents. Spend some time at the pool. I need to go shopping for something to wear tonight. Nothing I have will be appropriate." I thought about getting to an ATM and draining all of my money out of my account. I wanted to be cash only by the end of the night.

"You do not have to worry about what to wear, I bought you

something when I ordered the nightgown," he said, kissing my head. "It would set my mind at ease if you stayed on the grounds today."

"What did you buy me to wear?" I asked, thinking it was would be something I would hate. "Do I have veto power?"

"Tonight is going to be very important for our future. I need you to make a statement, and that means I need you dressed in a certain way and to act in a certain way. It would mean a great deal to me if you went along with it." He tensed for a fight.

"You make it sound like I'm not going to like it." I propped myself up on my elbow to look at him in the face.

"Well, I'm not sure you will like my idea, love." He brushed my bangs away from my forehead. "The best way for me to present you will be as my slave."

I took a deep breath and thought about it for a moment. "Please explain what I will have to do." I realized I had no other option if I wanted to leave with Vince tonight.

"You will have to be at my side constantly unless I tell you to do something. If I tell you to do something you must do what I say without question. At least on the outside. We don't want anyone to know about our mental connection or otherwise. Never speak unless you are spoken to, and the hardest part, I think, will be for you to pretend I have complete control over you," he said quickly, trying to get it all out before I could object to any of it.

"What are you going to 'make me' do?" I was not happy about that part.

"Hopefully nothing, but you never know what may happen." He ran his hand up and down my arm slowly. "Being able to think to each other without speaking is a huge asset, it should make everything much simpler I think."

"Well we have to do what we have to do," I said, then remembered pulling the mass out of my brain, I wondered if I was going to be able to speak mind-to-mind with him. *Can you hear me?* I asked. There was no reply, crap. "Should we get up?" How I was going to explain this new development.

"Yes, but before we do it may be a good idea to exchange blood again. Just to be on the safe side." I could tell he was not sure how I would take this idea.

I thought about it. It was the last thing I wanted to do but if he figured out I had removed his compulsion from my brain he might do something rash. I removed it once, I should be able to do it again but there was a question in my mind wondering if I would be able to or not. Getting rid of it later would be easier than explaining why I didn't want to share his blood now. "Do you want to go first?"

"We could do it at the same time," he said shyly.

"Okay, kinky." I was trying to sound excited. I was not going to be able to pass on the sex. Once we started, my basic human need would take over and no matter how much I didn't want to touch this man I was going to have sex with him, there was no way around it. I knew what that made me, and knowing that I would enjoy it made me feel worse than the slut I was becoming. Would I be able to look at myself in the mirror after the deed was done? "How?" I asked, taking a deep breath, and sacrificing what was left of this good little American girl my friends and family saw.

"Come and sit in-between my legs and rest your back against my chest," he said, pulling my hand toward him. I slid in between his legs and leaned against him. "Now I can drink from your neck while you drink from my wrist." He wrapped one hand around my waist to keep me from moving. He kissed the soft spot where my neck met the top of my shoulder. I felt him stiffen behind me and a low deep burning began to churn through me. "You have to remember to make me stop."

"I will," I said and heard something strong tearing.

His wrist was in front me, about to start dripping blood onto the sheet when he thought. *You start.* I quickly took his wrist in both hands and brought his wrist to my mouth. Blood filled it and I wanted to spit it out, but I had to do this. I swallowed and as my body tried to reject it, I overpowered the urge to vomit and continued to drink.

I felt Miguel bite into the spot he had just kissed and begin to suck the blood from my neck. I closed my eyes and we were no longer in a bright bedroom in Spain. We were floating in a field of stars where there was nothing but the two of us and far away pin pricks of light. It felt as though we were one.

He shifted us and penetrated me driving himself as deep as my body would allow him to, while he pulled the blood from my shoulder. I found myself withering on the edge of orgasm as he drove in and out of me. I never wanted it to stop. I wanted the orgasm that would be even bigger than the last one he had given me. There was no love, no hate, just the ecstasy of two bodies becoming one. There was no control only an animalistic need that demanded to be met.

After what felt like forever and no time at all, my release came and letting go of his wrist, I howled at the impact and pleasure of it. I was so caught up in my own pleasure I didn't even notice when Miguel had his. He let go of my neck after he came and we lay in the bed now naked, not sure how we got there.

Wow. I thought. *I didn't think making love to you could have been better but damn.* I felt my eyes fill with tears, but if I let them fall I was screwed. I blinked them away and reminded myself to play the game.

"What happened to our clothes?" I asked, looking around the room.

"I think what's left of them are scattered in pieces around the room. I'll have to get you a new nightgown." He reached down and lightly kissed my lips. "How are you feeling? Did I take too much?"

I sat up and the room spun for a moment but everything seemed clear, almost too clear to me. "I'm fine." I turned to look at him. He smiled looking worried but happy. "Hey you did great. I didn't have to ask you to stop or anything."

"Yes, well after I spent my seed I was feeling very full and very content. I was ready to stop," he said, looking pleased with himself. "It was a very simple task to complete."

"It was a great way to start the day," I said, getting up from the bed and heading toward the bathroom. "I'm going to get ready for the day and get some breakfast. Could you show me where the kitchen is so I can make something?"

"No, I will not have you cooking. I'll have Juan make you breakfast," he said, beating me to the bathroom door and sweeping me into his arms. *I love you.*

"You are amazing." I kissed him hard before pushing him away and closing myself in the bathroom.

That wasn't fair, he thought to me as I headed toward the shower and turned it on.

Every girl needs her privacy once in a while, I thought to him mostly because I wanted to make sure that letting him suck my blood and fuck me was worth it.

Yes, but I want no secrets between us, he thought and I heard him scratching at the door.

Believe me there are somethings you do not want to know about, I said stepping into the shower and letting the tears flow.

I will let you keep them, for now. I will meet you in the dining room, love.

At least it had worked, I thought to myself once the tears stopped. It had to be worth it, right? I scrubbed my body like I would never feel clean again. I did this to myself, I thought, I let him blind me with lies. I had to do this to get away from him. Right?

I looked at myself in the mirror after drying off. I looked the same but I felt completely different from the young woman who stepped off the train with the love of my life, or so I thought. I was never going to be that woman again. I was going to have to learn to live with myself, with what I had done. It was going to take a while.

After breakfast with Miguel, I was on my own since he needed to work. I didn't want to run into Lolita so I changed into my bikini and went back to the pool. After getting all of my essentials set up, I pulled my phone out and saw I had a text message from Vince and a missed call from my parents. I called parents back first and left a message telling them everything was fine, I would try to call them later, and I loved them.

I opened the messages from Vince:

'Hi hun, I talked to your mom last night. She is really proud of you. She wants me to help you out in any way I can. Are we still on for meeting this afternoon?'

Vince was good at the coded messages. I needed to take the message seriously, but I had to giggle too.

'You talked to my mom? That's great I am glad she wants you to help me. It has been a long morning; I am sitting at the pool right now. It's so awesome! Sorry I can't get away from the villa today. Miguel is worried about me and wants me to stay here. But we are going to the movie and after party tonight. Maybe I will see you there.'

I hoped he understood we were going to have to go with plan B. If I left again today after Miguel asked me specifically not to he would know I was up to something. We didn't want him to know I was leaving until we were on the plane out of here.

I checked my social media account and my email. I replied to the few messages I had. I kept up a good face; told everyone I was having the time of my life. It was easier to lie in text then it was in person.

I looked down at my miniscule top and the tan lines I had from my tankini. This might be the last day I got to spend outside if things didn't go to plan, it was time to be bold. I undid the top and took it off. I was in Spain after all and on a private estate. I didn't care who saw me. I lay back on the lounge chair, plugged my ear buds in and let the music carry me away.

Don't get a sunburn love, Miguel thought and I looked up at the windows smiling.

Thanks, I thought and rolled over. *How's work?*

I am getting caught up finally, he thought sounding bored. *Oh, Lolita wants to help you get ready for tonight. Can you be back inside by five?*

Wonderful, I thought looking at my watch, I had an hour of sunshine left. *I'll let you get back to work, and I will see you later.*

Enjoy love, he thought and went quiet.

I was hot and sweaty so I slipped in the pool to cool off. After my swim I lay back on my towel and air-dried. I pulled my phone out thinking I would try my parents again when I saw that Vince had text me back.

'I am not sure if they will let me in or not but I will try. Please be careful. See you later.'

He must be worried that Miguel would not let us see each other. I hoped with everything I had that Miguel would let him. Otherwise I wasn't sure how we were going to pull this off.

I looked at my watch. I wanted to get a shower before five. I didn't feel comfortable around Lolita without any clothes, or with clothes on for that matter, but I needed to stay on Miguel's good side tonight so I would do as he said. I shook my head, got up, gathered my things, and went back inside not looking forward to the next few hours.

Miguel met me in the hall as I was heading to our room to take a shower. He took me in his arms and gave me a massive hug. I could hear him inhaling deeply. "Do I smell that good?"

"Lovely, lilac, coco butter and sun, and you are glowing." He pulled back from the hug. "I wish I could talk you out of showering. Just so you would smell like this all night."

"Have to have a shower. I feel all sticky," I said as we began to move toward his room.

"I could help." He lifted his eyebrows and looked at me from the corner of his eye.

I smiled on the outside and gagged on the inside. "I think your sister would end up intruding on us." I looked at my watch. "It's already five."

"Your right, but I need a shower too," he said as he opened the door to our room. "What if I promise to behave myself?"

"It's not you I'm worried about." I grinned at him as I headed for the bathroom to escape. "I don't want to be late for your sister, besides it'll take you much less time to get ready then me," I said, shutting the door behind me.

In the shower I rinsed out my bathing suit and hung it on the door. I jumped when I saw Miguel leaning against the wall watching me. "What are you doing?" I asked, fighting the need to cover myself with my hands.

"Watching you," he said with a small smile on his lips. "Why don't you want to shower with me?"

"Like I said, I don't want to piss your sister off by being later then I already am." I turned around to pour shampoo in my hand and hide my face. I started scrubbing the chlorine out of my hair trying to pretend I was alone in the bathroom.

I heard the shower door open and close quickly. I went to turn and tell Miguel to get out but he pushed me up against the wall and held me there with his body. "What are you doing?" I asked, trying to squirm away from him.

"I just couldn't resist," he said and began to kiss my neck.

"Miguel, I am not in the mood right now." I was trying to be stern. "Can we please do this later?"

"No," he murmured, bringing his hand around and squeezing my breast hard enough to hurt. "I need you now."

"Ow," I yelled and tried to elbow him in the gut.

He let go of my breast and took a step back. Without saying anything he took my hands and held them over my head in one of his. I tried to keep my legs shut but between his muscles and the slickness of the floor he pried them apart and force his way into me.

"No, stop, please." Tears were running down my face as he pumped into me from behind.

"You are mine, Katie. I will take you whenever I want to, do you understand?" he asked before sinking his fangs into my neck.

There was no pleasure this time only blinding pain. I fought to dislodge him from my neck. I didn't want him to take any more blood, or have the bond grow any stronger but it was no use. I wasn't strong enough. I started hyperventilating. I couldn't get air into my lungs, when out of nowhere my dad's voice broke through the panic in my mind.

"If he is behind you, stomp on his foot," my dad had told me before I headed out on my first date. He wanted to make sure I would be able to defend myself.

I lifted my foot, up estimated where Miguel's foot was and stomped down hard. He jerked pulling his teeth out of me. "Stop," I yelled and tried to put as much power into the word as I could. He stepped back and I turned around. "Leave," I said, putting the same power behind it.

He took a step back and rammed his fist into my jaw, I saw

the floor coming towards me and blinked. When I could focus again, I realized I must have blacked out and putting power behind my words did nothing to him. The shower was still running but Miguel was nowhere around.

I made myself get up and scrub my body. I knew he was trying to take advantage of me but I never thought he would rape me. What was I going to do now? Could I run now? I wanted to, how far would I get? Would Vince even have time to get to me before Miguel, Juan or Lolita picked me up and brought me back to the villa?

What if the plan failed and we couldn't get away tonight? How was I ever going to get out of here? I shut the water off once my skin felt raw from scrubbing. I took a towel and slowly began to dry myself off. I didn't feel like I was really there, I felt like I was outside myself watching. I was depressed, how I had let me life come to this?

When I was dry I took the robe from the hook and wrapped it around myself. I walked into the bedroom with every intention of grabbing my daypack and running shoes and walking away, but Lolita was waiting for me.

I couldn't out run her so I just stood there waiting for her to tell me what she wanted.

"Katie, come and sit down," she said in an oddly gentle voice. "Miguel said you fell down in the shower and hurt yourself. Are you okay?"

"I'm fine," I said. With no way out of this room I went and sat in the chair; resigned to my fate.

"I am beginning to get tired of the noise you two are filling the house with," Lolita said, beginning to mess with my hair.

"Sorry," I murmured, only half listening as I stared at my

reflection in the mirror a bruise was forming on my jaw from where he hit me. I wondered if Lolita would be able to cover it with makeup.

"Don't be. I have never seen my brother this happy before, and I think you're happy for the most part."

"For the most part." I let out a breath trying to hold the tears in. I needed to act normal like nothing was wrong but I couldn't pull it off at that moment.

"Be calm Katie," Lolita said, standing in front of me and applying my foundation. "You are going to be fine. Wait till you see the outfit Miguel picked out for you, you are going to look like a total badass. You need to think of yourself as Miguel's Secret Service. You are there to see and hear. Only to be heard if asked. You are going to be fine especially since you can hear each other's thoughts. Hold still," she commanded as she applied the blush to my face.

I took a deep breath and tried to forget what was happening to me. Thinking about all the questions I had was not going to solve any of them. The best I could do is show her that she did not scare me.

Katie are you alright? Miguel thought to me and I fought back a scream and managed to ignore him. *Can you hear me? Do I need to come and check on you?* Fear spiked through me. I did not want to see him.

I can hear you, but I'm far from alright. Leave me alone, I thought to him, my hands balled up in fists so tight my knuckles turned white. I didn't know if I was strong enough to keep up the act.

"Katie, you need to relax or I am going to mess this up," Lolita said.

I took a breath wishing for a way out but seeing none. "That is better," Lolita said, continuing her work.

I want to give you the run down for tonight so you know what to expect. First we will go to dinner at one of my restaurants, then to the Fort for the final movie showing of the festival, then to one of my clubs for the after party. Please acknowledge that you got all of that, Miguel thought.

Yeap, I said trying to stay relaxed.

"Open your eyes," Lolita said, holding a tube of mascara in her hand.

I will not have you ruin my credibility tonight. What do I need to do to earn back your trust?

"Look down," Lolita said. "Good, now up, and we are done with the makeup. Time to get dressed."

I wanted to say take a long walk in the sun but that wasn't going to get me anywhere. I thought about it for a minute. If there was any chance he was going to let me out of his sight tonight I was going to have to make him think I forgave him. *An apology would help,* I thought back to him wanting to shove my hand down his throat and pull his heart out.

I am sorry I forced myself on you. I wanted you so badly I could not help myself. When you stepped on me instinct took over and I hit you. I promise it will never happen again.

Never again, I thought back to him.

"I don't know if it was worth the work getting these pants on," I said, looking in the mirror. They were black leather and it took me and Lolita ten minutes working together to get them on. They looked like they were painted on, and the shirt made me feel naked. It was a halter top, covered in sequins, very loose with a neckline going almost to my navel, and with an open back. There was no way to wear a bra with it and double-sided tape would have ruined the look of the shirt. I was going to have to be very careful not to have a 'wardrobe malfunction'.

I crossed my arms over my breasts while staring into the mirror. "Katie, put your arms down," Lolita said, from behind me. I did as she said and pulled my shoulders back. I did look a little badass. I could own this, I thought to myself. Lolita did a good job covering the bruise too, I only noticed it is because it hurt when I moved my face and the swelling made my face look deformed.

"You better go and find Miguel, he probably wants to leave soon," Lolita said, picking up her makeup bag and leaving the room.

I went to my daypack, pulled out my hidden money belt, and somehow got it around my waist under the pants. I put my passport, money, and credit cards in it, then I put my phone in the back pocket of the pants. In a few hours, with a lot of luck, I would be out of here for good. I looked at my backpack, I hated leaving everything here, but better to leave it and be free then to try and take it and become a prisoner.

I headed down the hall to find Miguel reminding myself to be nice and pretend like nothing happened in the shower. I was his love and he would treat me better then he would all else. It was a lot to swallow, but I was trying.

He was sitting at one of the settees in the living room. His eyes lit up when he saw me, and I could feel his need as he looked at me. His eye got bigger every time they went up and down my body.

You look like the goddess of seduction.

Thank you, I thought back to him. It would be hard to have sex tonight unless he ripped the pants off me. That was a good thing as far as I was concerned. "You don't look half bad yourself." Taking in his perfectly tailored outfit of black loafers, black slacks, and a white silk t-shirt.

"No one is going to see me with you standing next me." He kissed my bruised cheek lightly then offered me his arm. I took it and we walked out the front door to the waiting limo.

CHAPTER 34

"Do I look like your slave?" I asked once we were on the road. I was trying to make polite conversation.

"No, you look like a master who has her own slaves. Lolo did well making you look as though I tamed a wild beast instead of catching a hare in a snare." Miguel squeezed my hand. "Remember I want you to be strong but you will submit only to me."

"Yes, Master," I said in a sultry voice and ran my free hand up his pant leg to where it met his hip. I threw up a little in my mouth as I did, but I swallowed it back down reminding myself I was almost rid of him.

What did Lolita teach you this afternoon? He thought and moved my hand.

How to be a good slave, I answered. *Does this please you, Master?* I asked sarcastically.

"Not right now, let's keep our head in the game," he said as we pulled up to the restaurant. *Time to put your game face on. Remember to be strong and independent but enamored with me. You get out first then turn and wait for me.*

I stepped out of the limo looked around to see about a dozen people milling around the front of the restaurant looking preoccupied with themselves. I took one-step away from the door and turned to watch Miguel get out of the car. He took my arm and we walked into the restaurant.

"Good evening, Señor right this way," the maître d' said, leading us through the crowded main room to a small private room with a round table. Miguel went to the chair furthest from the door, looked from me to the chair on his left and I followed. The maître d' pulled out my chair, and I waited for Miguel to sit before I allowed the man to help me with my chair. "Would Señor like a bottle of the usual?"

"Yes, and a menu as well. My guest is hungry," Miguel said in a deep and authoritative voice I had never heard before. He gave Miguel the menu and left us to ourselves with the door closed. *What would you like to eat love?*

I'm not picky. I answered not sure if I could eat, my stomach was turning into a knot of fear but I kept my face calm and blank.

The maître d' came back in with a bottle of wine and an opener in his hand. As Miguel went through the process checking the cork, smelling, and tasting the wine, I thought about taking the corkscrew and jamming it in his eye. I wondered how far I would make it. Patience I told myself, his time would come. Finally, Miguel nodded that the wine would be fine and spouted something in Spanish. I hoped it was my dinner order.

The waiter paused at the door before leaving and turned. "Señor, there are a few patrons who seek your company this evening. May I send them in?"

"Yes, in a few minutes they may come," Miguel said in that voice he used when we were in the shower. The memory made me cringe. The waiter nodded his head and left shutting the door behind him.

I was just about to speak when he was in my head. *There are ears listening nearby. Let's keep as much as we can to ourselves.*

Is that your normal voice? Have you been pretending to be nice this whole time? I thought looking at him skeptically.

Attitude my love, he thought giving me a hard stare. *No, it is the voice I use when people need to heed my authority. It should instill fear in my followers and my slave but not my love. Don't be afraid.* He brought my hand to his lips and brushed them across it. "You are mine. No one can touch you without my permission." *Remember almost everything I say will be part of the act. You can do this.*

If you say so. I closed my eyes and took a deep breath. I squared my shoulders and thought about how badly I wanted to hurt Miguel and how good it would feel.

He stared at me for a moment and turned his head as if someone had knocked on the door, I didn't hear anything. *You look like such a vixen right now. Keep it up,* he thought winking at me. "Come," he said in his 'work voice'.

The door opened a female vampire walked in and glanced between us. Her mouth opened as if she was going to say something, but she reconsidered and closed it. She forced a smile on her face. "My Lord," she said, genuflecting before Miguel. I wanted to gawk at her for genuflecting. I had never thought of treating Miguel with such reverence. Why would I though? He was good looking, rich and all, but there was no way I would genuflect before anyone less than the

Pope.

I forgot to warn you. If you need to go to the ladies' room or anything, you need to ask for permission, genuflect when you leave and when you return.

"Isabelle," Miguel said, switching gears gracefully. "What can I do for you this evening?"

Couldn't I just bow instead genuflecting? It's so not me. I asked. This was going to get ugly I had a feeling.

"My Lord, may I ask who your guest is?" Isabelle asked, finally rising from the kneeling position and locking her almost black eyes with mine.

Was she trying to get into my mind already? *She is and yes you may just bow but make it a full bow from the waist,* Miguel thought. Crap, how had I sent that thought to Miguel? I was going to have to watch it.

"Isabelle, this is Katie my slave and I would appreciate it if you would stop trying to mind-fuck her," Miguel said in his scary calm voice.

"She's your slave?" Isabelle asked, looking even harder at me.

"Katie, please show her my mark," Miguel said, followed by, *the bite marks get up if you need to.*

"Yes, Master," I said, rising from my chair, and walking over to Isabelle who was about a foot shorter than I was. I tilted my neck and moved the collar of my shirt to show her the bite marks. She leaned in, looked carefully then took a step back. I turned, went back to my chair, and sat down.

"Satisfied, Isabelle?" he asked picking up his wine glass and draining it.

"Yes, Sire, congratulations on your new pet," Isabelle said as her gaze rolled over me in lust.

"Thank you," Miguel said and looked at me. "It took some time to tame her, but so far she has been well worth it." He pulled my face to his, pushed my neck back and licked it from my shoulder to my ear.

Was that really necessary? I asked but didn't change anything on my face to give my disgust away.

Good girl, he thought. *Keep it up we may have to do more as the night progresses.*

"It looks like she is a pussycat in your hands," she said, coming closer to me. "I wonder how she would do with me." She brought her face to my level, noisily smelling me.

Do I have to put up with this? You said I only had to be a slave to you right? I asked as Isabelle took her index finger and ran it down my jaw line.

Do what you will or I will step in. You are mine. He sounded angry even in his thoughts.

With the go-ahead from Miguel I took hold of the finger resting on my jaw and, using the element of surprise, I bent it backward as hard and as quick as I could until I heard the bone snap. "I'm Miguel's property. No one else's," I said as she withered and fell to her knees in pain.

"Isabelle, it would be smart to ask before you touch in the future," Miguel said. *Nicely done love. I did not realize you were so strong.*

Neither did I. Maybe it's your blood, I thought back at him. Why couldn't I have done that in the shower? I thought to myself trying to hold back a grimace.

"You bitch," Isabelle almost yelled, finally able to speak after resetting her finger. She crouched readying herself to spring at me when Miguel pushed his chair away from the table.

"Isabelle, you propositioned my human without my permission. You took your punishment. Now calm down or leave."

Isabelle gave a quick glance at Miguel then moved from her crouch to genuflecting again. "My Lord, I'm sorry. I forgot myself. Please forgive me," she said, not taking her eyes off her shoes.

I raised my eyebrows. *Wow, you must be a ruthless leader,* I thought resuming my calm demeanor.

Yes, I am. You have no idea what I can do, he thought as he pulled his chair back to the table. "Was there anything else, Isabelle? Our dinner is here," he said just as a soft knock came from the door.

Isabelle rose from her genuflect and smiled. "Nothing that should interrupt dinner. Will you be attending the film?"

"Yes, I would never miss the finale of the festival," Miguel said, sounding bored. "You may enter now," he said a little louder.

The waiter opened the door and pushed in a cart full of food. Isabelle backed up to the door, then turned and left. The waiter put the food in the center of the table and served a portion to both of us. He refilled the wine and was gone.

"Eat, you are going to need the energy," Miguel said, adding a few drops of blood to his wine and took a generous sip.

"Yes, Master," I said, trying hard not to sound like a smart ass, but I wasn't sure if I accomplished it.

I wonder who will pop in next, he thought and folded his hands on the table and settled in to watch me eat.

I didn't even look at what I ate. I needed the calories so I would have the energy I would need later when we ran. Who knew when I would get another chance to eat? We dined in silence. We did not think to each other or talk to each other, I enjoyed the silence.

What do we do now? I asked anxious, and ready to move on from the restaurant. I wanted to get to Vince so we could find a way to leave.

The movie starts in about an hour. I always skip the red carpet fiasco. I moved my chair back to get up but he put his hand on my arm to stop me. *Wait, someone is outside.* "Would you like to join us?" he asked in a voice no louder than if he and I were talking.

The door opened and at first, I thought an ogre was standing in the doorway. I did a double take and realized it was just another vampire. Great, what was this one going to do to me? He had to be close to six and a half feet tall, dressed in black biker leathers, with jet-black hair buzzed close to his skull. He had dark wraparound sunglasses on. He had an olive complexion that looked like it had been tanned by the sun in his human years. Was this the guy who started the Hell's Angels?

He came around the table, and not only did he fall into the ceremonial genuflect but he grabbed Miguel's hand and kissed it. "My Lord, I just saw Isabelle and came to you as soon as I could. Why didn't you call me?" he asked and his face fell into a hurt expression. It seemed amazing to me that anyone of this guy's size could have his feelings hurt.

"Theodore, I can take care of myself once in a while," Miguel said, pulling his hand back. "Katie, this is Theodore. He is my bodyguard."

Theodore rose, came over to me and kissed my hand. "A pleasure to meet you, Katie," he said and looked back at Miguel. "My Lord, I am sorry I was not here to keep Isabelle from touching your property."

"Katie took care of it quite well I think," Miguel said, looking like a proud parent. You would have thought I had just taken off on my bike without training wheels for the first time.

Theodore's expression changed from apologetic to one of jealousy. Was this guy for real? Why would he be upset because I can take care of myself?

He is very protective toward anyone he has sworn to protect. Since you are my property, you are an extension of me. I should not have to protect myself, in his mind, that is what he is for, Miguel thought. "But I'm sure it will not be the end of it Theodore, and I am depending on you to make sure Katie stays safe," he said as an adult speaks to a child.

"Yes, my lord," Theodore said, getting up and standing behind Miguel.

"Shall we?" Miguel asked, standing. I followed. *After you my love.*

We exited the restaurant quickly with me leading the way, Miguel in the middle, and Theodore bringing up the rear. The limo was waiting out front for us. The door was already open so I went ahead and got in. Just before I was going to turn and sit in the seat where my back would rest against the back of the driver's seat and as far from Miguel as I could get, I noticed there was someone already there. I adjusted my movement and went to sit by the door on the driver's side while thinking to Miguel. *We have company.*

The vampire across from me was the definition of tall, dark, and handsome from what I could tell in the dim lights of the limo. His hair looked long and was pulled back in a ponytail. His shoulders were broad and came down to a small waist. He was clean-shaven with a tan, but I could instantly tell he was a vampire. His eyes looked black in the darkness of the limo, his nose sharp, and his lips full. It was Vince.

It took everything I had not to grab his hand and escape through the driver's side door. I gave him a look that said *Please save me.*

What is wrong? He asked bringing his eyebrows together.

I glanced over to where Miguel was getting in the car and looked back at Vince. Miguel sat next to me and put his arm around me. "Vince," he said. *This one is very dangerous be careful and stay calm.*

I know you cannot tell me what is going on, but you will never have to see him again after tonight, Vince thought. *You can do this.*

Theodore got into the car and sat next to Vince. "Hi, Vince," Theodore said, stretching is long legs out in front of him.

"My Lord," Vince said, doing his best to bow but it looked awkward since he was sitting in a low seat. "Who is this?" he asked, motioning in my direction.

"This is my new pet, Katie, you remember the girl I had you follow," he said, making me sound like I was the new family dog and nuzzled my ear. I let out a small moan as his lips touched a spot right behind my ear lobe. *You are too good at this.*

He had you following me? I asked Vince but got no response.

"Katie, welcome," Vince said, ignoring the continued

nuzzling that was going on. "Oh yes, I remember now. That was a long day. Have you marked her?" he sounded as if he already knew the answer and licked his lips. *Yes, I followed you the first day under his orders but I did not tell him about your gifts or your tattoo. I have to play this up,* he thought to me.

Show him. Miguel thought pulling himself away from me. I leaned forward and moved the shoulder of my shirt again to show Vince that I was off limits. *Please help me,* I thought to him realizing he probably couldn't hear me since I hadn't had his blood. Damn, I thought to myself hoping Miguel did not hear.

Vince leaned forward and inspected the tooth marks satisfied, he leaned back in his seat and I did the same. *I am sorry; just keep the goal in mind. You are doing great.*

"Why are you here, Vince?" Miguel asked, not sounding thrilled to be in the car with him or maybe he was not thrilled that I was in the car with Vince.

"When Isabelle called me to tell me you had found yourself a pet I found it very hard to believe. I wanted to meet it. You always choose the most interesting pets," Vince said in a voice that made it sound like he didn't care.

"Vince, my old friend," Miguel said, sounding bored. He put one arm around my shoulders and the other indecently high on my thigh. "She's a special one. She is going to be with me for a while. After everything I went through to break her she better be everything I need."

"Isabelle said this one broke her hand for touching her," Vince said, still sounding uninterested. *Nicely done.*

"It was only a finger," Miguel said. "And she did not ask me for permission. Katie can do what she likes if I give her the go ahead."

The limo came to a stop and the door opened for us to get out. Theodore crawled over everyone to be the first one out; no doubt to make sure his Lordship was safe. Miguel went next followed by me, not giving Vince a backward glance. Miguel took my arm and began to steer me toward the entrance of Castillo de la Mota.

What is Vince's problem? I thought to Miguel remembering the plan, I had to have an instant dislike for Vince as far as Miguel knew. We passed by the cannons, other remnants of the fort, and spectators who were hoping to see someone famous. We walked toward a building where spotlights marked the entrance.

He is my second in command and wants to make sure I am looking after the interests of the city not wasting time with a human. Miguel thought as a guard opened the door for us.

"Katie! Katie!" A voice I knew too well called out from the crowd.

Forgetting my part of the act, I stopped and turned to look. *Oh, this is just great*, I thought. Mark was standing just on the other side of the rope that divided the spectators from the ticket holders, practically drooling at me. He looked drunk. Big surprise.

What is it? Miguel asked before he saw Mark trying to jump the rope.

What do we do? I thought looking at Miguel.

What do you want to do?

Give him to Isabelle to drain, but that would be too mean. I guess I should talk to him, but I don't want to mess anything up. I wondered how much worse this night could get.

Why don't you invite him up with us and we can have a private chat without listening ears? It will be fine. He thought to me then kissed me hard enough to bruise my lips, and forced his tongue into my mouth.

I kissed him back the best I could but he was being too rough. Finally, he let me go. *I will meet you upstairs. I am going to leave Theodore with you and he will show you where to find me.* Miguel turned to Theodore, said something in his ear then to the guards at the door and headed into the building like nothing was wrong. I took a deep breath and walked over to Mark.

"Mark, why don't you come inside and we can talk?" I asked, trying to sound collected and confident. I could feel Theodore behind me, and I was wondering where Vince had gone.

"Okay," he said, sounding small after he looked over my shoulder at Theodore. He stepped around me and helped Mark get across the rope without falling on his face.

Theodore put a hand on Mark's back and I followed them inside the building then up to the second story. It was a very rustic building. It had either been preserved very well or they reconditioned it to look like it did during the Spanish wars. The walls were plastered and the ceiling was tongue and grove with massive rough-cut beams holding up the weight of the roof.

Theodore stopped at a door down a long hallway and knocked lightly. He must have heard Miguel give him permission to enter because he opened the door and pushed Mark into the room. Following them in, I guessed it was one of Miguel's offices since he was sitting behind a desk giving Mark the evil eye.

"Theodore, you can wait outside," Miguel said and Theodore left shutting the door behind him.

Miguel got up and walked out from behind his desk and over to Mark. "Mark? Hi, nice to meet you I'm Miguel." I could feel the jealousy pouring off him. "Please have a seat." Motioning Mark toward the chair in front of the desk while he went back to the chair behind the desk. *You can be yourself in here love*, Miguel thought to me.

"You look like shit, Mark," I said, standing in front of him with my arms crossed over my chest. "What are you still doing here anyway? Weren't you supposed to leave this morning?"

"I was but when I tried to follow you the lady at the train station said you had canceled your ticket. I have been looking for you everywhere." He put his head in his hands and rested his arms on his legs. "I thought you were dead, Katie, and look at you. You look, wow, you look great."

I turned and paced away from him then back trying to find the right words for what I wanted to say. "You bastard!" I yelled at him. "Do you know the emails I had to answer thanks to you? Why did you leave poor old Mark? He is so worried about you. You lied to everyone we know. You know damn well why I left you, you bastard."

I glanced at Miguel. He was feeling very happy with how I was handling Mark.

"Katie, I'm sorry. I love you. I know this guy has money and all, but seriously what we had was special," he said, looking up at me.

I stood stock still for a moment and met Mark's eyes. "Go to hell, Mark. It was so special that you fucked around on me how many times? Oh, wait, you probably can't count that high. How many times since we got to Europe?" I asked and started to pace again.

"Those meant nothing to me, babe. You'll always be my

number one."

"Number one? Of how many, Mark?" I stopped again to face him I was so mad at him, and at myself for not seeing who he was sooner.

"There will never be anyone else, I promise." He stood up and walked over to me with his arms open for a hug. He thought I would just take him back after he made a tiny meaningless promise to me.

There was only one way I was going to get through to him. As he continued to walk forward, I cocked my arm back and punched him in the nose as hard as I could.

"Go to hell, Mark! If my friends or my family get one more email from you, even if it is one of those stupid jokes you send, I will have Theodore hunt you down and castrate you," I said, shaking my hand out to try to mitigate the pain radiating up my arm. *Sorry Miguel. I didn't mean for him to bleed on the carpet.*

God, I love you, he thought getting up and picking Mark up by his armpits. "I am giving you until sundown tomorrow to get out of town or I will give you to Theodore as a play thing. He loves boys," he said, opening the door and shoving him to Theodore. "Get him out of here." He closed the door, and looked back at me. *Are you okay?*

"No," I said and started pacing again and flexing my hand. I wanted nothing more than to turn and do the same thing to Miguel, but I needed to remember the goal. "But I will be in a moment. Damn, it's been a while since I've punched anyone my hand is killing me." I stopped mid-step and inspected it.

Miguel was at my side before I had fully stopped. He took the injured hand gingerly in his to inspect it. "It's swelling. We need to get some ice on it. Since you can move it, and there are no bones sticking out I do not believe you broke it." He kissed it very lightly and looked up to meet my eyes. I tried to show my badass persona but I do not think it worked.

"In the future I would appreciate it if you would not bruise my lips when you kissed me," I said, running my uninjured fingers over them.

"I think," he said, not wanting to finish, but knowing I wouldn't let it go. "I think I was jealous of him. I will try and watch myself if you are compliant, if you are not then there is no telling what I will do."

"Silly vampire, you had nothing to be jealous of," I said, remembering I had a part to play. Then he brought his lips to mine, and he kissed me with a hunger that only comes after a battle. I felt his lust, and it tried to stir me but my hate toward him won out. I was thankful for the leather pants, otherwise he would have already had them around my ankles.

"What's next on the agenda?" I asked, after pulling away.

"Well, I was just wondering how I could get those pants off you without destroying them, but you're right. Back to work. I believe it's time to take our seats to watch the movie."

"What's the deal with Vince? He seems more like a stalker than a vampire to me." I walked over to the mirror to check my face and hair.

"He wants you. The night we met, he caught your scent on the way to your hotel. I had to call him off, he hates authority, and I think the only reason he is still here is because we respect each other. I have never had to call him off a meal before and he hates it." Miguel rubbed his hands up and down my arms.

"What would he have done to me?" I asked, making sure I didn't let my feelings about Vince slip through. I would not believe anything Miguel said about him. I just wanted to keep Miguel busy and not thinking about having sex with me again.

"Let's not talk about it, love. I need you to put on that strong badass face of yours so we can face the minions." He pulled my chin up with his finger.

"Let's get this over with," I said, only thinking about ripping his finger off for a second.

I walked out of the office with Miguel's arm carelessly thrown over my shoulder, and he steered us to another door leading into the theater. We were in what appeared to be a long skinny box with two rows of six seats. They were all full except for two right in the middle. Vince was next to one of the empty chairs and Theodore was next to the other. I saw Antonio sitting behind Vince but let my gaze go past him. I had to play the part of Miguel's slave and saying hi to Antonio would not be something he allowed his slaves to do.

Miguel wasn't happy that Vince was sitting next to the empty chairs. It felt like he really wanted to sit next to Theodore, but he wasn't going to let me sit next to Vince, so we were stuck.

Are you okay? Vince thought to me as I took my seat next to Theodore.

I wanted to answer him but I couldn't, Miguel would notice even if I shrugged my shoulders. All I could do is look at the screen as the movie began to play.

As we filled out of the movie theater, I wondered if Miguel was going to leave me alone at all. Every time I moved during the movie, he grabbed my hand and squeezed as if I was going to run away. I wanted to but I knew I wouldn't get far.

Where is the party? I asked Miguel as made our way to the limo.

Actually it's at the same club where we first met, he thought smiling.

I smiled too, wondering if Vince had our exit strategy figured out yet.

We walked back out to the limo and climbed in as we had before taking the same seats. As far as I knew, there was no reason for Miguel to need a bodyguard. All he had to do was glower at someone; vampire or human, and they would fall all over themselves to do whatever he asked.

It was quiet in the limo. Miguel held my hand stroking it with his thumb as he looked out the window. Vince stared at me, but he didn't think anything to me. It was probably for the best since I wasn't sure I could keep a straight face. Theodore was twiddling his thumbs. I don't think I had ever seen anyone really do that before, it was almost entertaining.

After what seemed like hours the limo stopped, the driver got out and came to the back door. "Vince, you will be first out followed by Theodore, myself, then you my dear Katie, " Miguel said before the driver opened the door.

I wasn't sure why we needed to select an order to get out of the car, but I guess it made it easier then everyone going for the door at once. After everyone else was out, I exited the limo and thought about running for it. It would take Miguel at least thirty seconds to notice I was gone, but I vetoed the idea. Thirty seconds was nowhere near enough time for me to get away. So I trailed behind them as they made their way into the club. They went up a staircase guarded by a bouncer, who of course, stopped me from following the group up the stairs.

Miguel? A little help here, I thought to him. He stopped abruptly and the other members of the group had to catch themselves to keep from running into the person in front of them.

"Raul, let her pass. She is with us," Miguel said, turning, then continued up the stairs without making sure his order was followed.

Raul looked me up and down, frowned, and allowed me to pass. I just lost another chance, I thought to myself. I would have had a few minutes that time. I hurried up the stairs as quickly as I could in my heels, even a few minutes wasn't going to be enough time. I caught up with the group as they made their way to the balcony overlooking the dance floor.

Come to me, Miguel thought and I did as he ordered. He pulled me in front of him and made me face the dance floor filled with famous people and their entourages. He wrapped his arms around my middle, and slid his hands under my shirt, and up to my breasts. It startled me and I jumped. *Remember your place love. I get to do what I want when we are out in the open.*

I am not one for public displays of affection, I thought back to him. I tried to think about the end game. Vince and I were going to sneak out and catch a plane out of here tonight. I had to put up with Miguel's bullshit for a little while longer. Just pretend you are in the doctor's office, I thought to myself.

"It is time to go and sit down," he said, releasing my breasts and heading over to the table, leaving me to follow him feeling used and dirty.

He moved to the middle of a booth and indicated that I should sit on his left side. I moved into the seat. *What now?* I asked wondering when Vince would signal me that it was time to go.

Now we wait for them to come to us. What would you like to drink?

Vodka tonic, I thought back to him as a waitress came over to take our order.

You need to understand; I have a role to play just as you do. Right now, I need to concentrate on that role. He thought to me before the first of many visitors came to our table.

Each vampire would approach our booth, genuflect to their master, Miguel would introduce me as his slave, and they would give him a full envelope. For the most part, no one looked twice at me. The few who did, looked away as soon as we made eye contact. It was very boring. I found myself trying to find Vince with my mind, but there were so many vampires in the vicinity I couldn't find his wavelength.

After an hour and a few vodka tonics, I needed to use the bathroom. "Master, I need to use the ladies room," I whispered in his ear.

"Of course. Theodore accompany Katie to the restroom," he said, kissing my cheek.

I slid out of the booth happy to move again and followed Theodore to the door marked 'Señoras'. "I'll be right back," I said and went inside.

After using the facilities, I stood in front of the mirror and washed my hands. I wanted to hide in there for the rest of the night, but Theodore would come in looking for me before long. I smoothed my hair down and went out to rejoin Theodore so he could accompany me back to Miguel's table. We had just come out of the alcove the restroom doors were in when Vince approached us.

"He does let you out of his sight," Vince said, smiling.

"I'm not." I rolled my eyes, remembering my part. "He can see everything from his booth. He is probably watching us right now, and Theodore is escorting me." I looked from Vince to Theodore.

We will go soon, Vince thought his eyes darting back and forth.

"I need to get back to my master." I wished he could hear me when I thought to him as Miguel could. I think he understood what was going on. If Miguel knew Vince and I were friends, if that was what you would call us, he would kill Vince.

Bring him to me, Miguel thought. I snapped my head in his direction and nodded my head. "Miguel wants to see you."

"By all means," Vince said and offered me his arm.

I looked at it, rolled my eyes again and took off at an almost run towards Miguel wishing the whole walk that I took Vince's arm and let him lead me out of there. I slid into the both beside Miguel quickly, and he brought me in for a deep kiss. *Careful,* I thought to him wishing I had the guts to bite off his tongue.

He broke off and stared at Vince. "Stop drooling friend. What brings you back?" *Do you see what I mean?* He thought to me annoyed.

Yes, what's his problem? I thought trying to make it sound believable.

"My Lord," he said, genuflecting. "Nothing more than the company of a friend."

"Well, get up my friend and sit." Miguel smiled but it did not reach his eyes.

Vince slid into the booth next to me, and I slithered closer to Miguel, the prick.

"How was the rent?" Vince asked, ignoring me.

"The usual," Miguel answered, taking a sip of his wine, and eyeing me suspiciously.

"Good," Vince said.

I looked from one to the other neither of them were happy. Just as I was about to start talking about the weather Lolita appeared at the top of stairs. My jaw dropped when I saw what she was wearing. She looked like a goddess wearing a floor length, black sheer dress with sequins artfully hiding her intimate areas.

Miguel followed where my eyes were looking. *Pretend like you have no idea who she is.* He stood up and opened his arms to greet her. She almost fell into them just like the night she had arrived.

"Lolita looks the same as always," Vince said. *I am trying to find a way to get you away from them. Miguel is keeping a better eye on you than I thought he would.*

"Really? This is the first time I have seen her." I was trying to think of a way to let Vince know I was ready to go hours ago. "I wonder if she will be a distraction for him."

"If she had just shown up today then I would say yes." He took a sip of his wine. *But since she has been here for a few days they have some sort of a plan for this entrance.*

I watched Miguel make a show of gushing over his long-lost sister then glanced around the room. Everyone was watching them except for Theodore who was watching me. Not time yet, I thought to myself and drummed my fingers on the table. "Too bad," I murmured.

"Yes, I agree," Vince said, looking around the room and saw Theodore. *I am going to leave in a minute to move my car around to the front entrance so we can make a clean get away.*

"Well, we all do what we have to do." I was not sure how to respond. I still wasn't sure how we were going to be able to leave without someone seeing us.

"It will all work out in the end," Vince said, looking down at my cleavage.

"Katie," Miguel called. "Come and meet my sister."

Thank you. I thought and got out of the booth without saying anything more to Vince. Miguel took my hand as I approached and I bowed to Lolita.

"Lolo, this is Katie my new slave," Miguel said as I straightened myself.

"She is lovely, Miguel," Lolita said, looking at me from all angles. "Will you share?"

My body started to shake at the idea of being alone with Lolita, Miguel could feel it. *This is all part of the game, Love,* he thought to me.

"Of course, sister, how could I not share with you?" Miguel asked, looking at me with a smug grin. "Would you like to use my office or would you like to have your fun at my booth?"

Lolita's eyes widened and began to glow. "For my first taste of this one I think your office might be best." She took my hand. "Would you like to watch?"

"Yes, but maybe later. I still have some things to wrap up." Miguel kissed me hard. *You look like you need a break,* he thought to me. I felt the truth in his words but there was something underneath I couldn't put my finger on.

Thanks, I answered and followed Lolita to the wall opposite of the booth where there was a door leading to an office. Once we were inside with the door shut, she let go of my hand.

"So you already broke someone's hand?" Lolita went to the sofa, and sat down like a debutant.

"It was a finger, and she was being a bitch," I said in reply and began pacing the room. "Miguel said I could. I was actually surprised I had it in me."

"Isabelle has been chasing after him for a long time. It sounds like she wanted to share you in hopes of bringing them closer together. It doesn't look like her plan worked very well."

"What are we pretending to do right now?" I asked, stretching. I was so tired of sitting, and I was trying not to think about how Vince and I were going to escape.

"Fucking and I should be drinking your blood, but I already ate. Besides Miguel would not be too happy if we fucked even though he said I should try you." She looked at her long red fingernails. "Was that Vince you were sitting with when I came in?"

"Yes, what an ass," I said, choosing to let her comment about fucking me slide. *Miguel, why would you want to have your sister fuck me?* I thought to him instead. I didn't really expect an answer. He had fooled me worse than Mark.

"It has been a long time since I last saw him. He is fine. Maybe when we are done I will take care of that problem."

"What do you mean?" I asked, backing towards the door.

"I cannot allow you to live," she said, examining her

manicure. "Do you really think I would let 'The One' have power over me? I am the strongest female vampire in existence; I have worked hard and taken out many enemies to be where I am. I am not going to give it up to you."

CHAPTER 35

"If you do not want me to have the power why have you been helping Miguel with the prophecy?" I asked, making it to the door, and wrapping my fingers around the doorknob.

"You really are dense. I helped him in order to take care of you while you were still weak and easy to take down. With you gone Miguel will be lost. Either he will find a way to move on or he will end it. I do not need him anymore." She looked up to see where I moved.

I had to get out of here. *Miguel, I think your sister is going to try to kill me*, I thought to him. I didn't want to but this room was soundproof and if I yelled no one would hear me. He was the only one who may be able to stop this.

It was too late though, she was on me in the next heartbeat and I lost my grip on the door handle as her fangs pierced the skin on my neck and I let out a deafening scream. She was at my vein. Somehow, I knew she had nicked my jugular. I didn't need to be a doctor to know if I did not get help soon I would be dead. "Get. The. Fuck. Off," I yelled, trying to dislodge her, but she had me from behind. I couldn't shake her. I felt her jaws beginning to close, and I had a feeling she was going to take more than blood.

I tried to elbow her in the ribs, but she was standing too far away from me to reach her. I tried to stomp on her foot, but she was too quick. With nothing left, I screamed and pulled away. I felt flesh and muscle separate between her teeth. The pain was indescribable but I was loose.

I turned my hand, already in a fist, and put everything I had into a punch that connected with her jaw. It was like hitting a brick wall, but I knocked her back a few paces. I turned for the door, my hand was on the doorknob when there was a knock, and the handle began to turn under my hand. I jumped back and Miguel walked in looking upset.

What have you done? He bellowed at me in my head. "Lolita, what did you do?"

"I was going to change her for you brother." I heard her say as I ran to the only other door in the room, not caring if it was a closet or a bathroom I just wanted away from everyone who drank blood.

I opened it, went in, and closed it in a heartbeat. It was dark, so dark I couldn't see my hand in front of my face. I felt for the lock on the door, engaged it and began groping for a light switch. After fumbling at the wall a few times, I found it, flipped it on and found myself in a hallway ending a little way ahead.

With one hand applying pressure to my neck, I ran for it. I could hear Miguel yelling at Lolita, then a crash sounded behind me. Good, I thought with them fighting I would have more time to get away. Before I made it to the end of the hallway I heard someone banging on the door trying to break it down, but I forced myself not to look back. I had to keep moving forward.

My hand was slick with blood and I could feel it running down my arm to my elbow where it dripped to the floor. I needed help and I wouldn't get it from Miguel and Lolita.

At the end of the hall, there was a set of stairs leading down. Of course, Miguel would have an emergency escape path, I thought to myself. I concentrated on putting one foot in front of the other. At the bottom of the stairs, there was a door with a huge bar over it. It was going to be heavy, but I had to get out of there. I tried lifting it with one hand but it barely budged.

"Katie, come back, you're hurt." I could hear Miguel calling me. He was putting power behind the words, more than he had when he told me to suck his dick. I pushed the demands away, I was not his slave, damn it.

I didn't understand why he wasn't already here trying to save me. He could be faster than light when he wanted to be. Why was he not doing that now?

My flight instinct took hold of me. I bent down, positioned the bar over my shoulder, and forced my knees to straighten and lifted the bar on my shoulder. I took a step back and dropped it to the ground. I opened the door and tried to run away but I didn't get ten feet before a black sports car pulled up in front of me and Vince jumped out. I turned ready to run the other way. All I wanted was a hospital, not vampires who could go into blood lust at a moment's notice. I didn't care that we had planned on running away together.

Lolita stepped out of the door licking her lips. I turned back to Vince who was coming towards me. I started to run towards him and everything went black.

I was standing on the cliff watching the waves crash far below me. There was no pain, no inner turmoil, only peace. Had I died? Had I lost too much blood? Was Vince unable to save me? I asked these questions but I didn't care about the answers. I wanted to be left in peace.

I felt Mom grab my hand and pull me to face her.

"I'm sorry I failed you, Mom," I said with tears coming to the surface of my eyes and spilling over.

"Why do you think you failed me?" She took me into her arms for a hug.

"I couldn't save Miguel and now I think it's too late. I think I died." I squeezed her hard and buried my face in her neck.

"Saving Miguel was one of many options. Not all is lost with him yet. I am proud of you." She pulled out of the hug to look at me.

"Why? I pulled the binding out of my brain, but then I had to let him put it back so he wouldn't know I got rid of it. Our plan to run away failed. I ruined your plans."

"You were brave and strong, you looked deep within yourself to find the protector you need. You are going to be fine. Have faith, and remember I will always be with you," she said, backing up and disappearing.

I turned and looked back out at the waves. I hoped she was right.

CHAPTER 36

The pain in my neck woke me up. I put my hand to it thinking the pressure would ease it. What was the old joke? 'Doctor it hurts when I do this. Well, stop doing it.' The pain was twenty times worse when I touched it. I could feel a large piece of gauze over the wound but it felt smaller than it did the night before. I must have some stitches under the gauze.

Lolita had taken a chunk out me. I tried to remember where I was before I opened my eyes. I remembered Vince and Lolita coming towards me from opposite directions then I dreamt of my mom on the cliff.

I opened my eyes to a dimly lit room I had never been in before. The bed and bedding were a crisp white, as were the walls. The frame of the bed was black iron, and all of the furniture in the room was black as well. I tried to turn my head but it hurt too much. I noticed a tube hooked up to my arm. Looking up I could see it attached to a bag of what looked like blood.

I took a moment and thought. How in the hell had I lived through that? Then I wondered where I was. Did Lolita and Miguel have me at some super-secret hospital? Had Vince whisked me away? I really wanted to get out of wherever I was. In my mind nothing positive could come out of this.

I needed to leave now, but I had to figure out how. I was making an educated guess that I needed the blood being piped into me. The IV bag had to come with me. I looked under the covers with the hand was not attached to the IV. I could have guessed. I was naked which meant I was going to need some clothes if I wanted to get out of here. The next obvious question was, where was I going to go? Where was my money belt? It had been under my pants but since there were no pants, there was no belt. Was there a US consulate in this tiny town? I had no money, no passport, and no clothes. Well, I would just have to figure something out.

I sat up and the world swam for a second. When the world righted itself, I swung my legs off the bed, and I was still feeling all right. I looked down and saw the bag of blood, I did not know what else to call it, was on one of those towers with wheels. At least I would not have to hold onto the bag. I put my feet on the floor and tested the strength of my legs. They were a little shaky, I could move but I wouldn't be going anywhere fast.

I heard a door handle turn and the door opening. I hurried to get back in bed and cover up. I hope that whoever it was would not know I was trying to escape. I closed my eyes pretending to be asleep, and listened as footsteps came closer. I held my breath when the footsteps stopped and felt a cool hand on my wrist. They sat down on a chair close by and said. "I know you are awake. Let me know when you are up to talking. You are safe."

It was Vince. I wanted to be relieved I wasn't at the villa with

Miguel and Lolita, but Vince was still a vampire, and I didn't want to hang out with any of them at the moment.

"That's what all of you say isn't it?" I opened my eyes, and stared at the ceiling. Wow, it hurt to talk. "Why am I here? And where is here?"

"You are in my home. You are here because you were in need of medical attention that did not include you being turned into a vampire."

"What do you mean?" I croaked. "Could I have some water please?"

"Of course," he said, leaning towards the nightstand, and poured water from a pitcher into a glass. I sat up, propped my back against the headboard, held the sheet to my chest with one hand, and took the glass with my other. I gulped the water down letting it soothe my throat. "Lolita tore your jugular and without a doctor you would have died, or they would have turned you into one of us."

"That bitch needs to die," I said, thinking of everything Lolita had told me. Miguel did too after what he had done to me, but Lolita was the bigger threat. She would stop at nothing to take me out of the equation. She did not want to control me; she wanted to kill me. There would be a time and a place I knew, but I needed to think about the now. I needed to get out of this city.

"Why am I naked?" I was trying to keep the sheet over my breasts.

"When I brought you into the operating room last night you were covered from head to toe in your own blood. I had to undress you and clean the blood off. Would you rather I left you covered in it?" He sounded annoyed at my question.

"No, you're right. Thank you. Are you a doctor or something?"

"I have spent some time patching people up. I knew how to repair your artery and stitch you up, so I did."

"That was very kind of you," I said, realizing there was a bigger question I needed answered. "Why didn't you change me if I was so close to death?"

"It was not what you wanted and you are not ready yet."

"Thank you. You were right; I don't want to become a vampire, but what did you mean, I am not ready yet?"

"If you are to be queen you need to know everything you can about our world before you change. You will also want to be in optimal shape, so it will carry over to your next life. Everything you learn as a human will carry over into your vampire life, only you will be stronger and faster." He rested the ankle of one leg on the thigh of the other and folding his hands together.

"Why would I want to learn all of that?" I asked my mind still foggy.

"Do you think all of the vampires in the world will automatically bow down to you? There are many, including Lolita, who will want to strip you of your power. You are going to have to learn to defend yourself."

I pondered his words, my thoughts going back to the shower with Miguel then Lolita. "Will you teach me?" He looked like he could fight.

"If that is what you want, I will," he said with a ghost of a grin.

"I think I do. How much blood did I lose?" I asked, thinking about how weak I felt.

"About half. Once this batch gets into your system you should be full up again." He looked at the bag it was almost empty.

"Interesting," I said, looking at the bag and wondering about the bond. I closed my eyes and looked into my brain where the binding was located. It was still there but it looked weak and easy to remove.

I took the tweezers in my mind as I had before and began the process of removing it. I didn't need it anymore and I wanted it gone. It took longer this time. It looked weak but it was stronger than the last one. There were more tentacles snaking off it. I heard Vince talking from far away but I ignored him concentrating on my task.

I began to sweat from the pain. I felt Vince running something cool over my forehead. My breath was coming in short bursts and Vince was talking more loudly now. Almost there, I thought as I removed the last tentacle and pulled the mass out of my brain. I didn't even look at this time. I incinerated it and let out a scream as it burst into flames. I breathed; I let the pain wash over me then flow away. I needed to rest for a minute.

Katie, Vince thought. *Please wake up. Are you okay?*

I opened my eyes to find Vince hovering over me with a worried expression on his face. "Sorry, I had to pull the binding out, it was a lot harder this time."

"What do you mean, this time?" Vince sat back down in the chair.

"My mother taught me how to pull it out, so I did after my run, after the last time we talked. What day is it?"

"You have only slept for twelve hours so it is Wednesday," Vince said, wanting me to get on with the story.

"Anyway, I started wondering how to explain to Miguel that I could not speak to him mind-to-mind with the binding gone, so when he wanted to exchange blood again yesterday I agreed knowing I could pull the binding out again. It was a lot harder this time, but it's gone." I cringed inwardly thinking about the other things I did with him yesterday. I was going to want a shower every time I thought of it for a long time.

"The goddess told me you had taken care of the bond. She is not going to be happy you let it happen again."

"If I was smart I would have left with you the first night. I'm sorry I was difficult. You were right about everything: Miguel, Lolita, all of it. If I'd gone with you that night none of this would have happened." My eyes filled with tears, I didn't want to cry, but I was mad at myself for not seeing what was going on.

"Hey, it will be alright. I am going to make sure he never gets close to you again." He got up and went to the door.

"Did you say something about a goddess? Who is that?" I asked confused. "What are you talking about? Where are you going?"

"Asteria, your mother. You did not know that your birth mother is a Titan? I am getting your breakfast." He opened the door allowing a servant to bring in a tray of food. The smell of it made my mouth water. I was starving. The servant put the food on the table next to the bed and left without even looking at me.

"No, my mom isn't a goddess. How can she be? She died." I was at a loss of words. I looked at the food and at the sheet covering me. How was I going to eat without showing Vince my breasts? "Do you have a shirt or something I could borrow?"

Without a word he disappeared in the closet and reemerged

with a men's oxford shirt in his hand. "Will this work for the time being?"

"For the time being." I held my hands out for it. He gave it to me then turned his back towards me. "Thank you." I pulled the shirt on being careful not to let it touch my mutilated neck. Luckily the IV tube was long enough to come up my arm and out the neck hole. I started to button it noticing my right hand was swollen and my fingers didn't want to do their job. Was it from when I punched Mark or Lolita? I smiled despite the pain for a second. At least I fought back.

"How's it going over there?" Vince asked.

"I may need some help," I said as the pain in my hand shot up my arm. "My fingers are not working very well and they hurt," I explained, pulling the shirt together so he could not see what was underneath. Realizing what I was doing, I blushed. Hadn't this guy seen all of me last night?

"Blushing really? Here let me," he said, quickly buttoning the shirt without even trying to see what lay beneath. "You know you were wearing less last night then you are right now."

"I know, but different circumstances and all. Why do you think my dead mother is a goddess?"

"Asteria is the Titan of oracles, prophecies and dreams. Why do you think you only see her when you are dreaming?"

"Because my subconscious is using her as mechanism for me to explain all of the crazy things that have happened lately," I said, scooping up some eggs with my good hand.

"While that is a reasonable explanation, it still does not explain why you can hear vampire's thoughts."

"Ok I will go with it for now," I said, before taking another mouthful of food. "What does the prophecy say?"

"I am going to give you the English translation," Vince said, standing at the foot of the bed.

"Those of my begotten who have forgotten me will be made to heal by a woman bearing my mark.

She will be found on the east shores of the great ocean beyond the Pillars of Hercules, in a protected bay.

None will be able to deceive her as she will be able to listen to what is in the hearts of my creation.

Her powers will manifest as her knowledge of her kind grows.

Those who try to enslave her will reap the recompense of her exasperation.

The one who mentors her will be endowed with an accolade from the chosen one.

The one who changes her will be her consort and reign at her side.

She will bring my creation back into the fold."

"Really, it sounds like something out of a paranormal romance novel," I said, trying not to laugh, and bringing another forkful of eggs to my mouth.

"I am not familiar with paranormal romance novels," Vince said, grimacing at my comment. "But I promise you it is true. When you see the tapestry you will understand."

"So my tattoo has something to do with the prophecy?" I ate a piece of bacon.

"The prophecy says, 'a woman bearing my mark'," he pointed at my side. "The mark looks just like your tattoo."

"I will have to see it to believe it." I was trying to keep an open mind. "Why did Miguel try to enslave me if the prophecy says if they do, they will 'reap the recompense of her exasperation,' that sounds like a bad thing to me, but I would need a dictionary to make sure."

"The problem with the prophecy is that it was written down in ancient Greek, in a dialect very few can translate anymore. There are many different versions of the translation and everyone interprets it differently. The one I read to you is the most widely accepted. Miguel preferred a different one."

"What did his say?" I asked, done with the food, and putting the plate back on the nightstand.

"Something like, 'the one who enslaves her will control her' or some nonsense." Vince rolled his eyes.

Come to me, Miguel thought to me.

"Oh, shit," I said, bringing my hands to my ears momentarily forgetting about the wound on my neck and the swelling in my hand.

"Are you in pain?" Vince asked, coming to my side with his hand on my arm.

"Yes. I have a few wounds that do not like to be moved but the, 'oh shit' was because Miguel is calling to me, in my head."

"What is he saying?"

"To come to him. Since I can hear him doesn't that mean he is close by? Do you have somewhere else I can hide?" I asked, beating myself up for falling for everything Miguel told me. I wanted to shrink inside myself so I could no longer see how stupid I had been.

"This is the best place for you to hide. There is a reason why you are not in the hospital. He may be on his way here to discuss what happened last night, but he will call me first."

"What are we going to do?" I wanted to brush my teeth and shower before we had to run, but if we didn't have time I would be happy getting away from Miguel with dirty teeth and stinky armpits.

"It is the middle of the day. There is not much we can do. Stay here you need to rest. I will not let them find you." He meant what he said, but I couldn't help having doubts about getting out of here.

"If I am stuck here, I might as well get cleaned up. Do you have a shower I can use?"

"You cannot get your wound wet yet," he said, looking apologetic. "You can take a bath as long as you are careful not to get the bandage wet."

It sounded better than nothing. "Lead the way," I said, moving to get out of the bed.

"Let me get the IV out first." He quickly and painlessly pulling the needle out, placing a cotton ball over the puncture, followed by a piece of medical tape. "It should stop bleeding in a few minutes. There are towels, a robe, and a new toothbrush in the bathroom," he said, pointing to the door on the opposite side of the room.

"Thanks," I said, moving to get out of bed slowly so I didn't make myself light-headed. I pulled the shirt he gave me down to make sure I was covered up but there was no need to. He was so tall the shirt came down to my knees.

"I will go and find you some clothes. Try to rest. I will not let them find you," Vince said, leaving the room and closing the door behind him.

A few minutes later, I slid into the hot bath making sure my shoulders stayed out of the water. I leaned my head back on the porcelain and closed my eyes. I had to stop being stupid, I needed to gain some perspective, and not blindly follow a man just because they gave me some sense of security. I was smarter than that. I would learn from this. I was going to find a way to give myself my own sense of security.

What about Vince? How did I know Vince wasn't trying to accomplish the same thing Miguel wanted? Was I doing the same thing with him as I did with Miguel? How did I know if he was telling me the truth? I could hear him in my head too. It didn't mean I could trust him. I had better check myself for any new bite marks. After looking and feeling all over my body and finding none that weren't already there, I looked inside my head for anything that looked out of place. Everything looked good, Vince had not given me his blood, thank god.

I told myself there was no need to cry. Just be happy I was alive. What should I do? Did Vince have my wallet? Would he give it to me if I asked? I had to get it back. How far could I get without it? Did I want to be one of them? Did I have a choice? Maybe not but I wouldn't be a slave to anyone.

When the water started to cool down, I pulled the plug and carefully got out of the tub. While I was drying myself off I made a few decisions. I needed to learn everything I could about this prophecy before I left. No one was going to drink my blood from here on out. And, I needed to get out of town as soon as possible.

I thought about how I was going to accomplish these tasks while I brushed my teeth and hair. Vince seemed to know a lot about the prophecy. I needed to talk him into giving me all of the information he had about it.

How was I going to get out of town? Maybe I could call Antonio, but he was at the theater with Miguel. It was very likely he was Miguel's slave. One more thing I could beat myself up about. I would have to ask Vince. I didn't want him to know where I went, but unless he had my passport and credit cards I was going to be at his mercy.

Finished with my grooming, I went back into the bedroom and found it blessedly empty except for a pile of clothes. I went over to the bed and picked up a pair of black satin thong panties. You would think men would understand why a piece of string between your butt cheeks isn't comfortable but they don't. I put them on and picked up the bra, how had he gotten the right size? I wondered putting it on. The clasp was in the front, but it still took a few tries for me to clasp it with my injured hand and the pain in my neck. The faded blue jeans felt like heaven compared to the leather pants I had on the night before. They were a relaxed fit and big in the waist making them easy to button. The soft cotton t-shirt had a scooped neck so it didn't come near the stitches on my neck and as an added bonus, it made my boobs look good.

I looked around for some shoes. All I found were the heels I had on the night before. Not what I wanted but heels were better than barefoot if I needed to move around outside.

Finally dressed, I sat down in the overstuffed chair, took a deep breath, and closed my eyes. Was I ready to get on with this? No, but I had things to do and plans to make so I might as well get started.

I opened my eyes and went to the door. I turned the handle but it did not open. Locked? I looked for a way to unlock it, but was an old doorknob that required a key. Of course, there was no key. Why had Vince locked me in here?

CHAPTER 37

I went to the closed window shades and pulled them up. Maybe I could get out through the window. Sunlight streamed in, blinding me for a moment. When I could see again, I saw a lush green yard with a pool.

I ran my fingers around the window trying to find a way to open it but it was plate glass, built-in to the wall of the house. I would have to break it. Beginning to panic I ran to the night table and grabbed the lamp sitting on it. I yanked the cord out of the wall and headed back over to the window determined to break it. I brought my non-injured shoulder back and was just about to hit the lamp against the window when the phone rang.

I stood frozen thinking. Should I just get out of here and take my chances or find out what was going on before I overreact? After the third ring, I walked over and picked up the receiver. "Yes?" I asked, trying not to sound hysterical.

"Katie, this is Vince."

"Why did you lock me in this room?" I asked, trying to hold back my tears of fear and anger.

"Miguel and Lolita called, they are almost here." His voice was tight and low. "I did not want to disturb you, and I did not want you to wander out while they are here."

"Do they know I'm here?" I asked, unable to hide the panic in my voice now.

"No, they think you are at one of the human hospitals in the ICU. They cannot get into see you during the day. If he calls to you, remain silent, and they will not know you are here."

"Do you have my passport and credit cards?" All of my plans depended on him having them.

"No, I had to leave them at the hospital to ensure the illusion for Miguel. Don't worry I will take care of you."

"Great someone else promising to take care of me," I muttered. "When are they going to be here?"

"Any moment, they are taking the tunnels," Vince said, stopping short. "I have to go. This should not take long. Please rest and stay quiet."

"Okay." It wasn't like I had much of a choice but he had already hung up. Trapped, scared, and frustrated I looked longingly out the window at the beautiful day. I could break the window and run, but where would I go? No money, no passport, and no phone. I could go to the hospital and explain that the girl in the ICU wasn't me, and ask if I could please have my purse back? I didn't see it working, especially since I spoke almost no Spanish.

It felt like people I didn't know or trust were making all of my choices for me. Heck, they weren't even people, they were vampires. I wanted to do something, to move around, but I wanted to be quiet. I knew how good Miguel's ears were, and I didn't want to give him any reason to think I might be here. The only thing I could do was lower the shades back down, sit in the chair and make as little noise as possible.

Mi amor, are you here? Miguel's thoughts filtered into my mind. I froze.

I tried not to think, not to breathe, to just shutdown.

Lover, I am lost without you. Are you hurt? Is he holding you against your will? Let me save you. He thought sounding like the gentleman I had met at the beginning of all this. It was all an act. I wanted to hurt him so bad for what he had done to me, but I sat there on the chair and counted strands of yarn in the carpet.

I heard footsteps in the hall. They were quiet but I could hear them. They stopped outside the door. I held my breath and continued to stare at the carpet.

Katie, are you in there? Lolita asked. I was surprised because she had never spoken mind-to-mind to me on purpose before. Carpet. Keep counting the strands of yarn and do not make a sound.

After what felt like an eternity, I felt her move away from the door and continue down the hall. I didn't move beyond blinking and breathing. I didn't want anyone to hear me.

I must have fallen asleep at some point because I awoke to a cool hand on my cheek. I jumped out of the chair and assumed a fighting stance; at least what I thought was a fighting stance. "Vince?" I asked when I realized it wasn't Miguel or Lolita.

"Yes, they are gone." He took a step back to give me my space. "What happened?"

"They were trying to find me. They were both speaking, mind-to-mind with me. Someone came down the hall and stopped outside the room. I think it was Lolita." My eyes filled up with tears for what felt like the millionth time that day. "I was so scared they would find me. Lolita has had my blood too. Does mean she can track me?"

"It has been known to happen, but it is a special gift, not all vampires receive it. I do not know if it would even work on you since you are 'The One'." He reached out to comfort me but reading the look on my face he dropped his arms. "I am guessing she could not track you because she did not find you. Believe me, if she knew you were here she would have torn this place apart to find you."

"Are they mad at you for saving me last night? What did you tell them?"

"She saw me take you. As did a bunch of humans. I told everyone you must have been hurt falling down the stairs, and I would take you to the hospital. There was no other way of covering everything up. There were too many humans around for her to come after me." He paused, sitting down in the chair. I was still in my fighting stance and had no intention of moving until I knew he wasn't going to hurt me. "Miguel and Lolita still believe I took you to the hospital which is what we do when humans see the damage we cause. We typically spell the human involved into going along with whatever cover story we are using, and drop them off at the hospital as any Good Samaritan would." He leaned back in the chair and laced his hands behind his head.

"The woman I took to the hospital last night will not survive, and she has all of your information on her. A car hit her. A homeless prostitute with no family," he said with no sympathy.

My eyes burned with tears and they began rolling down my cheeks. "Did you hit her?"

"No, I happened to her on the way to the hospital with you. I saw an opportunity and I took it." He bent over and rested his elbows on his thighs.

"What am I going to do?" I felt bad he put his neck on the line to save me. I gave myself a mental slap. Stop thinking that way. He is helping you because you're 'The One,' and he wants to use you. Keep your guard up.

"Miguel knows everything about you. He will be able to track you by your credit cards, your passport, and your name. Believe me when I say he will not give up trying to turn you. You must go into hiding." Standing, he went over to the window and looked out through the edge of the curtains.

"Are you suggesting I leave my life behind? Let my family think I died and become someone else entirely?" I sat down on the bed and rubbed my face with my good hand.

"Yes, it is the safest way to keep you from Miguel, Lolita and the other vampires out there in search of 'The One.'"

"I know changing my identity can be done, but I have no clue how to do it." I did not want to ask him for help.

"I have already done it," he said, pulling a manila folder from the bedside table drawer, and bringing it to me. I flipped it open and found a passport, an airline ticket, an ATM card, and a black credit card. I shut the folder and felt the stress leave my shoulders. "Thank you, but you will still know who I am."

"I will not betray you to anyone. I have obtained a new identity as well. You can use it as insurance. If you feel you cannot trust me, all you will have to do is call Miguel, give him my new name and I will be as good as dead." He wasn't joking about any of this. "Or we can travel together. I can teach you about our kind and how to fight. Prepare you in the event you are turned.”

“There has to be another choice.” I turned my back on him. “Could we kill them?”

“It is an option, but I don’t know how it can be accomplished at this time. They are both so old they rarely have to sleep, and if they catch a whiff of either of us they will be on us in a split second.” He was doing everything in his power not to touch me. “With time and training you will be more powerful than both of them. Then you can exact your revenge.”

My life as Katie Hunter was over. Should I risk running on my own? With little to no knowledge of the monsters who hunted me or did I run with the monster who says he will protect me? Could I trust him? No, but what had he done to not make me want to trust him? Nothing. He had saved me from . . . from what? An untimely death or was it just putting off the inevitable? I need to leave as soon as possible, learn more about what the prophecy said, and learn to fight.

I could learn from Vince. He could teach me about how to keep myself safe from the vampires who would seek to turn me for their personal gain. With the first broken promise I will dismiss him, run from him as long as he could show me how to disappear first.

“What did Miguel and Lolita want?”

“They wanted to know what had happened to you last night, and why I took you away. They do not trust anyone right now. They are so swept up in you being ‘The One’ that they will stop at nothing to get you back,” he said, staring at my favorite corner of carpet. “They sent Antonio to the hospital to make sure you were alright, but since you were in the ICU, no one but your family would be allowed in.

After the sun goes down they can spell the nurses and they will know you are not there. In the meantime, they came here to threaten me with bodily harm worse than death if you died in the hospital."

"Lolita wants to kill me not turn me or control me," I said, relaxing my stance. "She wants to be the most powerful female vampire in existence. She could care less what Miguel wants."

"How do you know?" Vince asked, jerking his head up to look at me.

"She told me before she took a chunk out of me," I said, remembering the helplessness I felt as she bit down. "I don't ever want to feel that helpless again."

"She is an evil bitch," Vince said, looking down at the carpet again. "I will help you become strong enough to beat her."

"Thank you," I said in a small voice. Be strong, isn't that what my mother told me in the first dream? It was time to learn to be strong.

"So I run. It's what I was planning to do anyway," I said, beginning to shake all over with tears running down my cheeks. "I didn't think I would have to leave my life behind." I wasn't sure if I was crying for the woman who had taken my place in the hospital or for the loss my family must be experiencing. I shook myself. "What time is it?" I looked around the dimly lit room.

"Nine o'clock in the evening. We need to get moving before they find out you are not in the hospital."

"Where are we going to go?" I rubbed my eyes. I might as well learn everything I can. If he gets all psycho like Miguel, I would just have to run away from him, but this time I would be more prepared.

"I have everything in order if you will trust me," Vince said, reaching to take my hand but stopping and folding his hands together. "You have no reason to trust me except that I saved you from Miguel and his sister last night. They betrayed you, lied to you, and tried to turn you. He did it in a way that would have made him look like a savior instead of the traitor he is.

"I will be honest with you in all things. Your mother paid a visit to my dreams last night. She asked me to teach you and protect you. She asked I take you to her temple so you can look at the original tapestry and prophecy. I will do this not only because she asked me to, but because I have wanted to help you since the moment I caught your scent in the bar. I only wish to be your protector and instructor, nothing more."

"Thank you, as long as I feel I can trust you I will travel with you. There will be no, and I mean no, sharing of blood."

"Agreed," Vince said, without batting an eye.

"Great, where are we going, and when are we leaving?" I put my hands on my hips and turned to him. While I didn't like everything he just admitted to me, it did help me trust him more than before. Plus, I could feel the honesty behind his words.

"We are going to Greece. Where the prophecy was made; I know where the original text is located. We can study it then we will go and stay with my child." He smiled and walked toward the door.

CHAPTER 38

"That sounds like a good plan and it was on my list of places I wanted to visit," I said, following him to the door and down the hall, with the information on my new life clutched to my chest. "I would still like to see everything you have about the prophecy though."

"I have gathered everything about it on a flash drive. We can look at on the plane," he said, moving at a steady pace in front of me.

I almost had to run to keep up, but the sooner we were gone the better. "What will Miguel and Lolita think when you disappear?"

"They were not happy I ruined their plans with you. They would not have followed protocol with you and taken you to the hospital. They would have taken you back into the club and changed you. They banished me from the city. They gave me until midnight tonight to leave and not come back for a hundred years." He paused to laugh. "I only stayed here as long as I have to stop Miguel from gaining the power he wants from 'The One'. Now that you are ready to leave, so am I. The management is getting a little too high handed for me." He stopped in a large entryway to pick up a bag sitting near the door and look out the window. "The car is here. Are you ready to go?"

"Let's do it." I moved to his side.

He opened the door and we briskly walked toward the car. *Katie, where are you my love?* Miguel's voice said in my head and I stopped dead in my tracks.

"What is wrong?" Vince asked, holding the door open for me looking impatient.

"He's looking for me." I frantically looked around expecting Miguel to melt out of the shadows at any moment.

"Is he talking in your head again?" Vince asked, leaving the door open, and coming to my side.

"Yes, he's searching for me." I looked at Vince, terrified. Miguel was going to find me, kill Vince, and turn me into his creature.

"Let's move," Vince said as he pulled me to the car, helped me in and pushed me down to the floor boards. He got in on the other side and told the driver to go. "It is safer for you down there. I do not want anyone to see you."

Katie, my love I'm sorry. Where are you?

"Miguel knows I'm not at the hospital," I said with a twinge at the sound of his voice in my head.

"What is he telling you?" Vince looked out the rear window.

"He is sorry and he wants to know where I am." I tried to sink lower into the floor thinking it would keep me better hidden.

"He is trying to lure you back to him." He pulled a buzzing cell phone out of his jacket pocket, and flipped it open to answer it.

"Miguel, what can I do for you?" he asked then listened to Miguel's reply. "I left her right outside the emergency room. That is all I can tell you. There was a car coming up behind me at the time. I am not sure what they were doing, and in her state, I did not feel like I should stick around to make explanations." His voice was calm as he looked at me then out the windshield. He listened again for a moment giving me a worried look. "I am leaving before midnight as you dictated." I could feel his tension growing. "I am not sure yet. I will have to see what looks good when I get to the airport." He rolled his eyes at me. "Thank you and good luck finding her. I'm sorry I could not be more help. . . Very well." He flipped the phone closed.

"He is following us to the airport," Vince said, not taking his eyes off the window. "He says he has a going away gift for me." He pulled at the collar of his shirt nervously. He turned to his bag sitting on the seat, pulled out a leather travel wallet and handed it to me. "Put everything in the folder into the wallet." He turned to the man driving and spoke in rapid Spanish. When the driver replied, I recognized the voice even though I couldn't understand what he was saying.

"Antonio?" I asked, afraid of looking around to see if it was him.

"Hola, Chica," he said, sounding cheerful.

"Vince, I think he's Miguel's slave." I fear ratcheted through me. "He is the one who took me to the villa."

Vince chuckled. "Miguel thinks Antonio is his, but I converted him to me years ago."

"Are you sure?" I had a bad feeling about Antonio. He had been a huge help but there was something about him I never trusted.

"I am Vince's," Antonio said, smiling. "I am so glad I don't have to pretend to be Miguel's anymore."

"When we get to the airport I will walk back to Miguel's car. Antonio is going to leave the airport and bring you back around. It should give me enough time to get rid of Miguel. Just in case I cannot get rid of him quick enough, everything you need is in here. Check in for the flight and get through security as quickly as possible. If I do not make the flight I will get in touch with you on this." He pulled another phone out of his pocket and gave it to me.

"I don't want to go without you." I shoved everything from the envelope into the travel wallet without taking the time to look at any of it.

"I know. I do not want you to go by yourself either, but we must make him believe I have no idea what happened to you or we will never have a moment's peace. You can do this. Be that badass woman you were last night."

I tried to summon the persona, but as I did, my eyes filled with tears. I held the travel wallet to my chest, took a deep breath, and slowly let it out. I told myself I had to do this. There was no other way out.

"Thank you for saving me from them and for helping me find my way out of here. I hope you'll be able to join me at the gate." I wiped the tears from my face.

"Just be the woman I know you can be, and everything will be fine. Meeting you has been one of the greatest things to happen to me in my long life," he said as Antonio came to a stop outside the airline's curbside check in.

"Antonio, make sure nothing happens to Katie please." Vince opened the door and stepped out.

"Yes, sir," Antonio said, bobbing his head.

"My new alias will be Ares Charchalis. I will see you soon," Vince said to me before closing the door and hitting the roof once.

"I'm going to take you around the airport again and drop you off a little way from here," Antonio said, staring straight ahead before pulling back into traffic.

I stayed where I was on the floorboards, and looked out the window on the other side of the car. I could tell when we left the airport. I expected us to turn around to head back, but it looked like we were headed further and further away from the airport.

"Antonio, I thought you were going to take me back to the airport?" I popped my head up between the front seats of the car.

"I have other orders." He pushed my head back with one hand.

"What orders are those?" I asked with a sinking feeling.

"To take you back to Miguel's villa."

"So you are Miguel's slave after all?" I wondered how I was going to get out of this. I pulled myself off the floorboards and sat up in the seat.

"Yes, I always have been. Now maybe he will turn me." He pulled his phone out of his pocket.

I could not let him call Miguel. How was I going to get him to take me back to the airport? "Antonio, put the phone down," I said, mentally willing him to do as I said. "Turn around and take me back to the airport."

I don't know why it worked. Maybe because he was a slave, and he had ingested enough vampire blood to allow me to force my will onto him. Or he was strong enough to overpower the order Miguel had given him. I didn't care why it worked, only that it worked.

"Si, Señora," was all he said before he turned around and took me back to the airport. I relaxed back into the seat.

"Antonio, if you see Miguel or Lolita drive a hundred yards

past them before you pull over," I said, getting back on the floor of the car.

"Si Señora." I heard his phone start to ring. "It is Miguel."

I cursed inwardly. "Answer it and tell him I was not with Vince, and you have no idea where I might have gone." I remembered to put my will behind it.

"Bueno?" He answered, listening for a moment before answering in Spanish. Great I had no idea what he was saying to Miguel on the other end of the line. I really needed to learn some more languages.

After some back and forth Antonio hit end on the phone and threw it in the passenger seat. "What did you tell him?" I asked, keeping my will in the words.

"Just what you told me to, that you were not with Vince and I didn't know where you might go. We are almost there."

"Great you are being a really good friend, Antonio; I need you to do a few things for me alright?" I asked, keeping my will in place.

"Si," he said as he navigated through airport traffic.

"I need you to forget the new name Vince is going to be using. If anyone asks what name he is using, you tell them Vince."

"He only goes by Vince." His voice sounding far away.

"I need you to move out of San Sebastian as quickly as you can and stay away from vampires." He was creepy but he didn't deserve to live as a slave to vampires.

"Thank you," he said, sounding relieved. "We are here. Good luck, Katie." He pulled over and got out of the car to lean on the trunk. I heard him tap lightly on the trunk lid. I wiggled my way up the seat and looked out. It was busy. People were moving everywhere but thankfully I didn't see Miguel, Lolita, or Vince.

Taking a deep breath, I opened the door, untangled myself from the floorboard and stepped out on the curb. I squared my shoulders, and looking straight ahead, made my way to the sliding doors. I told myself to be that badass woman from last night. Pretend I didn't care what was going on around me.

I made my way inside and found my way to the bathroom where I locked myself in a stall and opened the travel wallet Vince gave me. I pulled out my new passport first. Thinking I had better learn my new name. Mary Anne Sims, from San Diego, California. Well at least I had been there, I thought to myself, but where had he gotten this picture? I found the ATM card and the black credit card with my new name on both.

I pulled out my airline itinerary; it was first class to Athens with a layover in Madrid. I put everything back in the wallet in a more organized way. I was just about to leave the bathroom when I noticed something hard and small protruding from the wallet.

I opened it again and found a hidden zipper pocket; I unzipped it and found a flash drive. Vince had just earned more of my trust. I had a feeling it included everything he had on the prophecy. I smiled, but I knew it would have to wait until I had a computer to see what was on it. Maybe there would be a cyber café at the Madrid Airport. If I made it that far.

Feeling a little better, I flushed the toilet and left the restroom with the same attitude I had when I entered it.

I found my way to the check-in counter and showed them my passport and ticket. "You will have to hurry Ms. Sims your plane is already boarding and you still have to get through security. May I offer you an escort to speed things up?" The woman behind the counter asked, putting my tickets in a paper sleeve and giving it back to me. I glanced around looking for Vince with no luck. "No thank . . ." I trailed off as I saw Lolita headed my way out of the corner of my eye.

Panic stabbed through me, but I fought through it. "Actually, that would be great. That women over there is stalking me, and I am afraid of what will happen if she gets me alone." I let the fear bleed through my badass demeanor. The woman looked over nodded and waved for a large man to come over.

"Bernard, will you please escort Ms. Sims to her gate? She is running late," she asked the man then looked at me. "Don't worry I will not tell her anything. Good luck."

Bernard opened his arms as a signal to follow him. "Thank you," I said and went quickly after him.

Where are you going little girl? Lolita asked in my head. I faltered for a step but kept moving. I would not allow that bitch to get me.

We made it to security and, of course, had to wait in line. I looked around nonchalantly and found Lolita standing back from the line. I had never been more thankful for airport security, but as I continued to look around, my gaze landed on Miguel who was making his way toward me. My stomach knotted. I really wanted to find the nearest trashcan to throw up into, but I forced the bile back down and moved up in the line giving the first security guard my ticket and passport.

Where are you going Katie? Miguel asked and I felt him trying to get into my thoughts. He was trying to use the bond that was no longer there to hurt me. I followed his brain pattern back to him. I found his brain and squeezed it with my minds-eye. I didn't know if it would work, but I didn't give up until I heard a crash. I turned to see him on the floor. Passengers and security people surrounded him trying to help.

I put my travel wallet in the plastic bin, took off my heels and put them in as well. I smiled, *back at you dickhead,* I thought to Miguel. I didn't care if he could hear me or not. The guard on the other side of the metal detector waved me forward, and I followed his command, walking slowly through the arch. He nodded when no alarms went off. I grabbed my wallet, and quickly put my shoes back on. Bernard and I moved down the concourse to my gate.

I could still feel Miguel's gaze on my back and I smiled knowing I would never allow another vampire to have power over me ever again. I didn't let myself look around until I was giving my ticket to the airline employee standing at the gate.

"You just made it Señora. They are just about to close the door to the plane," she said while I looked around. Miguel was nowhere in sight; I could only hope he had not seen where I was heading.

"Thank you," I said, taking my ticket stub, and turning to Bernard. "Thank you for escorting me. You just saved my life." I gave him a quick kiss on his cheek.

He blushed, nodded, and waited for me to hurry down the gangway to the plane. I walked on board and met the eyes of a flight attendant who gave me a dirty look then looked at her watch, the standard non-verbal for, you're late. I looked at my stub found my seat and the empty one next to it.

Panic rocketed through me. Where was Vince? What had they done to him? Was his going away gift a punishment worse than death?

I sat down in the seat next to the window, put my seat belt on and put my head in my hands. I was too worn out to cry.

"Señora, I need to see your ticket this is the first-class cabin," the annoyed flight attendant said. I shoved it to her and she nodded. "Forgive me but I am required to check. Can I get you anything before we take off?"

"Some water please." I looked at her and trying to sound pleasant. I looked around the cabin hoping to see Vince sitting in another seat, but he wasn't there. The attendant gave me a cold bottle of water, and I drained without taking it from my mouth. We were finally pulling away from the gate. I took a deep breath, listening for Vince in my mind but there was nothing but silence. I said a prayer for his safety, silently thanking him for all his help.

I opened the wallet again and pulled out the flash drive. He had been telling the truth when he said he would help me no matter what. He had given me everything I needed whether he was with me or not. I looked through the other pocket hoping for a note or something, but I found nothing but a few hundred Euros in cash. I closed the wallet and my eyes as we rocketed down the runway. Goodbye San Sebastian, goodbye Mark, goodbye Katie Hunter. There were too many goodbyes to make, but I refused to say it to Vince.

Dear Reader,

Thank you for reading Found by Vampires. I hope you enjoyed part one Katie's journey into the world of vampires. She escaped them for the time being but she is far from done dealing with them.

If you enjoyed this story please tell a friend and leave a review on **Amazon**.

Here is a sneak peek at the next book in the series, Trained by Vampires.

Happy reading!

Joy.

Joy Mosby
Trained By Vampires

CHAPTER 1

I waited outside the arrivals terminal at Ben Epps Airport in Athens, Greece, for the shuttle to the hotel I'd booked a few minutes after getting off the plane. I fingered the phone in my pocket willing it to ring and wishing I knew where Vince was. There was no way the 'evil ones' beat me here, even if they had known where I was going. But Vince knew. He could have found a way to meet me here or be arriving shortly, unless the 'evil ones' had done something horrible to him. I shivered and rubbed my arms, just thinking about them made my skin crawl.

The shuttle stopped in front of me a minute later, it was early in the morning, and it was empty except for the driver. "Kalimera," he said, after opening the door and coming down the stairs looking for my luggage.

"Good morning," I said, hoping I was responding in kind to his salutation.

"Where is your luggage?" he asked, switching to broken English.

Fumbling for an excuse. "It was lost." This man didn't need to know I had been forced to leave everything I owned at the 'evil ones'' villa in order to escape from them.

"I am sorry," he said, going back up the steps and taking his seat. "You look tired let's get you to your hotel."

"Thank you." I climbed the stairs and took the seat behind the driver. I let out a long breath and looked out the window. It was still dark, and even though the past twenty-four hours had been hell, a little jolt of excitement passed through me when I thought about where I was. My life had changed so much in the past week it was hard to believe I was alive, let alone in Greece.

Who would have thought leaving my boyfriend would lead me down a road I could never imagine? After leaving Mark I began to hear voices in my head. They weren't a figment of my imagination either. They were vampire voices. I had been manipulated by one, mortally wounded by another, and saved by a different one. I found out I am the prophesized savior of the vampire race, 'The One', though what they need saving from is beyond me. All I knew about the prophecy was on a flash drive in my wallet. It contained all of the information Vince, the vampire who saved me from slavery, had. I was exhausted, but the first thing I wanted to do was see what was on the drive and find out what being 'The One' meant.

"Here we are," the driver said as he pulled up to the hotel entrance and stopped the shuttle.

I got up and went to the head of the stairs. "Thank you," I said, before heading down the stairs and off the bus.

"Paracalo."

I went directly through the front door of the hotel to the front desk where a tired-looking older man sat behind the desk in a crumpled suit that looked like it had been slept in.

"Hi, my name is Mary Sims I just made a reservation for a room." I tried to speak slowly so the man could understand me. My name isn't really Mary Sims, it's Katie Hunter. Mary is the identity Vince set up for me to keep the 'evil ones' from finding me.

"Yes, you talked to me. I just need your passport and credit card." He looked down, and started clicking a computer mouse. "How long will you be staying with us?"

I hesitated at the question. I wanted to stay in Athens and wait for Vince, but every day I stayed increased the risk of the 'evil ones' finding me. Vince would be able to track my movements by the credit card he gave me. He would know how to find me. "Just tonight, if its's okay," I said, digging in my wallet, and giving him my passport and credit card.

"That should not be a problem," the man said, entering my information into the computer. "Where are you going from here?"

"I'm not sure yet." Even if I had known, there was no way I going to tell this guy. It would be too easy for the 'evil ones' to track me. "Do you have a computer I could use?"

"We have a guest computer," he said, pulling out a map and showing me how to get there. "You will need to use your room key to access the room."

"Thank you." Signed the credit card slip and took the key he gave me.

"Sleep well Ms. Sims."

When I reached the locked door outside the computer room I slid my key into the door, went inside and sat down at the computer. Letting out a deep breath I plugged the flash drive into the USB port and waited for the computer to read what was on the drive. My leg bounced up and down impatiently as the old machine whirled and spun. Finally, a window popped up with a document icon on it. I clicked on it and got an error message in Greek. I couldn't read it, but based on the version of the operating system, I guessed the computer couldn't open the document with the software on the machine.

Frustrated I opened the internet browser and tried to open the document with a program online but the internet was so slow it kept timing out. After twenty minutes of failure, I gave up, blinking back the tears burning my eyes. I needed sleep. I could find a computer the next day.

I went up to my room and opened the door. It was a standard room with a queen size bed. Everything about the room was typical with pastel color tones of tan, pink and blue. There was a desk in the corner with a chair, and a television sat on top a dresser.

I checked the closet, bathroom, and under the bed to make sure there was no one in the room with me. I locked the door and engaged the dead bolt before stripping off my clothes and going into the bathroom.

Since I didn't have any other clothes, I washed my panties in the sink with the hand soap provided by the hotel and hung them out to dry on the towel rack.

Looking in the mirror, I pulled back the gauze on my neck, where one of the 'evil ones' had taken a chunk out of me two nights ago. The wound was gone. I touched the angry looking, red puckered skin where the stitches had been the night before, how had I healed so quickly? I had stitches before, when I shut a car door on my hand and it took weeks to heal. My hand was better too. I bruised it when I punched first, my cheating ex-boyfriend, then one of the 'evil ones' in self-defense, the same night. When had that happened? I tried to think back to the last time it hurt. It was before we left Vince's house in San Sebastian.

Was this one of my new powers? Was I able to heal quicker then I used too? It had to have something to do with my mom and being 'The One'. As much as I thought this business with the prophecy was a myth, things kept happening to me that made me want to believe it might be true. I shook myself. Why would I be 'The One'? It still didn't add up for me. Without any answers I shrugged and got into the shower.

I took a long hot shower and cried the whole time. I cried for the loss of my former life. I cried for the pain my disappearing would cause my parents and friends. I cried at the pain I had suffered in the past twenty-four hours. I cried for Vince, hoping he was alright. Would he find me soon? Would he change me into a vampire even though I wasn't sure what I wanted? Did I have a choice? He thought I was 'The One' after all, my destiny was to become a vampire.

After I cried myself out, and left with more questions than answers, I went to bed hoping I would be able to leave all the bad thoughts behind and get some sleep. The drapes were pulled, the do-not-disturb sign was on the door, the deadbolt and the chain were engaged. I made sure the ringer on my cell phone was on and the volume was turned all the way up incase Vince tried to call me. I set my alarm clock for nine in the morning and I went to sleep, thinking I was as safe as I could be for the night.

ACKNOWLEDGEMENTS

Leah, I would have never had to courage to do this if you had not been there to read the first and second drafts and tell me that it was not crap, thanks little sister. I want to thank Amy, and Lesley for helping with the final edits. I feel blessed that I have two best friends willing to read and edit my books. My love, thank you for your unending support and reading my 'chic book'.

ABOUT ME

I love to write about the Heroines Journey in the paranormal universe, because writing about everyday life is boring for me (hence I am horrible at blogging). I love taking a character who thinks she is weak and showing her how strong she really is.

I live on forty acres in Northwest Colorado with two dogs (Ajax and Achilles), a few barn cats (Two-Face, Skeletor, and Silvester) and my amazing husband. I love not having any neighbors, being outside in the summer and inside in the winter. I have traveled to many places in the world, but I have many more places to visit before I am done.

When I am not staring at the monitor writing, I am staring at my Kindle reading, or spending time with my husband and animals.

Check out my website: Joymosby.com to find out about new releases and join my mailing list. I am not very good at updating it but bear with me I am working on it.

Visit Joy's website at: **www.joymosby.com** or follow her on social media: **https://www.facebook.com/joymosby81625**

Twitter: **@joy_mosby**